X

Just shoot her now.

Karleen thought the two little boys—twins, it looked like—were about four years old. Jumping around like that, it was hard to tell. God bless their mother, was all she had to say.

Then a Nordic god walked out from behind the truck, sunlight glinting off short golden hair and caressing massive shoulders effortlessly hefting a giant cardboard box, and Karleen's brain shorted out.

Not so much, however, that she couldn't paw for the pair of long-neglected binoculars on the bookshelf. She held them up to her eyes, letting out a soft yelp when the god's face suddenly filled the lens.

Lord, it was like trying to pick a single item off the dessert cart. The jaw…the cheekbones…the heavy-lidded eyes…the mouth.

Oh, dear God, the mouth.

Dear Reader,

From the moment Karleen Almquist walked on stage in *Playing for Keeps,* my single title for Silhouette Books, I knew she'd get her own story one day. What I didn't realize then was that she'd have to wait a few years, until Troy Lindquist showed up as Blake's business partner in *Marriage Interrupted,* my first story for the Special Edition line.

A more unlikely pair, you'll never meet. But what fun it was, letting these two completely opposite personalities find their way into each other's lives. And like my initial disbelief that this pairing could ever work, so do Karleen and Troy have a few things to learn about judging a person by the surface stuff—their taste in clothes or furniture or lawn ornamentation, for instance. Because when they dug a little deeper, they were surprised to discover their similarities were more numerous than their differences.

After all, it's easy to love someone who's just like you. But how boring is that?

Karen Templeton

PRIDE AND PREGNANCY

KAREN TEMPLETON

Silhouette®

SPECIAL EDITION®

Published by Silhouette Books

America's Publisher of Contemporary Romance

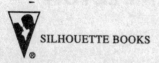

SILHOUETTE BOOKS

ISBN-13: 978-0-373-24821-6
ISBN-10:   0-373-24821-0

PRIDE AND PREGNANCY

Books by Karen Templeton

KAREN TEMPLETON,

a Waldenbooks bestselling author and RITA® Award nominee, is the mother of five sons and living proof that romance and dirty diapers are not mutually exclusive terms. An Easterner transplanted to Albuquerque, New Mexico, she spends far too much time trying to coax her garden to yield roses and produce something resembling a lawn, all the while fantasizing about a weekend alone with her husband. Or at least an uninterrupted conversation.

To Gail, for trusting me
To Jack, for believing in me
To Jane Austen, for inspiring me (and every other
romance writer who's ever trod the globe!)

Chapter One

By the time she was thirty, Karleen Almquist had signed three sets of divorce papers, at which point she decided to make things easier on herself and just get a hamster.

After all, hamsters didn't leave their clothes scattered all over kingdom come, watch endless football or stay out till all hours. And their itty-bitty paws were too small to mess with the remote. True, they weren't of much use in the sack, but then the same could be said of most of her husbands.

Unfortunately, also like her husbands, hamsters didn't exactly have a long shelf life. Which was why Karleen was burying yet another of the critters underneath the huge, gnarled cottonwood at the back of the large yard of the aging Corrales adobe she'd kept after her last divorce, seven years ago. Each tiny grave was marked by a minia-ture cast-stone marker engraved with the rodent's name, ordered from this place online that promised a two-day turnaround, if you were willing to pay extra for FedEx overnight service.

Karleen sank the marker into the soft soil, praying the neighborhood cats wouldn't disturb Mel's rest, although he was probably fairly scavenger-proof in the little metal floral can from Hobby Lobby. Then she stood, making a face as she peeled off her gardening gloves. Fond of Melvin as she'd been, it had taken the better part of an hour to glue on these nails and damned if she was going to ruin them for a dead hamster.

A cool, dry breeze shuddered through the veritable orchard of apple trees lining the far wall, sending a shower of white blossoms drifting across her dusty pool cover. The peaches, apricots and cherries would bloom in a few weeks. By mid-summer, the ground would be a holy mess with rotting fruit. But right now, her heart lifted a little at the sight of all those blossoms glowing against the brilliant New Mexico sky, the twittering of dozens of redheaded finches scouting out the assortment of brightly colored birdhouses suspended from the branches—

What was that?

At the giggling, she swung around in time to see a pair of pale blond heads vanish behind the low wooden fence separating her yard from the one next door.

"Boys!" boomed an off-stage male voice. "Get over here!"

Karleen zipped as fast as her beaded slides would carry her back to the house, dumping the gloves on a tempered-glass table on her flagstone patio as she went. Once inside, she scurried across the brick floor through the house, twisting open the slightly warped verticals in her living-room window to get a better view. And indeed, through the assortment of glittery, spinning porch ornaments hanging from the eaves, she saw a great big old U-Haul van backed in the next driveway.

The house was the largest of the four on their little dead-end road, a two-story territorial/adobe mutt centered in a huge pie-shaped lot crammed with a forest's worth of trees—cottonwoods, willows, pines, silver maples. The property hadn't been on the market more than a few weeks (the old owners had gone to live with one of their kids in Oregon or Idaho or someplace), so the new owners must've paid cash for it, for closing to have gone through that quickly.

The little boys—twins, it looked like—raced around the side of the van, roaring in slightly off-sync unison (and loud enough to be heard through a closed window), "Daddy, Daddy! The house next door has a *pool!*"

Just shoot her now.

Karleen thought maybe they were a little older than her best friend Joanna's youngest, around four or so. Jumping up and down like that, it was hard to tell. God bless their mother, was all she had to say.

Then a Nordic god walked out from behind the truck, sunlight glinting off short golden hair, caressing massive shoulders effortlessly hefting a giant cardboard box, and her brain shorted out.

Not so much, however, that she couldn't paw for the pair of long-neglected binoculars on the bookshelf crammed with paperbacks and doodads behind her. She blew off the dust, then held them up to her eyes, fiddling with the focusing thingy for a second or two before letting out a soft yelp when The God's face suddenly filled up the lens.

Lord, it was like trying to pick a single item off the dessert cart. The jaw…the cheekbones…the heavy-lidded eyes…the mouth.

Oh, dear God, the mouth.

She licked her own, it having been a long, long time since she'd had a close encounter with one of those. Although this mouth was in a class by itself. Not too thin, but not one of those girlie mouths, either. *Just right, Goldilocks,* she thought with a snort.

Karleen lowered the binoculars, shaking her head and thinking, *Well, doesn't this suck toads?* only to brighten considerably when she remembered there was, in all likelihood, a Mrs. God. So he was somebody else's problem, praise be.

While she stood there, trying to hang on to her newfound cheer, an SUV rumbled past, parking behind the van and disgorging a pair of dark-haired hunks. Or rather one hunk and one hunk-in-progress, a teenager not yet grown into his long arms and legs. The two men did the buddy-palm-slapping thing, then got to work unloading the van while the little boys concentrated on staying underfoot as much as possible and being cute enough to get away with it.

For the next, um, twenty minutes or so, she watched as plaid Early American wing chairs and sofas and brass lamps and sections of a dark wood four-poster bed and one of those bland landscape paintings people hung over their sofas marched from van to house. Occasionally she caught snatches of flat, midwestern speech and thought, *Yeah, that figures.* And as the minutes passed, she wondered…so where was this wife, already? Shouldn't she be flitting about, directing the men where to put everything?

About this time Karleen noticed the mail truck shudder to a stop in front of her mailbox at the edge of her yard. The carrier got out, took stuff out of the box, slammed down the painted gecko flag, stuffed stuff into the box, then walked around to the back of the truck and retrieved a package. Which, instead of carrying up the walk to Karleen's front door, she tucked into a nest of weeds at the base of the post. Oh, for pity's sake.

Karleen yanked open her front door and headed toward her mailbox, blinking at the dozen or so jewel-toned pinwheels bordering her walk, happily spinning in the breeze. Halfway down, however, she realized that all movement had ceased next door. While she had to admit she felt a little spurt of pride that, at thirty-seven, she still had what it took to render men immobile, there was also a ping of annoyance that she couldn't go to her damn mailbox without being gawked at. However, if she didn't say anything, she would be forever branded as The Stuck-Up Bitch Who Lived Next Door.

And that would just be wrong.

So she fished her mail out of the box and the box out of the weeds, then wound her way over to the fence through her ever-growing collection of lawn ornamentation.

"Hey," she said, smiling. "I'm Karleen. You guys my new neighbors?"

She might even have pulled it off, too, if it hadn't been for *the eyes*.

Bimbo.

The word smacked Troy between the eyes like a kamikaze bee. Followed in quick succession by *blonde, stacked* and *oh, crap*.

It wasn't just the eighties retro hair. Or the Vegas makeup. Or even that she was dressed provocatively, because she wasn't. Exactly. The stretchy pants rode low and the top rode high (and the belly button sparkled like the North Star), but the essentials were more than adequately covered. No cleavage, even. A delicate gold chain hugged her ankle, but that was pretty much it. She was just one of those women that fabric liked to snuggle up to.

Men, too, no doubt.

Beside him, Blake cleared his throat. Troy came to and extended his hand; Karleen shifted everything to one arm to reciprocate, an assortment of fake gemstone rings flashing in the sunlight. Jeez, those fingernails could gut and fillet a fish in five seconds flat, a thought that got a bit tangled up with the one where Troy realized that her breasts seemed a little…still.

"And I'm Troy. Lindquist." Her handshake was firm and brief and he suddenly got the feeling that she wished this was happening even less than he did, which irked him for some reason he couldn't begin to explain.

"You're kidding?" She hugged her mail with both arms again, her deep blue eyes snaring him like Chinese finger traps. "My maiden name's Almquist."

"Swedish," they both said at once, and everybody else looked at them as though they'd totally lost it, while Troy noticed that Karleen's mouth said *friendly* and her eyes said *pay no attention to the mouth*.

"Anyway," Troy said. "These are my boys Grady and Scott, and this is Blake Carter, my business partner, and his son Shaun."

She said all her hello-nice-to-meet-yous, very polite, very careful…and then she turned that glistening smile on the boys, and Definite Interest roared onto the scene, huffing and puffing. Because people tended to have one of two reactions when confronted with his sons: They either went all squealy and stupid, or got a look on their faces like they'd stumbled across a pair of rattlesnakes. Karleen did neither. Instead, Karleen's expression said, *Anything you can dish out, I can take and give back ten times over,* which Troy found disturbingly attractive and scary as hell at the same time.

"Hey, guys," she said in a perfectly normal voice, with a perfectly normal smile, which was when he realized she was around his age and that she hadn't had any work done that he could tell. Not on her face, at least. "Let me guess— y'all are twins, right?"

Scotty, slightly smaller than his brother, stuck close to Troy's leg while the more outgoing Grady clung like a curious little monkey to the post-and-rail fence separating the yards. Still, clearly awestruck—and dumbstruck—they both nodded so hard Troy was surprised their heads didn't fall off. Out of the corner of his eye, he caught Blake elbowing Shaun. *"Breathe,"* he said, and the sixteen-year-old turned the color of cranberry juice.

"How old are you guys?" Karleen asked, not looking at Shaun.

"Four!" they chorused. Then Grady leaned closer and asked, "You got any kids?"

Karleen shook her head, tugging a straw-colored hair out of her lipstick. "No, sugar, I sure don't."

"Then how come you gots all that stuff?" Grady said, jabbing one finger toward her yard. Which looked like an annex for Wal-Mart's lawn-and-garden department. And no, he did not mean that in a good way. Surely all those whirligigs and stone raccoons and such hadn't been there before? Was that a *gnome* over in the far corner?

"'Cause it's fun," Karleen said with a shrug. "I like sparkly stuff, don't you?"

More nodding. Then Scotty piped up. "You got a pool, huh?"

"Yeah," she said, wrinkling her nose. Disconcertingly cute, that. "But I haven't used it in years."

"How come?"

"*Okay*," Troy said, slipping a warning hand on the boy's shoulders. "Too many questions, bud."

"It's all right," Karleen said, meeting his gaze, apparently forgetting to switch from kid-smile to I'm-only-doing-this-because-that's-how-I-was-raised smile, and his lungs stopped working, painfully reminding him how long it had been since he'd done the hokeypokey with anyone. Then, thankfully, she returned her attention to the child. "It just got to be too much of a bother, that's all."

"Oh. Daddy said we couldn't have a pool 'cause we're too little an' he didn't wanna hafta to worry 'bout us. But if we learned to swim, then he wouldn't *hafta* worry 'bout us."

"Yeah," Grady put in with another enthusiastic head nod, after which, as one, both blond heads swiveled to Troy with the attendant you-have-ruined-my-life-forever glare. But then Troy pulled his head out of his butt long enough to realize that that was the most Scotty had ever said to anyone, ever, at one time.

Karleen laughed. A low, from-the-gut laugh. Not a ditzy, tinkly, bimbo laugh. Definitely not a laugh Troy needed to hear right now, not with this many neglected hormones standing at the ready to do what hormones do. He glanced over to see Blake looking at him with a funny, irritating smirk, and he shot back a *What?* look. Chuckling, Blake poked Shaun—twice, this time—to help him unload the leather sofa for the family room, as Karleen said, "Your mama must sure have her hands full with you two," and Troy thought, *Oh, hell.*

"We don't got a mama, either," Scotty said, but with less regret than about the pool. "She died."

Karleen's eyes shot to Troy's, even as her cheeks pinked way beyond the makeup. "I am *so* sorry—"

"It's okay," he mumbled. "They've never known her."

"But you did," she said, then seemed to catch herself, the flush deepening.

"Hey, Troy," Blake called from the house. "You wanna come check out the sofa, make sure it's exactly where you want it?"

"Yeah, sure, be right there." He turned again to Karleen, who was already edging back toward her house. "Really, it's okay," he felt compelled to say, and she nodded, said, "Well. It was nice to meet you, welcome to the neighborhood," and hotfooted it back across her yard.

"I like Karleen," Grady said, still hanging over the fence. "She's pretty."

"Yeah," Scotty said. "She's nice, too."

But Troy didn't miss that she hadn't said to feel free to ask if he needed to know anything about garbage pickup and the like.

He also didn't miss the lack of panty lines underneath all that soft, smooth, snuggly fabric.

A couple of hours later, he and Blake sat on Troy's redwood deck, legs stretched out in front of them, nursing a couple of Cokes as well as their sore muscles. The twins and Shaun were gone, off on an exploratory hike of the new neighborhood. If it hadn't been for the Sandia Mountains on the other side of Albuquerque peeking through the just-budded-out trees, he could almost imagine he was a kid again, on vacation at the Wisconsin lake where his parents would drag him and his brothers every summer. Letting his eyes drift closed, Troy took advantage of the moment to sink into the padded patio chair, soaking up the spring air, and the peace.

"That neighbor of yours is something to behold,"

Blake began in his Oklahoma drawl, and Troy thought, *So much for peace.*

He scrunched farther down in the chair, his Coke resting on his stomach. "I suppose. If you like that type."

"Not talking about me. Obviously. I got me my woman," his partner said with a noisy, satisfied stretch. "Now we need to start thinking about plugging up the gap in your life. And don't even think about giving me some crap about how you're just fine, the boys are all you need, it's not time yet, blah-blah-blah."

"I wasn't going to," Troy said quietly, his eyes still closed.

He could tell he'd caught Blake off guard. After more than ten years of working together, a rare occurrence.

"You saying you're ready to move on?" Blake finally said.

"You sound surprised."

"Try flabbergasted."

"Why? It's been four years." Giving up on dozing, Troy sat forward, his Coke clasped in both hands between his spread knees. "I loved Amy. I'll always love Amy. But I'm tired of being alone."

"And you miss sex."

Troy's mouth pulled tight. "Like you wouldn't believe."

Blake was quiet for a moment. Understandable, considering how wrecked Troy had been after his wife's death, how adamant he'd been that there'd never be anyone else. Even now, the pain still lurked, even if these days it tended to stay curled up in its corner, like an old, weary dog. But for every inch the grief receded, emptiness rushed in to take its place.

"Sounds like you've been chewing this over for a while," Blake said.

Troy held up his soda can, squinting at the shiny metal in the late afternoon light. "A year or so. Ever since we started talking about relocating the business down here." He lowered the can. "I don't know, I guess the change finally rattled something loose. That maybe I'd like to think about another relationship while my working parts are all still in order."

The dark-haired man crossed his arms, fixing Troy with a far-too-astute gaze. "Any idea what you intend to do about that?"

Troy released a weighty sigh. "None whatsoever. Amy and I were together for thirteen years. And she's been gone for four." He shook his head. "Saying I'm a little out of practice is a gross understatement."

"It'll come back to you, I'm sure," Blake said dryly.

"I'm not talking about that, dirtwad. I'm talking about dating. Starting a new relationship. It was bad enough in my teens when at least I had youth to hide behind. Now I'm supposed to know what I'm doing."

One side of Blake's mouth tilted up. "You're not exactly indigent and you still have all your teeth. My advice? Leave it up to the women. They're born knowing what to do."

Both men jumped when overloud country music knifed the silence; just as suddenly, the volume receded. Not, however, fast enough for Troy.

"Like that one, for instance," Blake said when Karleen appeared in her yard, practically hidden by an umbrella-sized straw hat. A minute later, she was walking back and forth, head down, pushing something—a spreader, maybe?— singing enthusiastic backup with the female vocalist. Her cell phone rang; she stopped, answered it, that damned low, warm laugh carrying over the fence on the slightly chilly breeze.

Staring, borderline miserable, Troy shook his head. "Why the hell not?"

"Her front yard?"

"At least there's no junkers on cement blocks. Or toilets."

"That we can see. Anyway, then there's the hair. And the nails. And the…" He rolled his hand. "Attributes."

Blake frowned. "I'm not following."

Her call finished, Troy waited until he heard the rhythmic groan and squeak of the spreader before he said, "The woman's not *real,* Blake, she's a hallucination brought on by sexual deprivation. And I'm not looking for a hook-up. Which is all that would be. If anything."

"Oh, believe me,-buddy, *anything* it would be." Blake took a swig of his soda, chuckling. "*Something* is what that would be. I half expected the grass between the two of you to ignite."

"That's crazy. And do *not*—" he jabbed his soda can in Blake's direction "—shake your heading pityingly at me."

"I'll shake my head any damn way I want. I'm beginning to wonder if maybe I should go back and double check the van, make sure you didn't leave your brain inside it. The woman's pretty, likes kids, seems reasonably conversant in the English language and looked like she had her tongue stuck to the roof of her mouth for a while there. No, wait—that was you." Blake pushed himself back on the chair, grinning. "Not real sure I see what the problem is."

"Just because she doesn't have kids doesn't mean she's single," Troy said before he caught himself.

Blake tapped his own wedding ring. "No ring."

"So she could still have a boyfriend, you know. But it doesn't matter, because I'm not interested. Oh, come on, Blake…you know as well as I do that 'opposites attract' stuff is a crock. Yes, she strikes me as a nice enough woman, but I'm looking for something with some sub-stance to it."

"Like you had with Amy."

"Exactly. What?" he said when Blake shook his head again.

Dark-brown eyes met his. "They call it *starting over* for a reason, dumb-ass. There's never gonna be another Amy, and thinking that's even possible isn't fair to anybody. Es-pecially you. But aren't you jumping the gun a little here? Thinking you're gonna find the next Mrs. Lindquist right off the bat without taking a couple of test drives first? Why limit your options by automatically tossing out any woman who doesn't immediately make you think wedding bells?"

"Because it's a waste of time? Because…" He glanced toward Karleen's house, then lowered his voice even further. "Because the enhanced look has never done it for me?"

"Must've been one helluva trick of the light, then, that poleaxed look on your face. And anyway, what makes you so sure they're not the genuine article?"

"Educated guess."

"Huh. Never realized MBA stood for Master of Boob Authenticity. Hey!" Laughing, he ducked when Troy threw his empty soda can at him, the crushed aluminum making one hell of a racket as it bounced across the wooden deck. Karleen jerked her head in their direction. They both waved. She waved back. A little reluctantly, Troy thought.

"And anyway," Blake said, "haven't you always wondered what fake ones feel like?" only to laugh again as he dodged Troy's smack upside the head. Then, hearing the boys' voices as they trooped around the side of the house toward the backyard, Blake stood, checking his watch. "I need to get back, I told Cass I'd be home by five. You ready to drop off the truck and pick up your car?"

"Might as well."

Which Troy had fervently hoped signaled the end of the discussion. Except, after the U-Haul had been returned and Blake dropped Troy and the twins back by their old apartment to pick up the Volvo, Blake called Troy back to his car.

"So, you gonna put out feelers with Karleen or not?" Blake said quietly over Shaun's hip-hop on the stereo, and Troy glared at him.

"This is payback for all the grief I gave you when you were trying to get back with Cass, isn't it?"

Chuckling, Blake put the SUV in reverse, then gave Troy one final, concerned glance. "No. But I am wondering how you think looking for another Amy is being open to possibilities. Just something to think about," he said, then backed out of the driveway.

Twenty minutes later, Troy pulled up in front of his new house, the boys springing themselves from their car seats the instant he cut the engine. "Stay in the backyard!" he yelled out the window, a moment before they vanished in a cloud of dust and giggles. Then he sagged into the leather seat, his head lolling against the rest as he looked at his new home, waiting for the dust storm of memories to settle inside his head.

Several years before, when Troy had finally felt confident enough that the business wasn't going to disintegrate out from under him, that he and Amy could actually apply for a mortgage with a straight face, they'd driven the poor Realtor in Denver nuts, looking at house after house after house. But it had been their first and it had to be perfect. Especially since they'd start raising their family there.

Meaning, the minute they'd walked inside, it had to say *home.* And the way his and Amy's tastes had dovetailed so perfectly had almost been spooky. They'd both craved clean lines, openness, light woods and walls—a house nothing like their parents' slightly disheveled, suburban two-story pseudo Colonials. The house they'd finally fallen in love with had smelled of fresh plaster, new wood, new beginnings, even if they'd filled it with the comforting, muted colors and traditional styles of their childhood.

After Amy's death, Troy had assumed he wouldn't be able to bear staying there. He'd been wrong. Instead, the familiar, the routine, had succored him in those first terrible weeks, months, after the unthinkable had happened. The house, and their beautiful, precious babies, had saved his butt. And his sanity. Leaving it hadn't been easy.

So after the move, he'd again taken his time, driving another Realtor crazy, looking for a new home for him and his boys. Another new start. He could have bought pretty much any house he wanted in Albuquerque. But he hadn't wanted any house; he'd wanted the *right* house. Only, who knew "right" would be this quirky, lopsided grandmother of a house, mottled with the patina of mold and memories? That his new definition of *home* would include bowed wooden floors and a wisteria-and-honeysuckle choked *portal,* weathered corbels and windows checkered by crumbling mullions and pockmarked wooden vigas ribbing the high ceilings?

Damn thing was twice as big as they really needed, even after getting everything out of storage. And he'd have to buy one of those John Deere monsters to mow the lawn. Still, he thought as he finally climbed out of the car, hearing the boys' clear, pure laughter on the nippy breeze, this was a house that exuded serenity, the kind that comes from having seen it all and surviving. A house that begged for large dogs and swing sets and basketball hoops and loud, boisterous boys.

Troy walked over to inspect what turned out to be a loose, six-inch thick post on the porch, shaking his head. And, because he'd clearly lost his mind, smiling. The house needed him. Right now, a good thing.

A flimsy wooden screen door whined when he opened it, the floorboards creaking underfoot as he walked through the family room to check on the boys in the backyard. The French doors leading outside were suffocated underneath God-knew-how-many coats of white enamel paint; Troy dug his trusty Swiss Army knife out of his pocket and scratched through to the wood: maple. Maybe cherry. Pocketing the knife, he pushed the doors open, his lips curving at the sight of the kids chasing each other around and around the trees, their yells competing with doves' coos, the occasional trill of a robin.

"You guys want pizza?" His voice echoed in the half-empty house, the emptiness inside him.

"Yeah!" they both hollered, running over, their faces flushed under messy, dirty hair. *Find towels,* he thought. *Wash kids.*

"C'n Karleen eat wif us?" Grady said, five times louder than necessary, and Troy thought, *What?* even as he stole a please-don't-be-there glance at her yard.

"She probably has other plans, guys. You go back and play, I'll call you when it gets here."

God, kids, Troy thought as he tromped back into the house, thumbing through the phone book for the nearest pizza delivery. After ordering two larges—one cheese, one with everything—a salad and breadsticks, he soldiered on upstairs to the boys' new room. Since it faced the back, he could work and still keep an ear out. Blake and Shaun had helped him set up the bunk bed, but the boxes of toys and clothes and heaven knew what else had clearly multiplied in the last two hours.

Shaking his head, he got to it, only to discover a couple boxes of his junk among the kids. After another glance out the window at the boys—huddled together underneath a nearby cottonwood, deep in some kind of twin conspiracy, no doubt—he stacked the boxes and carted them to his bedroom across the hall, no sooner dumping them on the floor at the foot of his (unmade) bed when his cell rang.

"Just called to see if you were settled in yet," his mother said in his ear.

"In, yes," he said, shoving one of the boxes into a corner with his foot. "Settled?" He glowered at the pile of boxes sitting in front of him, silently jeering. "By the time the boys graduate from high school, if I'm lucky."

"Which is where a woman comes in handy. Although listen to me," Eleanor Lindquist hurriedly added, as if realizing her gaffe, "I've still got unpacked boxes in the garage from when we moved in here when you were five! At this point, I think we're just going to leave them for you and your brothers to 'discover' after we're dead."

"Can't wait."

Eleanor laughed softly, then said, "I'm sorry, Troy. About the woman comment—"

"It's okay. Forget it."

A brief pause preceded "Anyway. Your father and I are thinking about coming down there for a visit. In a couple of months, we thought."

Troy stilled. "Oh?"

"We've always wanted to see the Southwest, you know—" News to him. "But we thought we might as well wait until you got your housing situation straightened out.

Of course, we can certainly stay in a hotel if it's inconvenient—"

"No! No, of course not, there's plenty of room here."
Good one, Mom. "But…how's Dad? Is he up to the trip?"

"Of course he's up to the trip, it's been more than five years, for goodness sake!"

The doorbell rang. Wow. Domino's must be having a slow night. "Pizza guy's at the door, I've got to run," he said, digging his wallet out of his back pocket as he thundered down the stairs. "My best to Dad." He clapped shut his phone and swung open the door, only to jump a foot at the sight of Karleen on his doorstep.

Bookended by a pair of slightly smudged, grinning, yellow-haired boys.

"Lose something?" she said.

Chapter Two

Troy allowed himself a quarter second's worth of sexual awareness—the perfume alone was enough to make him light-headed—before the hindsight terror thing kicked in nicely and he grabbed two skinny little arms, yanking the bodies attached thereto across his threshold.

"What's the big idea, leaving the yard? You *know* you're not supposed to go *anywhere* without a grown-up! *Ever,*" he added before Scotty could snow him with the pouty lower lip.

"We didn't cross the street or nothin'," Grady said, his defiance trembling at the edges. "We only went to Karleen's.'"

"Why on earth did you do that?"

"'Cause we wanted her to come over, only you said she prob'ly had plans. 'Cept she doesn't. Huh?" Grady said, twisting around to look up at her.

"I am *so* sorry," Troy said, following his son's gaze, which was when it registered that Karleen was wearing one of those painted-on exercise outfits that left little to the imagination, and that her skin was flushed—From exercise? From being pissed?—and her lipstick was eaten off and she'd pulled her hair back into a ponytail, leaving all these soft little bits hanging around her face and her eyes huge underneath her bangs and—

"We were coming right back," Scotty said softly, cruelly derailing Troy's train of thought.

Kids. Right.

Troy straightened up, forking a hand through his hair. Giving them the Dad-is-not-amused face. "That's not the point. You're too little to be by yourselves, even for a minute."

Grady's little forehead crumpled. "Then how come you always tell us what big boys we are?"

"Yeah," Scotty said, nodding, looking impossibly tiny and vulnerable. Not for the first time, responsibility walloped Troy square in the chest.

So he pointed a hopefully stern finger in their faces. "You're not *that* big," he said, just as a compact sedan with a Domino's sign clamped to the roof screeched up in front of the house, and the kids started hopping around like grasshoppers, chanting, "Piz-za! Piz-za! Piz-za!"

"No, wait," he said to Karleen as she made her getaway (he couldn't imagine why), breathing an oddly relieved sigh when she stopped, biding her time while Troy paid the pizza guy. After the very well-tipped teen loped back toward his car, Troy focused again on Karleen. Her arms were crossed underneath her breasts, her lips curved in a Mona Lisa smile as she watched the boys. The sun had begun to go down in earnest, soft-edging the shadows, leaving a chill in its wake. He wondered if she was cold…

"Good Lord, honey…how long has it been?"

Troy's head snapped up. "What?"

Bemusement danced in her eyes. "If you stare at my chest any harder, my bra's gonna catch fire."

"I—I'm sorry, I don't usually…" He blew out a breath, his face hotter than the pizza. "I didn't mean…" She laughed. Troy sighed again. "Okay, so maybe I did. But I'm not a letch, I swear."

"Oh, don't go gettin' your boxers in a bunch. You're just bein' a man, is all. No harm, no foul. It's kinda cute, actually."

Cute. Not exactly the image he was going for.

Oh, God. He was staring. Again. Not at her breasts, at least, but still.

"Uh…thanks for bringing the guys back," he said, shifting the pizzas.

One eyebrow lifted. "I hadn't exactly planned on keepin' 'em."

"More's the pity," Troy muttered, then shook his head. "Honestly, I have no idea what got into them, they've never gone off like that before. But you really are welcome to stay. If you haven't eaten, I mean." He hefted the two boxes, which he now realized were slowly melting his palms. And probably the salad on top. "There's plenty. I'll even promise to behave," he said, remembering to smile.

Now it was apparently her turn to stare, in that thoroughly assessing way women had that made men feel about six. "So the boys really came all on their own? You didn't send them over?"

Troy jerked. "*What?* No! Why would you think that?"

"Sorry. I just…" For one small moment, wisps of regret floated between them, only to spiral off into nothingness when she said, "Thanks for the offer, anyway. But I can't."

She pivoted and again started back toward her house.

Let her go, let her go…

"Another time?"

Karleen turned. "You're not serious?"

"Well, yeah, actually I am." *What?* "Was. I mean, we're neighbors and everything…" He shrugged. Lamely.

"Yeah, well, it's the *and everything* part of that sentence that worries me."

"Figure of speech," Troy muttered, fighting another blush. *Bad at this* didn't even begin to cover it. "I promise, Karleen, I'm not coming on to you."

"Well, no, you haven't reached salivatin' stage yet, maybe. But you are definitely coming on to me."

Troy snagged the *Really?* before it got past his lips, then thought, *Hey, maybe this is easier than I thought. Or maybe she is.*

Then he remembered she was the one walking away.

"And…that would be inappropriate because you probably have a boyfriend or something."

"Or maybe I'm not interested."

"Or that."

That got a head shake, which made the ponytail, if not the breasts, bounce. "You know, you really are sweet," she said, and again those wistful wisps cavorted in the chilly early evening air, more visible this time, although no less phantasmagorical. "As it happens, I haven't had a *boyfriend* since I was…" She cleared her throat. "A long time."

"You're into other women?"

She burst out laughing. The kind of laugh that made him smile, even around the size thirteen in his mouth. "Oh, God, you are too much! No, honey, I just meant *boyfriend* sounds kinda…juvenile or something. I've had lovers, and I've had husbands—"

"Husband*s*?"

"Three, if you must know. And three is definitely this girl's limit. Anyway. I'm trying to make a point, here—no, there's nobody in my life right now. By choice. Because if you ask me, it's all far more trouble than it's worth. Which is why I'm turnin' down your invitation. For tonight or any other time. Because you are sweet and there's no use pretending we're not attracted to each other, but some things just aren't meant to be."

She nodded toward the boxes. "Your pizza's gettin' cold, sugar," she said, then spun around, this time making it all the way across his yard.

Troy stared after her for several seconds as it all came flooding back. The part about how much it sucked to get rejected. Even when the woman wasn't someone you really wanted to get tangled up with, anyway.

He went inside, slamming the door shut with his foot, and called the boys to dinner.

"What's his name again?"

"Troy Lindquist," Karleen tossed in the direction of the speakerphone while she pedaled her butt off on her exercise bike. It had been two days since Troy and his Tiny Tots had moved in next door. Two days since Karleen had walked away from an invitation that she'd known full well had included a lot more than pizza, Troy's insistence otherwise notwithstanding.

Two days since she'd answered her doorbell to find a plastic-wrapped Chinet plate on her doorstep, heaped with two slices of pizza—one cheese, one supreme—a breadstick and salad. And taped to the top, a note:

It'll only go to waste. Enjoy. T.

And in those two days, she'd put in enough miles on this bike to give Lance Armstrong a run for his money. If nothing else, she was gonna have thighs you could bounce a rock off.

Slightly crackly, fuzzy clicking filled the room as Joanna tapped away at her computer keyboard, the rhythmic sound occasionally punctuated by her dog Chester's barking, the occasional squawk, scream or "Mo-om!" from one of her four kids. Clearly ignoring them all, Joanna said, "Huh."

"*Huh,* what?" Karleen said, panting and daubing sweat from her neck and chest with the towel around her neck. Of course, she could have Googled the guy herself, but Joanna beat her to it.

"Blond, you said? Late thirties? Blindingly gorgeous?"

"That would be him. Why? You find something?"

"Well," Jo's voice croaked over the speaker, "there's a photo of some blond hottie named Troy Lindquist, with a dark-haired hottie named Blake Carter—"

"Yes! He was there, too!"

"Yeesh, I'm surprised your retinas didn't melt. Anyway, there's a caption under the photo—oh, for God's sake, Matt, let the baby have the ball, already! And put the dog back outside, his feet are all muddy!—about their company. Ain't It Sweet."

"I don't know. Is it?"

"No, Ain't It Sweet. The frozen desserts people?"

Karleen stopped pedaling, her heart beating so hard she could hardly hear herself talk. "As in, The Devil Made Me Do It Fudge Cake?"

"The very same."

"Troy *owns* it?"

"Apparently so. Well, he and this Blake person are partners. It says here…" Karleen waited while Joanna apparently scrolled. "They recently moved their headquarters from Denver to Albuquerque…. Main ice-cream plant still in Denver…holy moly."

"What?"

"'Analysts say, with its steadily increasing sales figures and healthy profit margins, as well as a huge projected franchise growth within the next three to five years, Ain't It Sweet is poised to bolster its North American market share by as much as fifty percent, with plans to increase its overseas distribution in the works. Already, this upstart company is routinely among the top five high-quality frozen confections brands Americans name when polled in market surveys.'"

"It sure as hell's the brand I think of when I think of…whatever you said."

"Yeah," Jo said. "Me, too. Their Yo-Ho-Ho Mocha Rum Truffle cheesecake…"

"Oh! And their Everlasting Latte Cinnamon Swirl sorbet…"

Stupid names. Fabulous stuff. Holy moly was right.

"Hot *and* filthy rich," Joanna cackled. "And single, you say?"

"Don't go there."

"*I'm* not going anywhere. You, on the other hand, have an unattached, lonely, rich hottie living on the other side of your west wall. A single, lonely, rich hottie with a direct link to the best ice cream in the entire freaking *world*."

Rolling her eyes, Karleen climbed off the bike and grabbed the phone from its stand, walking out to her kitchen for some water. "Why do you assume he's lonely?"

"I can see it in his eyes in the photo." Which, coming from anybody else, would have sounded weird as hell. But Jo was like that. And besides, much as it pained Karleen to admit it, she'd seen it, too. Up close and personal. "For God's sake, Karleen, pay attention! Ice cream! Sex! Money! *Ice cream!*"

She had to laugh. "I got it, Jo. I'm not interested."

"Are you *insane? I'm* interested, and if I were any more happily married my brain would explode. Maybe you better check your pulse, make sure you're still alive."

Karleen released a long, weary breath. "And you do know you are beating a very dead horse, right?"

After a pause, Jo said, "You never used to be like this."

"I think that's the point, honey," she said softly. "And yes, I'm very aware of how attractive he is. And nice. *And* he's got two adorable little boys. But his expression when he first saw me far outweighed whatever hormones were playing dodgeball between us—"

"There were hormones playing dodgeball?" Jo said on a squeak, and Karleen rolled her eyes.

"Jo. Even if I was thinking about followin' through, these lashes do not flutter at someone who looks at me the way Troy Lindquist did. You could practically see the 'trailer trash' lightbulb go on over his head."

"Karleen. Blond hair and a Texas accent do not trailer trash make."

"The boob job comes pretty damn close."

"Then half of L.A.'s trailer trash, too. And would you stop beating yourself up over that? You were thrilled when Nate gave them to you for your birthday."

"Uh-huh. Until I realized what's gonna happen at some point when they'll have to come out and I'm gonna end up with a pair of deflated balloons on my chest. I'll be regretting them for the rest of my life. Just like my marriages."

"Okay, that's enough," Jo said in a voice Karleen had heard far too often since the first day in seventh grade when they'd sat next to each other in Social Studies, and for some bizarre reason the daughter of a hotshot attorney and one of Albuquerque's most successful car dealers had taken a liking to a little hick from Flyspeck, Texas. "Dammit, Kar—you're smart, you've got your own business, you don't owe anybody anything. So your marriages didn't work out. It happens."

"Three times?"

"So you've had more practice than most people. Big whoop. But if being alone is what you really want, hey…go for it—"

Karleen's call waiting beeped in her ear. "Sorry, I'm waiting on a client's call, I need to take this. I'll talk to you later, honey, okay?"

At that point, she almost didn't care who was calling. That is, until she heard "Leenie? Is that you?" on the other end of the line.

A fireball exploded in the pit of Karleen's stomach. The phone pressed against her ear, she wobbled out to the family room, dropping onto the worn Southwest pastel sofa. Well-meaning friends, rich hunky neighbors, all forgotten in an instant. Not even the glass menagerie sparkling on the windowsill—usually a surefire defense against the doldrums—could withstand the all-too-familiar tsunami of irritation and guilt.

"Aunt Inky?"

"Well, who else would it be, baby? Shew, what a relief, I was afraid you might've changed your phone number or somethin'!"

Definitely an oversight on her part. Karleen resisted the impulse to ask her mother's younger sister what she wanted. Because she only ever surfaced when she did want something. "Well. This is a surprise."

"I know, I've been real bad about keepin' in touch. And

it would've been hard for you to contact me, since I've been doing so much, um, traveling and all."

"Uh-huh." Inky didn't sound drunk, for once. But then, it was only ten o'clock in the morning. The slurring wasn't usually noticeable until mid-afternoon. "So where are you now?"

"Lubbock. Been here for a couple months now. It's okay, I guess. God knows I've lived in worse places." A pause. "You take up with anybody new yet?"

Karleen shut her eyes. "No, Aunt Inky. I told you, I prefer being alone."

"What fun is that?"

"It's not fun I'm after, it's peace. You should try it sometime."

"Well, each to his own, I suppose," her aunt said. "You doing okay, then? Money-wise, I mean?"

Ah. Karleen had wondered how long it would take. "I get by."

"Well, that's good. You always were a smart little thing, though—sure as heck a lot smarter than your mama or me—so I guess I shouldn't be surprised. You still livin' in the same place, that house with all the trees around it?"

Ice immediately doused the fire in her belly. And oh, she was tempted to lie. If not to pack her bags and make a run for it. Except Inky was the only family she had left, for one thing. And for another, Karleen was done running, done believing that whatever she needed was always right over the horizon.

"Yes, I'm still here." She hesitated, then added, "It's all I've got, really," even if that *was* stretching the truth a little.

Sure enough, Inky came back with a soft "Then I don't suppose you could spare a couple hundred dollars? Just a loan, you understand. To tide me over until I get back on my feet."

Karleen nearly laughed, even as she again resisted temptation, this time to point out to her aunt that if she spent less time in a horizontal position—either in the company of men of dubious character or out cold from cheap booze—she might actually stay on her feet for more than five minutes. But it wasn't like Karleen had a whole lot of room to talk, so who was she to judge? And anyway, it had been nearly a year this time, so maybe this really was an emergency.

"I guess I can manage a couple hundred. As long as you pay it back," she added, because she wanted her aunt to at least think about it.

"Of course, baby! Let me give you my address, I'm stayin' with a friend right now—" *oh, brother* "—but I should be here for a while...."

Karleen scribbled the address on a notepad lying on the coffee table. "Okay, I'll send a check for two hundred dollars in the next mail—"

"Could you make that a money order, baby? And if you could see clear to maybe make that two-fifty, or even three, I'd really appreciate it."

Karleen sighed. But, she thought after she hung up, at least her aunt hadn't asked to come stay with her.

A thought that made her feel prickly all over, like the time she'd lifted up a piece of wood in the backyard after a rainstorm and a million great big old waterbugs had scurried out from under it. Even though it had been probably twenty years since she'd spent any significant time with her aunt, just talking to the woman disturbed a swollen, never-quite-forgotten nest of skin-crawling memories.

Karleen sucked in a lungful of air, then glanced over at

the big mirrored clock by the entertainment center. Plenty of time before her afternoon appointment to do some digging in the garden, work off some of this negative energy.

She traded her bicycle shorts for jeans, shoved her feet into a pair of disreputable sneakers, plopped her silly straw hat on her head and went outside, where she was greeted by that brain-numbing music Troy liked so much. She half thought about going back inside, only to decide she couldn't become a recluse simply because her new neighbor made her uncomfortable in ways she didn't want to think about too hard. The music, though, might well drive her right over the edge.

So she rammed a Garth Brooks CD into the boom box on the deck, hit the play button and tromped over to her shed. Honestly, she thought as the metal doors clanged open, she doubted Troy was even forty yet. How he could like music that reminded Karleen of meat loaf and black-and-white television, she had no idea. Eighties rock, she could have understood. She wouldn't 've liked it any better, but at least it would've made sense.

But then, there was a lot about Troy Lindquist that didn't make sense. Like why, if he was so well off, he'd bought a fixer-upper out in Corrales when he could've easily bought one of those flashy McMansions up in the foothills. Why there didn't seem to be a nanny or housekeeper in the picture.

Not that any of it was her business, but it was curious.

After shaking out her thickest gardening gloves in case somebody with too many legs had set up housekeeping inside, she yanked them on, then batted through a maze of cobwebs to find her shovel, which she carted over to a small plot that, unfortunately, was next to Troy's fence. But that was the only spot in the yard that wasn't in shade half the day, or plagued with cottonwood roots.

The pointed steel bit into the soft soil with a satisfying crunch. By the third thonk, two little pairs of sneakered feet suddenly appeared on the lower rail, followed by two little faces hanging over the top. Two little eat-'em-up faces that she bet looked exactly like father's when he'd been that age.

"Whatcha doing?" the shorter-haired twin, clearly the appointed spokesperson of the duo, now said. The babies reminded her of leaves fluttering in the breeze, never completely still.

"I'm gettin' the soil ready so I can plant a garden."

"Whatcha gonna plant?"

"Tomatoes," she said, breathing a little hard as she jabbed the shovel into the soil. Most people would use a rototiller and be done with the chore in no time flat, but Karleen liked doing it the old-fashioned way. "Cucumbers. Squash. Maybe cantaloupe." For some reason, she couldn't grow flowers to save her soul, but vegetables, she could handle.

"C'n we help?"

"Yeah," the second, smaller one said, his voice like a butterfly's kiss. "C'n we?"

"Oh, I'm not planting anything today," she said, secure in the knowledge that by the time she did, they would have in all likelihood forgotten this conversation. "It still gets too cold at night. So not for weeks yet."

"Oh," the first one said again. "But when you do, c'n we help?"

Then again, maybe she'd have to plant by moonlight this year.

Then the littler one said, his eyes like jumbo blue marbles in a face that was all delicate angles, "Yeah, we never, *ever* had a garden before."

Oh, Lord.

"Tell you what," she said, straightening up and shoving her hair out of her face with the back of her wrist, which was when she noticed Troy, his damp T-shirt molded to his torso, standing on his deck, watching her as intently as a cat stalking a bird. "When it's time, you can ask your father, and we'll see," which of course sent both boys streaking away shouting, "Daddy! Daddy! C'n we help Karleen plant her garden?"

Troy swung the first child to reach him up into his arms, making the little boy break into uncontrollable giggles as he blew a big, slurpy kiss into his neck. Chuckling, he squeezed a few more giggles out of the kid before setting him down to scoop up his brother and repeat the process. "You two are going to be the death of me yet," he said, the top notes of amusement and exasperation in his voice in perfect harmony with the deep, almost unbearably tender melody line of unconditional love.

The ache that bloomed inside her was so sweet it clogged her throat, even as, from thirty feet away, she caught the apology in his eyes. "It's okay," she pushed out, but he shook his head. He said something to the boys, who scampered off to the other side of the yard, before he stepped inside his house. A second later he reappeared and headed her way, a bottle clenched in each fist.

Karleen jerked her head back down and plunged the shovel into the soil again like she was inches away from striking oil.

Chapter Three

Troy'd been watching Karleen off and on for ten minutes or so, going after that poor plot of dirt as though it had offended her deeply. Especially after the boys had accosted her. Not that he could hear the conversation over that god-awful country caterwauling. But after more than a decade of dealing with bank managers, suppliers, advertising agencies and potential investors, he was no slouch at deciphering body language.

A dialect in which his new neighbor was particularly fluent.

The cold, wet bottles soothed his heated palms as he crossed the fifty feet or so. A good thing, since the closer he got, the more agitated her digging became. Well, tough. She still wasn't his type, but he wasn't the bogeyman, either. And it bugged him no end that she seemed to think he was. So, okay, maybe he wasn't exactly racking up the bonus points by invading her space, but considering she'd come out of her house looking ready to bite somebody's head off, he sincerely doubted he was more than a fly on an already festering wound.

The brim of her hat quivering, she glanced up at his approach. And sure enough, worry peeked out from behind the aggravation simmering in her expression, and he thought, *See? Told ya,* followed by the inevitable pang of empathy whenever confronted by someone in trouble. Amy used to tease him unmercifully about it, about his always getting far more personally involved in other people's messes than he should. Some things, he thought as he held out one of the bottles, can't be helped.

"It's hotter than it looks. You'll get dehydrated."

"Thanks, but I'm good," she said, stabbing the dirt again. Her jeans sat intriguingly low on her hips, allowing an occasional glimpse of that sparkly belly-button stud, companioned by one of those stretchy tops that were basically just big, blah bras. Although on her, not so blah. In fact, the way the sun licked at the moisture sheening her skin…

Nope. Not blah at all.

"It's a bottle of water, Karleen. Not my fraternity pin."

Panting slightly, she shifted her gaze toward him again; fireflies of sunlight danced over her face through the straw brim. He wiggled the bottle. She reached over and snatched it out of his hand. "Fine," she said, twisting off the top and taking a swallow. "*Now* will you go away?"

"Not until you tell me what's wrong."

Surprise flickered across her features, followed by a head shake. "Nothing's wrong."

"Bull."

Now her brows lifted, as well as one corner of her mouth. "You don't know me from Eve. Why would you care?"

"Consider it a character flaw."

She met his gaze with a startling intensity that jolted his sex drive awake like a fire alarm. Underneath her T-shirt, her sigh took her breasts for a little ride.

"It's not you," she said after a moment, breaking the spell before his tongue started dragging in the dirt. Jeez. "I got a phone call that rattled me, is all." She shrugged, then set the bottle down by the fence before she went back to work. "Family stuff, nothin' too serious, and not to put too fine a point on it—" she attacked a particularly obtuse dirt clod "—but it's none of your business."

The haze nicely cleared now, Troy took a sip of his own water, then propped the bottle on the top rung of the fence. "Okay, so I didn't come over here soley to make sure you wouldn't die of thirst."

A tiny smile made a brief appearance. "No?"

"No. You were right the other night, when you made that comment about it having been a long time for me. I haven't even gone out with another woman since my wife died."

The dirt clod exploded like a supernova; her gaze touched his. "You're kidding?"

"Nope."

She stilled, clearly on the alert. "And what does this have to do with me?"

"Well…Blake—the guy who helped me move in?—suggested that maybe I needed someone—a woman, I mean—to practice on before I plunged back into the dating scene." He lifted the bottle in her direction. "And since you live right next door, he thought maybe you might be that woman."

Karleen barked out a laugh, then said, "And I can't believe you're dumb enough to say that to a woman with a shovel in her hands."

"I mean to *talk* to, what did you think I—? Oh." His

mouth flatlined. Maybe the haze hadn't cleared as much as he'd thought. Good to know the hormones were still flowing, but the perpetual leaky faucet sucked. "Sorry. That didn't come out exactly the way I heard it in my head."

She stabbed the shovel into a hard section of ground, balancing on it like a pogo stick until it sank. "Well, if that boneheaded attempt you just made is any indication, your conversational skills could definitely use some fine-tuning. But why me, exactly? Besides the convenience factor, that is."

"Because I figure if I can handle a conversation with you, I can handle one with anybody."

That got another laugh, this one a little less scary, and the faucet started dripping harder. After living with a woman for nearly ten years, not to mention four years of celibacy since, Troy knew damn well he wasn't one of those men who thought about sex 24/7. But as he watched Karleen bend over to snag the water bottle and his eyes went right to her soft, round backside, he realized that it definitely hummed in the background like a computer operating system—unseen but always on.

Her lips glistened from her sip of water. Yeah, that was helping. "You mean to tell me," she said, "that you haven't so much as talked to another woman in all this time."

"Not in the man-woman sense, no."

"And what's really pathetic," she said with a smile that only underscored her words, "is that I actually believe you."

"Thanks. I think."

"Although…you're not doing so bad right now."

"Yeah?"

"Yeah. Got off to a bit of a bumpy start, but you recovered nicely enough." She took another swallow of the water, then made a face. Troy frowned.

"It's bottled water, how bad can it be?"

"It's not the water, it's that wussy music you're listening to."

"What's wrong with it?"

"Other than I keep thinkin' somebody's about to say, 'The doctor will see you now'? Not a thing. Music's supposed to get your juices flowin', sugar, not put you to sleep."

Troy let out a slightly pained laugh. "Trust me, between my work and keeping track of my sons and…other things—" *uh, boy* "—my juices flow just fine, thank you. I want something to calm my nerves," he said with a pointed glance over at the loud country music issuing from her patio, "not frazzle them more than they already are."

She'd picked up her shovel again; now she leaned both hands on the end of the handle, striking a pose that could only be described as *sassy*. Troy didn't do sassy.

He didn't think.

"You got somethin' against country?" she said.

"When it's loud enough to rattle windows in Phoenix? Yeah."

Karleen looked back over her shoulder, considering. "I suppose I could turn it down. But…" Then she glanced up at him, the sassiness half melted into something that, once again, sent all those crazy hormones running for cover. "The CD's almost done, you mind if I let it run out?"

"No, of course not."

"Thanks. But tell you what…how about we agree not to play music outside at all? Unless the other one's not around, I mean?"

"Deal. Oh, and sorry about the kids earlier." When she frowned, he prompted, "About the garden?

The shovel stabbed at the dirt, but she glanced up from under the hat's brim. "They're just bein' little kids, it's no big deal. And anyway, since it's not even an issue for at least another month, I'm not worried."

"You should be. Trust me, those two take bugging to a whole new level. They work as a team—one stops to take a breath, the other one effortlessly fills the gap."

She laughed, then straightened up, looking in the boys' direction. "Which one's which?"

Troy studied her face for several seconds, as if to commit what he saw there to memory. Deciphering could come later. Then he followed her gaze. "Grady's the bigger, more outgoing one. The instigator. Scotty's always been more cautious. Unlike his brother, he tends to at least think about things before getting in trouble."

"Aww...they sound a lot like my friend Joanna's twins. Real different personalities." She twisted around, one hand clamped around the handle, the other pointing to a spot a few feet away. "How about we give them their own garden, over there? They could plant a pumpkin vine, kids always get a kick out of that."

Troy frowned. "You don't have to do that. I mean, it's a great idea, but I could easily do a garden for them, too. It looks like the former owners had a plot over against the back wall."

"Forget it. That soil's crap, they could never get anything to grow. And I don't mind. Really. It'll be fun."

The conversation stalled. She kept digging. Troy picked up his water bottle. "Well, I guess I'll be going," he said, turning away.

"You tryin' to dig up those old roses along the back?"

He wheeled around far more eagerly than he should have. "*Trying* being the operative word." The ancient bush had sent out dozens of treacherous, thorn-smothered runners into the yard. "I'm beginning to think nothing short of napalm's going to work. But things growing wild bug me. And I want to get as much done around here before I have to go back to work next week."

She tossed him a funny look, then said, "I was wondering how somebody in your position was able to take so much time off." When he frowned, she shrugged and said, "Google. And a nosy best friend."

"Ah," he said, then responded, "state-of-the-art home office. And besides, I can take so much time off now because I had basically no life for the first five years we were trying to get the business off the ground." Then boldness struck and he asked, "And what do you do?"

One shoulder hitched. "I'm a personal shopper."

"Really?" He looked at her house, which while much smaller than his, still wasn't exactly a mud hut. The over-zealous outdoor kitsch notwithstanding. "You must do pretty well yourself."

Her eyes followed his. "I do okay." Her brows knitted together for a moment, then she said, pain faintly pin-pricking her words, "Ex Number Three apparently decided letting me stay after the divorce was worth bein' rid of me."

"He didn't like country music, either?"

A laugh burbled from her throat, producing a small glow of triumph in the center of Troy's chest. A second later, the boys popped up on either side of his hips, positively caked with dirt and looking damned pleased with themselves about it.

A grin, this time. "You sure those're your kids?"

"Heck, I'm not sure they're *kids* at all," Troy said, using the hem of his T-shirt to wipe the top layer of dirt from

Scotty's forehead. "Mud puppies, maybe. Hard to tell until I hose them down."

The boys giggled; then, hanging onto his hands, they launched into the we're-gonna-starve-to-*death* moans, and Troy looked down into two sets of trusting blue eyes, and his chest twinged, as it did at least a dozen times a day. When he met Karleen's gaze again, however, the clouds had rolled back across her expression. Heavy, leaden things that promised days and days of unrelentingly miserable weather.

"I think Nate and I had more issues than differing musical tastes," she said, and her eyes touched his, and a great, big *whoa* went off in his brain.

A *whoa* he'd only heard once before, when a certain sleek-haired brunette had glided across his path in front of Northwestern's library, nearly two decades before.

A certain sleek-haired brunette who wouldn't have been caught dead with bleached hair, or her midriff exposed, or a belly-button stud, or listening to country music.

"Go feed your babies," Karleen said softly, jerking Troy back to Planet Earth.

"Uh…yeah. Would you like to—?"

"We'll talk about the garden when it gets warmer," she said, then turned her back on him, ramming the shovel into the dirt so hard he could have sworn the ground vibrated underneath his feet.

At 6:00 a.m. three days later, Karleen had stumbled out of bed, slammed shut the window against the din of birdsong and stumbled back to bed. Where now, at eight, daylight sat on her face like an obnoxious cat, prodding her to get up.

Then she remembered that Troy still lived next door and she grabbed her pillow and crammed it over her head, only to realize it was impossible to suffocate yourself.

She tossed the pillow overboard, frowning at her beamed ceiling. Of all the houses for sale in Albuquerque, Troy Lindquist had to buy the one next door to hers. Was that unfair or what? Good-looking, she could ignore. Sweet, she could ignore. Sexy…she could ignore. But all three rolled into one? Lord, she felt like she was running to stay ahead of a raging wildfire—one trip, and she'd be barbecue.

Oh, sure, she could go on about her resolve to stay un-attached until her tongue fell out, but neither history nor biology were on her side. Because the whole reason Karleen had ended up with the three husbands—not to mention an appalling number of "gap guys" in between—was her complete and total inability to resist a handsome, sweet-talking, testosterone-drenched male. Especially considering her very healthy sex drive. Which had been sorely neglected for far longer than she'd thought was even possible.

Yeah, it was definitely easier to keep replacing the hamsters. But now she wondered if her singlehood had less to do with any resolve on her part and more to a lack of any real temptation.

And that, she decided as the sun continued its relentless ascent, must've been why Mr. My-Mouth-Says-One-Thing-but-My-Eyes-Are-Saying-Something-Else-Entirely had moved in next door. You know, to test her. See if all her talk about reforming was only so much hot air. Still, maybe she couldn't undo the past, but she sure as heck could learn from it. Although the neglected-sex-drive thing could be a problem.

Especially if it got too close to Troy's neglected-sex-drive thing.

Karleen kicked off the wadded-up floral sheets and

dragged herself out of bed, tugging at her boxer pj bottoms as she padded to the bathroom. Her cheek was creased, her eyes were puffy and her hair stuck up around her head like it'd been goosed. Lovely. She grabbed her toothbrush and squeezed out enough toothpaste for an elephant—

Wait. Was that a knock? She stepped out of the bathroom, toothbrush in mouth.

Rap, rap, rap.

Karleen quickly spit and grabbed her robe, yelling, "Who is it?" as she stomped down the hall, pulling the sash tight. One of these days she was really going to have to do something about fixing the doorbell—

"It's Troy," came from outside.

She made a silent Lucille Ball face, rammed her hands through her nutso hair and opened the door. And yep, there he was, even taller and more solid and—dammit—cuter than she remembered. And here she was, looking like a half-molted canary with overachieving hooters. The Volvo was parked in her driveway, full of twins. Who both waved to her, the little buggers. She waved back.

"Oh, hell," the father of the twins said, "did I wake you?"

"Uh-uh," she said, yawning, searching his face for signs of revulsion. Revulsion would be good. Revulsion had a way of dampening libidos. And things.

"Sorry to bother you," Troy said, not looking terribly revulsed, "but I've got a huge favor to ask…no! Not to take the kids," he said when her eyes darted back to his car. "But I've got an appointment to check out the Bosque View Pre-school and the Home Depot guys were supposed to deliver the new washer/dryer this afternoon, only they called about five minutes ago and said they were coming this morning instead, and I don't know if I'll be back by the time they get here. So I wondering if you could possibly let them in…?"

Then a breeze made her shiver, and two layers of thin jersey were no match for the Twin Peaks on her chest, and Troy didn't even try to avert his gaze and Karleen didn't even try to pretend not to notice, and his eyes lifted to hers and things got real quiet for several seconds while everybody contemplated what was going on here.

"It's—" She cleared the dozen or so frogs out of her throat. "It's okay, scandalizing the Home Depot deliverymen isn't on my list this morning," she said, and he said, "Their loss," and she said, "I don't have any appointments until after lunch, so it shouldn't be a problem."

Silence. Then: "You're a lifesaver."

"So I've been told," she said, and they stared at each other until one of the kids yelled, "Dad-*deeee!*" and Troy seemed to shudder back from wherever men go when their blood has shifted south and said, "I just didn't want to rush things. Checking out the school, I mean."

He glanced back at the boys, totally reverted to Daddy-mode. The mixture of worry and adoration in his expression made her tummy flutter. Or maybe that was hunger. Then his gaze returned to hers. Nope. Not hunger. Not that kind, anyway. "This will be their third day-care situation in six months," he said, reeking of guilt. "I'm hoping this one will be the last until they start kindergarten. They've been real troupers, but I know it's been rough on them, constantly having their routine disrupted."

A philosophy to which Karleen's mother had obviously not subscribed, she thought bitterly.

"Did you say Bosque View?" she now said. "Joanna's got her youngest there, he loves it. If that makes you feel any better."

"It does. It sucks, being the new guy in town."

Tell me about it, she thought as Troy dug a house key

out of his pocket and handed it over. "I've left a note on the door that you'll let them in," he said, backing away. "The machines go in the garage," he called out, then ducked behind the wheel, and she waved, and then they were gone and she stared at the Troy-warmed key in her hand and felt that wildfire about to singe her pj bottoms right off her butt.

The Home Depot truck was still in Troy's driveway when he returned, sans children, around ten. Meaning that, he presumed, Karleen was still there, as well.

One of those good news, bad news kind of things.

Troy sat in the car for a good ten seconds, his chin crunched in his palm, mentally ticking off all the reasons why he needed to get over this idiotic attraction to the woman. Why acting on some chemically induced urging was pointless. If not downright stupid.

He glanced back at her pinwheel-and-stone-critter-infested front yard. The plastic roses stuck incongruously along the base of the front porch. The birdhouses. The five million sparkly, twirly things dangling from her porch. And he shuddered. Mightily.

Then he remembered the sight of her fresh out of bed this morning, all rumple-haired and makeup-free, her sleep-graveled voice, and he shuddered again. Even more mightily.

Okay, he thought, getting out of the car and slamming shut the door, so she was cute and sexy and helpful, and she wasn't holding silver crosses up in front of the kids, but he didn't know anything about her, except for her penchant for excessive lawn ornamentation and that caution muddied her eyes. And besides, she wasn't interested, he wasn't interested (okay, so he was interested, just not that interested), end of discussion, case closed.

He could do this, he thought as he walked inside his open garage and through the maze of boxes and crap he'd yet to figure out what to do with, and there was Karleen, in some kind of flippy little skirt and a soft, hip-grazing sweater practically the color of her skin, and she was wearing a pair of backless, high-heeled shoes that were like sex on a stick, pink ones, with glittery, poufy stuff across the toes, and his mouth went dry. She looked about as substantial as cotton candy.

Only five times tastier.

And she was clearly driving the poor, mountainesque delivery guy insane as she made him put both machines through their paces.

"Okay," she said as she took the clipboard from him, "I just wanted to be sure, because the last time I got a new washer—not from y'all, but I'm just saying—they didn't hook it up right and I ended up with a lake on my garage floor…. Oh! Troy! You're back! Sign," she said, thrusting the clipboard at him. And that first, full impact of her perfume, the vulnerability trembling at the edges of her self-confidence, nearly shorted out his brain.

He gave the machines a cursory glance to make sure they were indeed the ones he'd bought before scribbling his signature on the bottom of the form. The delivery guy tore off his receipt, said, "Have a good one," and lumbered off, leaving Troy staring at a pair of control panels clearly modeled after the space shuttle.

Karleen stepped up beside him, her arms crossed. Her perfume nanny-boo-boo'd him. Her still hanging around confused the hell out of him. Way too many whys and whatchagonnadoaboutits floating around for his comfort. Then she reached out and—there was no other word for it—caressed the front of the washer, sliding two fingers along the smooth, cool porcelain edge, and Troy's mind went blank.

"I hate to admit this," she said on a soft rush of air, "but I am having serious appliance envy. My washer's one step up from a rock in the river."

"Right now," Troy said, forcing his attention to the gleaming white appliances in front of him and away from the fragrant blonde at his elbow, "a rock in the river isn't looking half-bad."

He could feel her bemused, incredulous stare. "Please don't tell me you've never used a washer before."

"Only three times a week for the past four years," he muttered. "But believe me, my expertise begins and ends with shove clothes in, dump in detergent, turn machine on, take clothes out." He squinted at the panel. "I'm guessing I'll never have to use the delicate cycle."

"Not unless you've got silk boxers."

"Uh...no."

She giggled, and his insides flipped. "Stick with normal and you'll probably be okay."

"Always been my motto," he said, and turned, and she was far too close, and it had been far too long, and it was far, *far* too soon to be feeling this far gone.

"How come you're still here?" he asked softly, and her gaze flicked to his before she shrugged. Just one shoulder. Sadness radiated from her like sound waves.

"Where're the kids?" she asked.

"Still at the school." Troy leaned one hip against the dryer, his arms folded over his chest. Watching her not looking at him. Trying like hell to figure out what was going on here. "They wanted to stay for a little while, so I'm picking them up after lunch. If all goes well, they'll start full-time on Monday. It seems like a great place."

Another quick glance. A small smile. "Feel better now?"

"A bit. It's a challenge, doing this on my own. I worry constantly about whether I'm making the right choice."

Her silence enfolded him, half soothing, half unnerving. "At least you *do* worry about them."

"That's what parents do."

"Not all parents," she said, the sadness turning more acidic. Without thinking, he slipped his hand around hers. Her head jerked up, her eyes wide. But not, he thought, particularly surprised.

"Thanks," he whispered, frozen, staring at her mouth. "For, you know. Being here."

"No problem," she said, equally frozen, staring at him staring at her mouth. "Um…don't take this the wrong way, but are you thinkin' about kissing me?"

"Don't take this the wrong way, but I'm thinking about doing a lot more than kissing."

Outside, birds twittered, breezes blew, gas prices continued to yo-yo. Inside, life-altering decisions hovered on the brink of being made.

"What happened to just wanting to *talk?*" Karleen finally said.

"Apparently, I've moved on."

The planet hurtled another few thousand miles through space before Karleen at last lifted her hand to trace one long, pale fingernail down his shirt placket.

"So I guess this means we're gonna have sex."

Somewhere, way in the back of his buzzing brain, Troy heard a resignation in her voice that, under other circumstances, might have tripped his sympathy trigger. At the moment, however, the safety on that particular trigger was firmly in place.

As opposed to other triggers, which were cocked and very, very ready.

"That's bad, isn't it?" he said. Still not moving. Away, at any rate.

"It sure as heck isn't good."

"Because…of everything you said." He lifted one hand, cupping her neck. Her breathing went all shaky. So did his.

"Uh-huh." She made a funny little sound in her throat when he touched his lips to her forehead.

"One of us should walk away," he whispered into her hair, which was a lot softer than he'd expected.

"I know," she said, and tilted her head back, and he lowered his mouth to hers, and his entire body sighed in relief, as though he'd been waiting for this moment for five years instead of five days. He knew it was wrong and foolish and pointless and he didn't care, didn't give a damn about anything except that brief shudder of surrender when their mouths met, the soft heat of her tongue against his, the softer, hotter press of her breasts against his chest. And, of course, the ever-popular collision of her pelvis against the aforementioned good-to-go trigger.

In fact, he was enjoying the whole kissing-pressing-colliding thing so much, it took a while before it sank in exactly where all this kissing and pressing and colliding was going on.

"For the record," he said, "I don't generally go around seducing women in my garage. Especially ones I've only known for less than a week."

"Somehow," she said, trickling her fingers down his arms, "I knew that."

His pulse thudding nicely in several crucial pressure points in his body, he took her face in his hands. "So how come you're *not* walking away?"

"Because…" Six inches from his face, her breasts rose as she sighed. "I guess I figure, since you have moved on, you may as well do that moving on with me."

"O-kay…" Troy shook his head, but the ringing was still there. "But why?"

Karleen linked her hands around his neck, toying with the bristly hair at the nape, and little flickers of happiness erupted all over his skin. "Because I can handle this for what it is—a man who's gone without for too long who needs…an outlet. Somebody to take the edge off, to ease you back into things." She shrugged, and the little flickers flickered more earnestly. "The way I see it, I'm actually doing the women of Albuquerque a favor. So when you go out there for real, you'll be able to see what you're actually looking for without sex cloudin' your brain."

She had a point. Except that, as murky as things definitely were in the old gray matter, he wasn't so far gone that he didn't catch the *tiniest* hint of self-deprecation in her voice. "How…altruistic of you," he said, letting his hands slide down to cup her sweet little backside.

She snorted. "Not exactly. Because it's been a while for me, too, so I'm not gonna lie, I want this as bad as you do. But, see, I'm not lookin' for anything serious, and you're not lookin' for somebody like me—and don't deny it, you know it's true—so this way, we both get what we need out of the deal. And anyway, we could both tiptoe around this thing for God knows how long until one or the other of us combusts…" Her gaze lowered to his neck, which she stood on tiptoe to—oh, *man*—lick. "Or," she murmured, her breath cooling the moist spot, "we could get this out of the way and be done with it."

He gripped her ribs, bringing her startled gaze up to his.

"I'm overdue. Not desperate. Trust me, there's not going to be anything *quick* about this."

One eyebrow arched before, slowly, her mouth stretched into a smile that was pure challenge.

"Guess we'll have to see about that," she said, then took him by the hand and led him back to her house, as his garage door groaned closed behind them.

Chapter Four

If nothing else, nobody could accuse Karleen of not being able to think fast on her feet.

Because, even after Troy'd kissed her, and her blood had gone all syrupy in her veins, she'd realized she was in far more control of the situation than she'd expected to be. Or that she'd ever been before. That she could have walked away, if she'd wanted to. And that her *not* wanting to had nothing to do with her being powerless, or weak, or over-sexed; it had to do with realizing she had a duty to pry open this guy's eyes before things got out of hand.

Because, she thought as clothes flew about her bed-room, once they got over the momentary sex crazies, he'd remember his mission, which was all about finding someone to share the rest of his life with. And Lord knew, that wasn't gonna be her—

Mouths crashed, tongues tangled, bedsprings creaked

as they fell backward onto the unmade bed she'd pulled together only an hour before.

—because, see, she'd taken a little peek into his house while she'd waited for the Home Depot guys. Not that she'd gone upstairs or done any serious snooping or anything, only enough to confirm what she'd pretty much figured, which was that Troy Lindquist liked things safe and predictable and traditional to the point of mind-numbing. Lots of browns and beiges and tans, relieved by the occasional splash of navy-blue. She wouldn't last five minutes. So she figured—

"Condoms, top drawer," she murmured when he unhooked the front clasp to her bra, but he said, "Thanks, but I'm in no hurry."

—she, uh, figured…where was she? Oh, right. She figured one good look at her place would pretty much wipe the goony look right off his face. Although it might take a while before he noticed much of anything except what was going on between them right at the moment, men not being generally known for their ability to multitask. In fact, right now, all he was getting a good look at were her breasts. With, it pained her to notice, an expression not dissimilar to the one he'd been giving the washer control panel a little while ago.

Oh, hell. He knows.

Karleen straddled him, still in her pale pink embroidered silk high-cuts. Then she leaned over (shyness in these situations having not been an issue for a very long time), knowing the hazy sunlight filtered through the lace curtains showed the darlings off to perfection. "I got the good ones," she said. "Trust me, they won't leak, deflate or pop."

Troy frowned. "Are you sure?"

"Oh, for pity's sake—" She grabbed his hand, planting it on her boob. His mouth pulled into a *not bad* expression before he tentatively gave it a little squeeze, and she went slightly cross-eyed.

"So…I'm guessing you can feel that?"

"Of course I can feel that, I'm not a blow-up doll. Think of this like…booster seats for breasts. The same, just taller. So could we please get on with it?"

He laughed. And cupped the other breast, flicking his thumbs over her nipples, and it was like first sinking into a warm bath. With candlelight. And Elvis crooning "Love Me Tender" in the background. "What's the rush? I'm having fun—" clearly getting into things now, he moved on to light plucking "—right here." He grinned. "Aren't you?"

"Mmm, yeah." Hissed breath. "But we only have an hour."

"Oh, honey," he said, flipping her onto her back, "you'd be amazed what I can accomplish in an hour."

"You bragging?"

"No. Warning." Troy shifted to lean his head in his hand, circling one nipple with his knuckle. "I have to admit, they're very pretty."

Karleen started to look down again, only to remember she got a terrible double chin when she did that. "They should be, considering how much they set Nate back," she said, and he laughed and tugged her in for another kiss. And oh, my, the man could kiss, like he wanted to get to know each nerve ending one at a time…and then he started on a lazy, meandering journey, nibbling and kissing and licking and sucking his way up…and down…first one rarely explored back road…then another…and another…

And she thought, *Hmm, not what I expected,* and from somewhere down by her knees, he said, "Why are you so tense?" which of course tensed her, even as she said, "I am not!" and he chuckled and moved up, stroking the insides of her thighs, cupping her bottom, lowering his mouth, and she was gone.

"Not tense now," she said a minute later, and he said, "Where are those condoms again?" and she limply flailed one arm toward her nightstand, vaguely considering when she'd last restocked. Although she didn't suppose it was that big a deal, since she seriously doubted disease was an issue and she'd just finished her period a week ago and besides, nothing had ever happened before....

Then Troy grinned, and she thought, *What now?* and he sat up, settling her in his lap, filling her to somewhere around her eyeballs, and she gasped, startled, even though by rights she should have been way past being startled. But the skin-to-skin was good, *he* was so good, his gentleness breaking her heart, bringing unexpected tears to her eyes.

And they stilled, him inside her, her surrounding him, each reflected in the other's eyes, and she thought, *I don't even know this man,* and he wrapped her up tight, and she felt safe, and thought, *Damn.*

He moved, still gently, still pushing, and she pushed back, not so gently, and they didn't so much find their rhythm as it swallowed them alive, swallowed up everything, everyone, that had come before. She hung on like she was almost afraid of being thrown, as the sweetness built and built and built and *built*....

Karleen arched, cried out, collapsed...and he tangled his fingers in her hair and brought their mouths together in a hard, fierce kiss, all the nerve cells colliding in a victory rumble, and another shudder of need ghosted through her, like the gradually diminishing thunder from a finished storm. Then she carefully lifted herself off, and after he got up to take care of business, she wrapped the sheet around herself, oddly self-conscious, although she could not have said why.

Well, that was different, she thought, although she couldn't pinpoint that, either.

And for sure there was nothing even remotely Muzak about the way the man made love, a thought that sent a shiny, tender green garden snake of regret slithering through her, that they wouldn't be doing this again.

Sitting tangled up in her sheets, she watched Troy—not a drop of self-consciousness in his veins, obviously—stroll back to the bed, naked as the day he was born and with a look on his face like he was half contemplating jumping up on something and beating his chest. Brother.

He sat beside her, slinging one arm around her shoulders and tugging her close to rest his cheek in her hair. "Thank you," he whispered, and Karleen heard herself ask, "What was your wife's name?"

Being sensitive was one thing. Clairvoyance was something else entirely. So while Troy had pretty much figured out that Karleen's tough-girl persona was so much BS, he had no clue what was behind it. So he'd watched, in the reflection from her bathroom mirror, as she'd pulled that sheet around herself, seen an almost pained confusion crumple her features, thinking, *What the hell?*

Then she'd asked about Amy and he thought, *Ah.* He planted a kiss in her messed-up hair. "I'm not comparing you."

"I didn't think you were," she said, predictably stiffening. Then, also predictably, she got up, mincing across the room like a character from *The Mikado* to perch on the end of a wicker chair covered in a leopard-print cushion.

In front of a window crowned in a poofy, purple valance.

Beside a small table on which crystal teardrops winked below the fluffy feather edging on the ugliest lampshade on the tackiest lamp in the known universe.

Sun catchers of every variety dotted her windows; on every surface, crystal figurines shared space with cutsy, overdecorated…stuff. And as the postcoital fog lifted, it began to register than the inside of Karleen's house was no less insane than the outside. The woman's penchant for tchotchkes knew no bounds.

"And I'm not asking because of what we just did," she said, tucking her feet up under her, hugging her pride close, and Troy's bric-a-bracaphobia eased off. Slightly. "I'm asking because in all likelihood we'll be living next door to each other for a while, and it would seem weird *not* to know her name. That's all."

Troy glanced at the clock by her bed. Only twenty minutes before he had to go pick up the boys. "Amy," he said, grabbing his boxers off the floor.

"You two had a good marriage?"

As annoyed as he was for her dragging his dead wife's ghost into their afterglow, Troy's chest still clenched at the wistfulness bleeding through the weak spots of her nonchalance. He pulled on the boxers, then his jeans. "Yeah. We did."

"How long were you married?"

He glared at her. "Is this your way of pushing me away?"

A slight smile curved her mouth. "How long?"

"Nine years," he said, shrugging into his shirt. Trying to shrug off oddly hurt feelings.

"Wow," Karleen said, bracing her feet on the edge of the chair to hug her knees. "That's longer than all three of my marriages put together. So," she continued before he could comment, "you must've been pretty young when you met?"

"Junior year of college. We didn't get married until we were twenty-five, though."

"How come you waited so long?"

Troy focused on his shirt buttons, his hands not as steady as he'd like. "According to Amy, she was ready by the time we graduated. Took me a little longer to catch up. Or catch on."

"What was she like?"

"Karleen—"

"Please?"

He jammed the tails of his shirt into his pants. "Tall. Light-brown hair. Blue eyes—"

"I'm not talking about what she looked like."

No, he didn't think so. "Four years, I've struggled to forget. And now you—"

"I know what I'm doing," she said, a hard-edged intelligence standing firm in her eyes, and Troy blew out a breath, then thought, his brow crumpled.

"She was…incredibly calm. Very little ruffled her. Probably because she was about the most together, organized person I've ever known. She didn't like leaving anything to chance, if she could help it. And she hated clutter. A dish left in the sink drove her nuts."

"But in a calm way."

His lips twitched. "Yes. In a calm way."

Karleen's expression didn't change. "What was her favorite color?"

Weird question, but what the hell. "Blue," he said. "But not just any blue, this kind of gray-blue. Like…" He looked around the room, but there was nothing in here even remotely close. So he shrugged.

"She get along with your folks?"

"They adored her. And they were wrecked when…"

"She died?"

"Yeah."

"What happened?"

Although as gentle as what he'd always imagined an angel's touch would feel like, her words knocked the stuffing out of him. And the resistance. Because most people were far too uncomfortable asking about things such as how a person's wife died, so if they didn't already know, they never asked. Troy sat on the edge of her bed— whoever thought foot-wide lavender roses were attractive should be shot—to tie his shoes, but by now his hands were full-out shaking.

"Something went wrong when the boys were born," he said, amazed that he could say the words without feeling as though his chest would cave in. "During the C-section." He took a deep breath and looked across the room at the first woman he'd made love to since his wife's death, trying to wrap his head around the significance of that milestone. "Amy died barely a week later."

He saw Karleen's eyes fill with tears, felt his own sting in response. "How on earth did you get through that?"

"For a long time, I wasn't sure I would. Forget day by day, it was all I could do to get through one minute at a time. But I had two babies who needed me. They wouldn't let me give up. Neither would my family. Or my friends." He looked up at her. "A lot of people thought I should sue."

"But you didn't."

"What would have been the point? To drag an already wrecked doctor—someone we'd known for years, one of the best in her field—through the mud? Yeah, I was a mess, and I was angry, too angry to understand anything they were saying at first. And hurting way too much to be even remotely objective about any of it. There I was, caught in the middle between the hospital needing to cover its butt and everybody insisting somebody needed to 'pay.' Hell, during those first few days, *I* wanted somebody to pay, too. Out of the blue, my wife was dead. You just don't accept something like that, something that makes no sense whatsoever."

Troy yanked the second lace tight, then dropped his foot to the floor. "But the fact is, life doesn't always make sense. And sometimes things go wrong. Even during a supposedly 'routine' procedure." He lifted his eyes to her. "Was I nuts, not going forward with the suit?"

Why had he asked that? Why had he asked *her?*

After a long, assessing moment, she said, "I doubt most people would've have been that noble."

"Believe me, this wasn't about being noble, it was about preserving what little sanity I had left. Money wasn't going to turn back the clock, and I couldn't see wallowing in all that negativity and bitterness for God knows how many years when I had two little boys to raise and a business to keep going. Speaking of whom…" He stood, feeling hideously awkward. "I need to go get them."

"Right." Karleen struggled to her feet as well, where they stood half a room apart, eyeing each other. Until Karleen broke the silence. "Please don't feel you have to say anything. This was what it was, nothing more."

"A one-time thing, you mean."

"That's what we agreed on."

After a moment of careful weighing, Troy said, "That was before," but she shook her head.

"Nothing's changed," she said softly. "Neither one of us is interested in going down some dead-end road. Which is what this would be. Not that I didn't thoroughly enjoy being the one to get you back in the saddle, but that's it."

"You're sure?"

"Positive. I still don't want to get involved. And you know full well you don't really want to get involved with *me*. Be honest, Troy. Because that's all we've got going for us. Bein' honest with each other."

The honesty of their recent lovemaking still imprinted in his memory, his reawakened libido, Troy glanced around, at the animal prints, the bilious floral sheets, the atrocious lamp. "We could—"

"No. We couldn't."

Troy watched her for a long moment, standing there all flushed and cocooned in her sheet, her sparkly toes peeking out from the folds puddled around her feet, and he knew she was right, that he wasn't interested in some dead-end road, and that continuing the affair—as tempting as the idea was—would only interrupt his quest to find someone who would fit in with his life, not agitate the hell out of it.

He walked over to her, though, clasping her bare, warm shoulders in his palms, leaning over to kiss her open-mouthed, long enough to—hopefully—get the point across exactly how much the morning's activities had meant to him. How much he genuinely appreciated—no, *liked*—her, even if he knew it would never work out.

Then he walked away before he could change his mind.

Hours later, however, as Troy hacked the heck out of the rangy lilac bush at the corner of the house and the boys *vroomed-vroomed* their Tonkas in a patch of dirt on the other side of the yard, he found himself in a very sour mood, indeed. Physically, he was feeling no pain. Emotionally was something else again.

Why, *why,* couldn't he have been born a callous bastard who could simply get his jollies and then walk away without a backward glance?

True, he hadn't put that chronic wariness in her eyes. Nor was it up to him to remove it. But it went against his nature, turning his back on something broken.

Even if he didn't have the right tools to get the job done.

He glanced up at the hum of a sleek, sand-colored minivan pulling into Karleen's driveway; a minute later, a redheaded, hippie elf climbed out, her wooden-soled clogs crunching into the gravel, her body lost in her billowy denim dress. As she bent over to spring an equally redheaded little boy from his car seat in the back, Troy caught a glimpse of crazily patterned socks.

Baby elf in hand, Mama Elf headed toward Karleen's front door. Like magic, the twins appeared at his side.

"Who's that?" Grady asked.

"Have no idea," Troy said, yanking a clipped branch out from the tangle. "They weren't exactly wearing name tags."

"They're coming over," Scotty said, as the woman yelled, "Hello?"

Troy looked over to see her standing and waving on the other side of the post-and-rail fence. "Damn." Both boys scowled at him. "Sorry," Troy mumbled, grabbing his T-shirt off the grass and wiping his face and chest with it so he wouldn't gross out the poor woman.

Underneath a thousand crazy curls, green eyes flicked over his torso before veering back up to his face. Not an elf, he decided: a Raggedy Ann doll. "Hi, I'm Joanna, Karleen's friend? She asked me to come over, only she isn't home. You wouldn't know where she is, by any chance?"

"'Fraid not." *Joanna, Joanna...* Why did that name sound familiar? "I, um, saw her drive off earlier, but that's all I know."

"Oh." The redhead flashed him a quick smile. A smile, Troy thought (hoped?), devoid of suspicion and/or curiosity. "Okay, guess I'll have to wait for a bit. What is it, honey?" she said to the little boy, who was tugging at her skirt.

"They gots trucks." He pointed. "C'n I play wif 'em?"

Grady immediately ran down to a wide spot in the fence and beckoned. "You can crawl through here!"

"Oh, Chance, honey—"

"It's okay," Troy said, smiling. "You can wait here, too, if you like. I'm Troy, by the way."

"Yes, I know. Karleen mentioned you. And your boys." Clutching fistfuls of fabric, she climbed over the fence with the grace of a woman used to chasing small boys, losing a clog in the process. As she wriggled her foot back into it, the light dawned.

"You're the Joanna whose boy is at Bosque, right?"

"That would be me." She tromped over the grass beside him. "Are you sending yours there?"

"Probably. They had a test run this morning." *While I was shagging your best friend.* "It seems like a really nice place," he said, hoping she'd think his flush was due to exertion and sun.

"It is. Chance loves it. Your two must be around the same age?"

"They turned four right before Christmas. Yours?"

"Three and a half." They'd reached the portal, where Joanna plopped down on the edge, yanking the dress to her ankles before turning a very warm, but completely unthreatening, smile on him. "My other kids are all much older, and they're usually with their father on the weekends. So other than when he's at school, Chance doesn't get much opportunity to play with kids his own age. Especially boys." She chuckled, nodding toward the three, all shoving around trucks in the dirt. When she linked her hands over her knees, a very impressive diamond and wedding band flashed on a short-nailed, sort-of chewed-up-looking left hand. "He's in heaven."

Troy smiled back, then remembered his manners. "Can I get you something to drink…?"

"Oh, no, I'm fine. And don't let me keep you from whatever you were doing, I'm sure Kar will be along soon." Troy picked up the clippers as Joanna said, "Her appointments sometimes go longer than she expects them to."

"She said she was a personal shopper?"

"Do I detect a note of incredulity in your question?"

"Not a bit of it."

That got a laugh. A shaft of sunlight caught in her wild red hair, slashed across her angular, makeup-free face. A pleasant-looking woman, but not what you'd call beautiful. "Kar's personal style might be a little out there, but she's got an uncanny knack for zeroing in on her clients' preferences. But then, that's just Kar," she said with a shrug. "She might come across as a bit on the prickly side from time to time, but deep down she's one of the most selfless people I know."

Troy grunted an acknowledgment, whacked another branch out of the lilac. Joanna went on.

"She started the business a few years ago. On a whim, really, shopping for my mother. An attorney. Loves clothes, hates to shop. Anyway, before Kar knew it, the whole thing mushroomed and now she has as much work as she can handle." From the other side of the yard, all three boys got to giggling about something; Joanna laughed softly. "I've got twin boys, too. I feel your pain."

Troy dropped the clippers, leaning over to grab a rake off the ground. "Same here," he said, smiling. Searching for something to say, he came up with "You've known Karleen for a while, I take it?"

"Since we were kids, actually. One of those strange things."

"Strange?"

"How we've remained so close, even though we're so different. I gave up trying to figure it out a long time ago." She paused, then said, "Kar's a good person. You could do a lot worse." When Troy's gaze darted to hers, she smiled and said, "For a neighbor, I mean."

Uh-huh. "She strikes me as the kind of person who doesn't take any crap off of anybody."

Joanna's brows lifted. "So you've talked to her?"

You should only know. "A couple of times." He shook the bush to loosen any stray pieces, then fixed his gaze on Karleen's *friend*. "Enough to know you're treading on very dangerous ground."

Joanna twinkled. "And from where I'm sitting, the risk is more than worth it. Oh! There she is!" she said as Karleen pulled up alongside the minivan in a valiantly shiny Toyota 4Runner that had been new three administrations ago. Joanna stood, brushing the back of her dress as she called her little boy.

All three kids ran over. "Does he hafta go?" Grady said, slinging a possessive, grubby arm around his new friend's shoulders.

"Yeah," Scotty piped up. "We're havin' fun!"

"I'm so sorry, sweeties, maybe another time—"

"Oh, let him stay for a while," Troy heard himself say. "We're not going anywhere, why not?"

"You sure?" she said as Karleen got out of her car, a small

pet-store box dangling from one hand. She was dressed in the same outfit he'd helped her remove earlier. Yeah, like he needed *that* particular memory prod. She probably would have walked straight into her house without acknowledging him, except she'd gotten distracted with glaring at Joanna. Troy instinctively took a step back from the redhead. Because, like riding a bike, some things you never forget.

Even if *somebody,* he thought, willing her gaze in his direction, seemed determined to keep that particular bike locked up good and tight from now on.

"Positive," he finally said, returning his attention to Joanna, who was doing the tennis-match head-swing thing between him and Karleen. "The boys could use some fresh blood. That is to say," he added, "somebody besides each other to play with."

On a yell, the boys took off again across the yard. Joanna grinned. "I knew what you meant. If he gets to be a pain, though," she said as she backed away, "just bring him over."

"Can I bring mine, too?" he said, and she glanced over her shoulder, laughing.

Karleen, however, was not laughing. In fact, Karleen looked ready to eviscerate anyone dumb enough to come within range of those claws of hers.

The very claws that had left marks on his back.

Damn. Instant recall was a bitch.

"Don't even give me that look," Joanna tossed at Karleen the minute they got inside her house. "What the hell was all that about?"

"What was what all about?" Marching straight back to her kitchen, Karleen set the PetSmart box on the counter. A tiny quivering nose peeked out from first one airhole, then another.

"The zippity-zap stuff between you and Troy. Outside. A second ago."

"Yeah, about that." Karleen batted that particular birdie right back over the net. "Getting a little chummy with my neighbor, weren't you?"

Since Joanna was blissfully married to her hunky baseball player, this wasn't about one woman encroaching on another's territory, and they both knew it. It was, however, about one woman sticking her cute little nose in where it most definitely did not belong.

"Oh, lighten up," Jo said, hitching herself up onto a bar stool. "You were late, and the boys took to Chance, so Troy invited me over to wait for you."

"No, you were early, since I'm right on time. *And* you have a key to my house!"

"Okay, so maybe I did get here a little early. They were out in the yard. I put out a few feelers. So sue me. You got any tea?"

"In the fridge. And you are so dead."

"Better dead than stupid," Jo said, sliding back off the stool to haul out the jug of sun tea from Karleen's twenty-year-old, the-icemaker-in-the-door's-just-for-looks refrigerator. "Holy catfish, that picture does not do the man justice. Besides which, he seems like a real sweetheart." Jo grabbed a glass out of the drainer and filled it. "One of those big, strong, protective Saint Bernard types. But less hairy. And I cannot believe you got another hamster."

Karleen took the pitcher of tea from her "friend"— at the moment, she wasn't so sure—and poured herself a glass. "Seeing as I've got all this hamster crap, it seemed a shame to not use it. And you're right, Troy's very nice."

"So I repeat, what was up between the two of you a minute ago?" Jo said, taking a sip of her tea.

Only to nearly choke on it when Karleen looked up at her, not even trying to keep the misery out of her eyes.

"Already?" Jo squeaked out. When Karleen nodded, Jo slammed her chin into the palm of her hand. "Jeez, Kar—that has to be some kind of record, even for you."

"Hey, you were the one who wanted me to get to know the guy."

"I was thinking more along the lines of, I don't know, inviting him and the kids over for lunch or something. At least *first*."

Karleen knocked back half her glass of tea, then picked up the hamster box, carrying it over to an elaborate series of tubes and chutes and multicolored plastic "rooms" in one corner of the breakfast nook. She popped open the box and lifted the soft, squirmy little critter out. She was blond and plump and Karleen was calling her Britney.

"It was a one-shot deal," she said, lowering Britney into her new home. The little animal speed-waddled from spot to spot, nose blurred in frantic excitement.

"Which you called, no doubt," Jo said.

Karleen latched the top to the cage. "It was mutual. Although I may have encouraged things to go in that direction. Or not, in this case."

"Because it was one of those sizzle-without-the-steak kind of things?"

One side of Karleen's mouth pulled up. "No."

"So let me get this straight," Jo said. "The guy's cute, nice, rich *and,* we now know, good in the sack." She frowned. "Am I missing something?"

Karleen walked over to her sink to finger the soil of the Philodendron That Ate Albuquerque threatening to take over the entire east wall of the room. From the sun catcher in the window, distorted rainbows danced over the striped leaves.

"Yeah. That it would never work."

"A conclusion you've come to after five days and one apparently noteworthy toss in the hay. Yeah, that makes perfect sense."

"And you, Joanna McConnaughy, are gettin' to be a real pain in the can."

"Only because I don't like what's happening to you. At all."

Karleen's head whipped around. "What's that supposed to mean?"

Jo stared at her tea glass so long Karleen briefly wondered if she'd imagined the comment. Until her friend finally hauled in a huge breath, then again lifted her eyes to Karleen. "Okay, when things fizzled between you and Nate, I understood why it took you a little longer to get your feet underneath you again. Still, I've never known you not to bounce back. Eventually. You'd take some time to lick your wounds, sure, but…" Jo's curls shuddered when she shook her head. "But over the past few years, it's like…you're losing altitude. Yeah, you're doing fine, with your job and everything, but…"

She glanced down, then back up. "When did the hope die, honey? When did you give up?"

Jo's words nearly knocked Karleen over. But not for long.

"The only thing I've *given up*," she said, her arms tightly folded over her quaking stomach, "is the idiotic notion that I can't function without a man. Took me long enough, but I finally got it through this thick head that it didn't work for my mother, and it didn't work for me, and the sooner I accepted that and got on with my life, the happier I'd be."

Not surprisingly, Jo didn't back down one iota. "Not needing a man…" She gave her a thumbs-up. "Turning your back on something potentially terrific…" The thumb emphatically jabbed toward the floor.

"Screw *potential*, Jo!" Karleen said, slamming down her glass. "This was sex! That's all! Just two adults relievin' a little pent-up tension. When I saw his house, heard him talk about his wife…" She shook her head. "Troy and I have absolutely nothin' in common. *Nothing*. And you of all people should know that being good together in bed does not a solid relationship make."

Jo made a face, but Karleen knew she couldn't argue, considering how her friend's first marriage, to a charming, sexy man who was still struggling with the concept of adulthood, had fared. Not that Troy was anything like Bobby, but the upshot was the same. Then Jo cocked her head, her brows drawn.

"He talked about his wife? While you two were…?"

"No! After. And I brought it up."

"God help me, but I have to ask…why?"

"Because my going-in-blind days are over. And besides, once we did that, it made it a lot easier for him to face facts. I know what you're thinking, that I cut this thing off at the knees before it even had a chance. But I prefer to think of it as, for once, avoiding the trap *before* getting caught. I'd call that progress, wouldn't you?"

Their gazes warred for several seconds before Jo slid off her stool, mumbling something about needing to get Chance.

Her arms crossed, her stomach churning, Karleen trailed her down the hall. But when Joanna reached the door, she turned and said, "It's only progress if you're moving forward, Kar. Treading water doesn't count."

Karleen yanked open the door. "And you know damn

well how long it's take me to feel like I'm actually in control of my life, and my choices. If you can't be happy for me about that, I'm sorry."

Worry crowding Joanna's eyes, she shook her head, then left.

Alone again, Karleen went to check on Britney, who was still snuffling around her new digs. At the sound of her cage being unlatched, the little furball sat up on her haunches, whiskers twitching. She didn't even try to get away when Karleen reached in to scoop her up, nestling her against her collarbone.

Yeah, she thought, stroking the tiny, trusting body with one finger, it really was better this way.

Chapter Five

"Daddy, how come we never see Karleen anymore?"

Troy wrestled the visor down to block out the overly cheerful early morning sun, glancing as he did into the rearview mirror at Scotty's screwed-up expression. "No real reason," he said levelly, returning his attention to the road. "Everybody got busy, I suppose."

"We're not," Grady said, which got an echoed, "Yeah, we're not," from his brother.

Waiting for the light to change, Troy rubbed his scratchy eyes—between still being half-asleep and a through-the-roof pollen count, he was surprised he could see at all—then let his wrist bang back onto the steering wheel. Two weeks since he'd slept with Karleen. Two weeks in which, between work and the house and the boys, he'd barely had five seconds to collect his thoughts. But in those five seconds, guess where those thoughts had wandered?

The light turned green; Troy pulled out onto the main drag. "Maybe. But you've both conked out right after dinner every night. And you went to play with Chance last weekend, remember? And we went to the zoo on Sunday?"

Silence ensued while they apparently pondered this. Four-year-olds' memories were bizarre things: Despite a million reminders, the boys couldn't remember to flush the toilet to save themselves, but they could call up details from their third birthday that Troy had long since expunged from the old data bank. So where the play date and field trip fit in, he had no idea. And where Karleen fit in, he had even less.

Ha. There was an understatement.

"When're we gonna get a dog?" Grady now asked.

Troy pulled up into the preschool's nearly full parking lot. "Soon," he said over the sound of slamming doors, harried parents' urging their kids to hurry up, the occasional wail of dissent. "Next couple of weeks, I promise."

"How long's that?"

"As long as…well, it's the same amount of time that we've been in the new house."

"*That* long?" Scotty said as Troy got out of the car, opened the back door. Both boys had already unhooked their car-seat latches; Troy had nearly had a cow when he'd discovered they knew how to spring themselves a couple of months ago (what one figured out, he was only too happy to share with his brother), but at least they didn't seem interested in performing their new trick when they were going seventy-five on the interstate.

"Okay, maybe this week," he said, which got dual squeals of glee from the two little boys, one dangling from each of Troy's hands as he guided them toward the school's door. Thank God *this* had worked out, was all he had to say.

As opposed to Karleen, who now avoided him like Ebola.

So he should be glad. That she'd let him go. Off the hook. Given him her blessing to go forth and date other women, put out an APB for the next Mrs. Lindquist.

So why wasn't he? Glad, dating, whatever.

He was still chewing this one over when, a half hour later, Blake knocked on Troy's half-open office door. Troy looked up from his computer.

"You're back."

"In all my glory," his partner said, sinking into the black, glove-leather chair in front of Troy's gleaming glass-topped desk. He squinted slightly from the glare coming from the giant picture window that framed sky, sprawl and the shadowed mountains at the city's eastern edge. Even though it was only eight-thirty in the morning, Blake was already loosening his tie. Still, compared with Troy's chamois shirt and jeans, his partner was dressed to the nines.

"Good trip?" Troy now asked, referring to Blake's two-week-long jaunt to personally check on their West Coast franchises. While they had eyes and ears aplenty to keep tabs on things, both men liked to keep a personal hand in the business they'd built up from a single little store selling handmade ice cream, back when they'd had no clue how high the odds had been stacked against them.

"Yep." His mouth stretched, Blake crossed his ankle over his knee and leaned back in the chair, his cheek propped on his knuckles. "Gave some of 'em a real thrill. Although not nearly as much of one as I get every time I pull up in front of one of the stores and realize, hey—that's *us*—"

Troy's direct line rang. Holding up one finger, he answered, only to feel his forehead knot. "No, Ray, I told you, I want to see the sketch for the new packaging before you go forward with the prototype…. I know, I know…just humor me, okay?"

He hung up, frowning at the phone for a moment.

"Ray's been designing our packaging since the beginning," Blake said mildly. "He hasn't steered us wrong yet."

"And it's our names behind the product. So since when did our input become optional?" Then he sighed and said, "You were saying?"

Blake eyed him for a moment, then said, "That it's good to be back. Although now I'm not so sure," he added, and Troy grunted. "I did miss the kids, though." He grinned. "And my wife."

Troy grunted again. As happy as he was that Blake and Cass had worked out their problems, right now Blake could take his domestic bliss and shove it. So naturally Blake asked, "Everything okay on the home front?"

Pretending he thought Blake meant the business, Troy said, "More or less. You see the new Web site?"

"I did. Looks real good."

"Yeah? I still think it's too cutsy, but I was overruled."

His partner flicked something off the heel of his boot, then looked at Troy again. "Marketing knows what it's doing, big guy," he said, then crossed his arms high on his chest. "But I wasn't talking about work."

And here Troy had been grateful that Blake hadn't brought up the subject—meaning, Karleen—since that first day. Actually, there'd been a time when neither one would have dared pry into the other's personal life beyond what was absolutely essential. Boundaries that, by some unspoken mutual consent, were fading more and more as time passed. Still, both men knew when to push, and when to let things ride. Judging from Blake's expression, he was in pushing mode.

Too bad for him.

"Things are fine," Troy said, returning his gaze to his computer screen, hoping Blake would get the hint.

"So you get cozy with your pretty new neighbor or what?"

So much for that. "I—or rather, the boys—invited her to have dinner with us the night we moved in," Troy said, not looking at Blake. Jocks in a locker room, they weren't. "She turned it—me, us, whatever—down."

"And that's it?"

Troy glanced over, then focused once more on the computer screen. "Well, let's see…she let in the delivery guys for my washer/dryer. And we had a chat over the back fence one morning, about maybe letting the boys have a little garden at one end of hers."

"Wow. Exciting stuff."

"We're neighbors, Blake. *Exciting* isn't part of the contract."

And you actually said that with a straight face.

Blake tapped his fingers on the desk. "She know you're rich?"

Troy shot him a look. "Excuse me?"

"You heard me." At Troy's snort of disgust, Blake said, "It's bait, that's all I'm saying—"

"And I hope to hell things haven't degenerated to the point where I have to wear a sandwich board advertising my net worth to get a woman to go out with me. But to answer your question…yes. She knows. Although not from me."

"Then how'd she find out?"

"Apparently we're plastered all over the Internet. Not our actual income, although I wouldn't be surprised if someone with sufficient know-how couldn't find that out, too. But I imagine once she saw I was CEO of AIS, it was a pretty short leap from there."

"And she *still* turned you down?"

"Yeah. Go figure."

More finger tapping. Then he said: "I'm disappointed in you, buddy."

"Hey. You said I should give it a shot. I shot. The target's out of range. End of story."

He could feel Blake's gaze on the side of his face for several seconds before the other man finally unfolded himself from the chair. "If you say so, buddy," he said, then zipped out of Troy's office before he could throw something at him.

The target, however, made a beeline for Troy the minute he pulled into his driveway that evening. Despite her agitated movement, her breasts remained immobile underneath a tight black tank top with—he could see as she got closer—"Grumpy Chick" spelled out in rhinestones. Judging from her expression, the shirt did not lie. Judging from how tight his jeans suddenly were—an unfortunate reaction to her also wearing short shorts—staying out of each other's paths had done nothing to dull the roughly five thousand extremely X-rated images that had instantly popped into his head.

And yes, at this point it was still mostly about the sex. Somewhere in the neighborhood of eight-five, ninety percent, he was guessing. Because he was male and not dead and he didn't know her well enough to override the hormones on a regular basis. Which was not to say the not-about-sex ten to fifteen percent wasn't making its voice heard, too. Her laugh, her wacky sense of humor, even her highly personal sense of style…he wasn't immune to those, by any means.

But mainly, it was about the sex.

Eventually, Troy realized her hands were full of mail.

His mail, apparently, if he read her gesticulations correctly. The second he turned off the engine, the boys were unlatched, out of the car and swarming the poor woman, yammering about the dog they did not yet own, their new school, was it time to plant the garden yet, and—oh, yes— how come she never came out in her yard anymore?

"I've haven't been around much, sweeties," she said, smiling but not touching them, he noticed (as far as Troy was concerned, they were like little magnets, but then, they were his kids). Then she tilted her head at Troy, now out of the car and standing in the driveway and looking down into her pretty, if grumpified, face. Her mouth, specifically. Speaking of magnets.

She held out the mail. "Yours," she said, then crossed her arms over the "Chick." "It was mixed up with mine. How on earth the carrier can screw up a street with four houses is beyond me."

"Thanks," he said, then yelled out to the boys to stay where he could see them as he strode back down the driveway to his mailbox. Which, yes, was empty.

"And what's this about a dog?" Karleen said as he walked back toward her, flipping through his mail. Nothing but the usual suspects, he mused, her words taking a second to penetrate. He glanced up, frowning.

"Is that a problem?"

"Not for me. Might be for the dog, though. Because the fence isn't secure?"

"Yeah, I'd thought about that. I'll probably build a large dog run along the other side of the yard."

She nodded. "What'd you have in mind? Kind of dog, I mean?"

"Something big the boys can't hurt."

That got a laugh, and Troy thought, *Oh, hell,* and

without thinking reached for her hand. "We need to figure this out," he said, and her eyes widened.

"There's no *this* to figure out. Which I thought we'd already discussed."

"I don't mean *that*," he said, nodding toward her house and all it represented. "I mean—" he dropped her hand, held up the mail "—*this*."

The space between her brows knotted. "Me bringin' over your mail?"

"Us being neighbors. Sharing a fence."

"Seems to me we're already doing that."

"No, what we're doing is avoiding each other."

"Not going out of my way to run into you's not the same as avoiding you."

On what planet? he thought, but all he said was, "Then why didn't you simply leave the mail in the box?"

"I—" Her gaze skittered away, as pink washed over her cheeks. "It didn't occur to me, okay? So don't go readin' more into it than there is."

"I'm not. Believe it or not, a repeat performance isn't my objective."

"Uh-huh."

"Well, okay, it's not like I'd turn it down. That strong, I'm not. But pretending each other doesn't exist…how is that a good thing?"

Karleen tucked a strand of hair behind her ear, making a face at the tops of her glittery, rope-soled shoes. Then, frowning, she looked back up at him. "Thought you were supposed to be lookin' for a wife?"

"Right now," he said, "I've got all I can handle looking for a dog. And anyway," he said when she chuckled again, "it shouldn't be a hunting expedition, you know? I mean, Amy…" He rubbed his mouth. "She was just *there*, and it felt right, so we ran with it. If it happened once, why couldn't it happen again?"

Two, three beats passed before she said, "I can't decide if that makes you real trusting, or lazier than all get out."

A smile stretched across his face, as he deliberately let his gaze meander from her mouth to her breasts, over the sliver of midriff peeking out above the waistband of her shorts, then back up. Behind her, her personal, miniature amusement park gyrated and twirled and sparkled in the breeze. "Oh," he said quietly, "I don't think anybody can accuse me of being *lazy.*"

To her immense credit—and his profound relief—she laughed again. "Lord, you are something else."

And in that moment, tenderness once again nudged aside lust, evening out the sex-to-other-stuff ratio a little more. "Karleen...obviously we don't know each other very well. And you have no reason to trust me. But you're safe with me. I swear."

One brow slid up underneath her bangs. "Exactly how do you figure that?"

"Because I miss more than sex."

She crossed her arms again, her mouth pulled down at the corners. "So what're you saying? That you want to be friends?"

"It's not unheard of."

A few feet away, the boys squealed at a lizard darting across the driveway. Karleen looked over, amusement and pain colliding in her eyes. "And if they start thinking of me in terms of Mama?" Her gaze touched his. "Then what?"

"Then I'll tell them how things stand, and they'll deal."

"And what if it's not *them* I'm worried about?" She waited until her words registered, then added, "Now do you understand?"

Troy watched her walk back to her house. Oddly, not even the sight of her adorable, taunting little rear end was enough to cheer him up.

Karleen peeked in on Britney, snoozing peacefully in a magenta tube, then took a last, mortifying check in the hall mirror before heading out for her morning appointments. Okay, that's it—the minute she got back home she was chucking all the chips and cookies and Little Debbie snacks in the trash before her butt qualified for its own zip code. Yeesh.

Once out the door, force of habit prompted her to glance over at Troy's driveway. It had been a week since his "What I really need is a friend" nonsense, but still. A girl couldn't be too cautious.

No car, no man, no kids, she thought on a relieved breath as a little voice whispered, *Um, isn't it a little late for* cautious?

She slid in behind the wheel and checked her mirrors, as she always did, then rearranged her boobs inside her too-tight push-up bra, which she'd been doing an awful lot lately. Maybe she should cut back on the Triscuits and cheese before bed, too.

Windows down, music blaring, she backed out of the driveway, wondering why she didn't feel more relaxed. Because clearly, Troy had gotten the message. Finally. Not that they were being stupid about it—they'd chat for a minute if they happened to pull up into the driveway at the same time, or wave to each other if they were both out in their backyards. And God knew she didn't have it in her to shut out the boys, who'd helped her plant the pumpkin garden over the weekend. Little Scotty, especially, who followed her around like a puppy, chattering nonstop. God, he was cute. But even with the baby Troys, she kept things light and casual, never mind that she itched so badly to hug the stuffing out of both of them, her heart hurt.

It was the giggling that most got her, though. She'd hear them going at it with Troy, out in his yard, and she'd well right up.

And what was with that, anyway? For heaven's sake, she'd practically helped raise Joanna's babies, but being around *them* never got the waterworks going. All she could figure was she was feeling extra tetchy these days on account of being so tired all the time. Which made no sense, because she was sleeping like the dead for nine or ten hours every night, and half the time needed a nap in the afternoon.

Anyway, whatever caused what, she'd been in no mood to listen to Aunt Inky's most recent sob story when she'd called earlier, ending with—big surprise—another plea for Karleen to "help her out," which would make the second time in less than a month and consequently set off every alarm Karleen possessed.

"Just until I get on my feet," Inky had sniffled into the line.

Only this time, Karleen somehow found the gumption to say, "Help you out, my fanny. *Bail* you out, is more like it. For pity's sake, you are fifty-three years old, it's high time you learn how to take care of *yourself!*"

And she would have slammed down the phone, if her aunt hadn't called Karleen on her cell. Slamming down a cell was generally not a good idea. Of course, Karleen knew by nightfall she'd be feeling all remorseful about being so mean to her aunt, who wasn't a bad person, only a weak one. And although on one level Karleen figured if *she'd* gotten over her dependency on men and found a way to support herself, in theory there was hope for pretty much anybody, she also knew everybody had to find their own path to salvation.

Except before a person can go down that path, their eyes have to be open to see it to begin with. And unfortunately, you couldn't pry another person's eyes open for them. Sad, but true.

From time to time, Karleen wondered what Troy's reaction would be to Aunt Inky. Not that this was something she needed to worry about, their ever meeting being highly unlikely. But somehow, Troy didn't strike her as the type of person to have an Aunt Inky in his family.

Halfway to her first appointment, she suddenly got so hungry she thought her stomach was going to turn inside out. Strange, because she'd had a good breakfast—eggs and fruit and toast—not two hours before. Up the road, a Blake's Lotaburger sign caught her eye, and her stomach started growling even louder. Even a Mickey D's would be better; at least they had salads. Although she knew this was one of those times when a salad wasn't gonna cut it, her spreading butt be damned.

"Lotaburger with green chili, large seasoned fries, chocolate shake," she called into the drive-through mike, then sagged back against the car cushion and thought, *What are you* doing?, only to jerk when the garbled voice told her to pull around to the window. She paid, then sat, chewing on a hangnail, at the window (at 10:30 in the morning, there was nobody behind her) practically snatching the white, heavenly scented bag out of the woman's hands and shoving a half-dozen hot, spicy fries into her mouth before she'd even pulled away. Five minutes later— if that—there was nothing left but a few shreds of lettuce and a couple of grease spots. She'd even eaten the onions, and she *hated* onions.

Unreal.

* * *

She'd coordinated the day's appointments so that all the morning ones were in the same large, downtown law firm where Glynnie Swann, Joanna's mother, worked. At the beginning, she wasn't sure who'd been more skeptical of her talents—the women or Karleen herself. But in the past seven years, her client list had grown to rather impressive proportions. By Albuquerque standards, at least, where "dressing up" like as not meant tossing on your Navajo silver with your denim and calling it a day.

Still, even here there were occasions where denim wouldn't work, and women with more money than time. Women who'd gladly pay somebody like Karleen to do their dirty work for them. God knows, being a personal shopper would never put her in the same league with Bill Gates or Oprah. But it was the perfect job for somebody who'd always envisioned heaven as a giant, never-ending mall where they always had "it" in your size and every store had a Half Off sign out in front. And the best thing was, all she'd needed to get started was a keen eye, common sense and a genuine ability to get along with almost anybody. Especially if the anybody was paying you a helluva lot more per hour than you'd ever make peddling burgers and fries.

So, most days she was pretty much convinced she was the luckiest woman in the world. Most days, it didn't bother her at all when one of her regulars rejected one of her suggestions, or when she didn't click with a new client. That was just the nature of the beast. Today, however, when her third appointment of the day—a newbie—was a total flop, Karleen found herself on the brink of tears as she stuffed a half-dozen outfits back into their vinyl shrouds.

"I'm sorry this didn't work out," the buxom brunette

said, thereby cutting off Karleen's offer to try again. Not that there'd be much point. The woman had hated everything. "Glynelle speaks so highly of you, I guess I just expected...more."

Thinking very un-Christian thoughts, Karleen hefted the bags off the portable rack she carried with her and fixed a smile to her face. "Don't worry about it," she said, laying the slippery bags across the small conference table in the corner and collapsing the rack.

The woman stood. "Well. I have your card." She extended her hand, so Karleen had to awkwardly shift everything to one arm in order to shake it. No offer to pay her for her time, she noticed. Yes, the first consultation was "free," but most clients were courteous enough to at least give her something for her efforts. Karleen briefly clasped the woman's hand—not even wincing when the wonker anniversary ring bit into her palm—then wrestled with bags, purse, rack and door for a good thirty seconds before finally making it out into the hall.

Which is when she realized she had to pee so badly she thought she'd pop. There was a public restroom at the end of the hall, but Glynnie's office was a lot closer. And, thank God, the door to her outer office was open, her secretary apparently at lunch. Karleen dumped everything on the reception-room sofa and rapped on Glynnie's door, nearly knocking the hummingbird-sized woman down when she opened it.

"Too much coffee, dear?" Jo's mother said when Karleen reemerged a minute later.

"Must've been." And damn, she was hungry again. "Sorry I dumped everything outside, this'll just take a sec...."

"Honey...are you okay?"

Karleen busied herself with setting up the rack so Glynnie wouldn't see her reddening face. From the moment Karleen had set foot in the Swanns' comfortable, stable house all those years ago, Glynnie had—to the best of her ability, at least—shouldered at least some of the burden Karleen's own mother had more or less abdicated to lethargy and booze. As busy as Jo's mama had been with her career and all, however, she'd barely had enough scraps left over for her own daughter, let alone some needy little stray Jo'd dragged home. And anyway, Karleen had learned a long time ago that while people might *say* they wanted you to feel you could open up to them, nine times out of ten they didn't really mean it. So while Karleen never doubted for a minute that Glynnie's concern was genuine, neither had she ever felt completely comfortable about dumping her problems on her best friend's mother.

"Yes, ma'am, I'm fine," she said, knowing Glynnie would be rolling her eyes at the *ma'am*, a habit she'd never been able to break Karleen of, even after twenty-five years. "I just…didn't sleep too well last night." *And my aunt is going to drive me insane and, oh, yeah, it's about my new neighbor who I slept with who's now stuck in my brain like a tick on a hound dog?* "And, well, it doesn't look like Doris Montoya's gonna work out."

The bags suspended from the rack, Glynnie had already unzipped one and removed the shell-pink suit from it. Karleen didn't miss the brief frown, but her first and best customer walked out to the middle of the reception area, holding up the suit under her chin to look at her reflection in the large, ornately framed mirror over the butter-colored leather sofa.

"I was afraid of that," Glynnie said on a sigh, masses of straight-from-the-bottle, strawberry-blond corkscrew curls quivering around her cheeks. "Doris isn't exactly known for being easygoing. But when she asked where I got the blue silk suit, and I told her about you, she insisted I give her your number. So I figured, what the hell..." She turned, still frowning, still clutching the suit to her chest. "You really think this color will work on me?"

"I really do. But don't take my word for it. Go try it on."

On a sigh, Glynnie vanished into her private bathroom, not bothering to shut the door all the way while she changed. "So. You and Jo still not talking to each other?" she called out.

Damn. Karleen knew there was a reason why she'd been dreading this meeting. She rubbed at the crease between her eyebrows that was going to become permanent if she wasn't careful. "Glynnie, you know I love you to pieces, but Jo's and my relationship isn't anybody's business but ours."

"Don't be ridiculous," came the disembodied voice, punctuated by the slither of fabric and an occasional soft grunt. "My daughter's been cranky as a witch with piles for the past three weeks. Which is the longest I can ever remember the two of you going without speaking. So the question is, who's going to tell her pride to take a hike first?"

She swung open the door. The suit fit like it had been custom tailored. But Glynnie's pale brows were still dipped over her little button nose.

"You still don't like it?" Karleen asked.

"What? Oh, the suit?" Glynnie gave a dismissive wave. "The suit's perfect. As usual." She glided over to the rack to paw through the offerings, selecting another suit, a dress and a charmeuse pants outfit in an eye-poppingly bright floral print, all of which she hauled back to the bathroom. "Jo misses you."

"I miss her, too, Glynnie," Karleen said softly, leaning against Glynnie's desk with her arms crossed. "But she overstepped the bounds of friendship."

"Meaning what?" floated out from the bathroom. "That

she said how things looked from where she was sitting and you took offense?"

Karleen bristled. "She told you what we talked about?"

"Only that she was worried about you, that she didn't like how you've changed. And I hate to say this," Glynnie said, sticking her head out the door, "but I have to agree with her. It's like you've made this nice, cozy little burrow for yourself where you've decided to spend the rest of your life."

"That is so not true!" Karleen cried as the redhead vanished again and an image of Britney plugged into her tube sprang to mind. "Y'all make it sound like I've become a total recluse! I get out! I do stuff!"

She heard what sounded like a snort. "Such as what? Shopping for a bunch of rich bitches? And don't take this the wrong way, sweetie—" out popped her head again "—but you look like hell on a bad day."

Karleen refused to rise to the bait. "Did you try on the pants outfit yet? I'm dyin' to see how you look in it."

Glynnie was far too shrewd not to know when she'd been purposely nudged—or in this case, shoved—off topic, but she sighed and ducked back inside. A minute later, she came out and did a graceful twirl.

Karleen pressed her hand to her chest. Except her boobs hurt so she removed it. "Oh, wow. It looks even better than I thought it would."

"It's gorgeous." Glynnie patted Karleen's cheek. "I can always count on you to make me look less like the sixty-year-old hag I am."

That, and enough Youth Dew to float a tanker. "Never happen, Glynnie. And never will." As opposed to Karleen's own mother, who before she'd died—at thirty-eight, only a year older than Karleen was now, she realized with a start—

had looked positively used up. In fact, when she'd taken her mother into the hospital that last time, the nurse had actually asked if the birth date on the chart had been a mistake.

"And for that," Glynnie said, disappearing into the washroom again, "I'll take the other suit and the dress, too. I love them all."

"I brought shoes, too."

"Shoes?" Jo's mama shot back into the room, handing the clothes to Karleen to rehang. "Where?"

"In the Dillard's bag."

Her face lit up like a kid's at Christmas, Glynnie sat on the edge of a flame-stitch chair, reverently lifting first a nude-colored, mesh-and-patent pump from its tissue-paper bed, then a pair of coppery sandals. "Ohhhh…I think I'm in love."

"They'd just gotten them in, and you know there's always only one pair of five-and-a-halves. So I grabbed them before anybody else could. I thought the light ones'd look good with the pink suit."

"You, sweetie, are a miracle," Glynnie said, then went behind her desk, pulling her handbag out of a bottom drawer to get her checkbook. Karleen laid the receipts for the clothes and shoes on her desk; after adding them up on her checkbook calculator, Glynnie looked at Karleen over the tops of her reading glasses. "And your hours?"

"Two. I swear," she said at Glynnie's raised brows. "Since I was shoppin' for three other people at the same time."

Glynnie nodded, then wrote out and handed over the check. Karleen frowned. "This is too much—"

"I added something extra to make up for Doris. The woman may be a crackerjack attorney, but she can pinch a penny hard enough to make snot come out of Lincoln's nose. She didn't pay you, did she?"

"Well, no, but…" At the other woman's glare, she tucked the check into her purse. "Thanks," she said, then involuntarily recoiled from the overpowering scent of Glynnie's perfume. Whew. She must have reapplied it after she'd changed back into her own clothes.

"Kar? What is it?"

"Nothing!" Somehow, she didn't think mentioning to her best client—not to mention her best friend's mother—that her Giorgio was about to make her hurl was a good idea. "Is it warm in here?"

Glynnie gave her an odd look, then said, "It is a bit stuffy, now that you mention it. Why don't we get out of here, go have some lunch? My treat."

At the mention of food, Karleen recoiled again, even as she was nearly overcome by the urge to strip a barbecued chicken clean in five seconds flat. Bizarre.

"I'd love to, but I've got more shopping to do for tomorrow's appointments. Maybe next time, okay?"

She gathered up the rack, the leftover dress bags from the Doris Montoya fiasco, her purse, and headed for the door, Glynnie following. When she got there, Jo's mother opened the door for her, then crushed Karleen and all her paraphernalia into a huge hug. Then she held her back, her hazel gaze both stern and kind. "I know it's never been easy for you to let other people worry about you, but there's nothing you can do to stop it. So deal."

At the unexpected expression of affection, Karleen got all choked up. Again. Honest to Pete.

"Thanks," she said, then beat a hasty retreat before she really gave Glynnie something to worry about.

By the time she finished up her shopping at five-thirty, she felt like she hadn't eaten in a week. But here was the weird thing: She'd fully intended on picking up something in the mall's food court, only she couldn't come within twenty feet of it without wanting to puke. How could she be so hungry and not be able to stand the smell of food?

Hopefully she could at least face the grocery store. As long as she stayed away from the deli section and the fried chicken, anyway. Yeah, yeah, shopping when you're hungry was a hugely bad idea, but oddly enough the moment she set foot inside the supermarket, all she wanted was good stuff. Veggies, fruits, whole grain bread. *Brown rice,* for God's sake. Meat, however…uh-uh. It was like that whole side of the store was giving off some sort of weird repelling vibes.

"Kar!"

In the midst of groping a cantaloupe, Karleen looked over to see Joanna rushing toward her, Chance in the cart's kiddie seat, happily gnawing on a bagel. His grin when he saw his "auntie"—not to mention the expression on Jo's face—twisted Karleen up inside. They hadn't been apart this long since Glynnie and Roger had taken Jo to Europe when she was sixteen.

The two women looked at each other for a moment before they both said, "I'm so sorry!" at the same time, then fell into each other's arms, babbling their apologies and earning them more than a few strange looks from other shoppers.

"God," Jo said after they pulled apart. She dug tissues out of her purse, taking one for herself and handing another to Karleen. "Are we the stupidest two women in the world or what?"

Karleen gave a soggy little laugh. "Your mother called you?"

"I'm betting before you'd reached the elevator. Although I'd already decided to put an end to this idiocy." Jo blew her own nose. "And of course I had no idea I'd find you here, I was planning on stopping by later. Or calling, or something."

"Yeah, me, too." Karleen dabbed underneath her eyes. God bless whoever thought up waterproof mascara, was all she had to say. "Sorry about being such a b—" She glanced at Chance, then back at Jo. "Brat."

"You had every right to be, I was totally out of line—"

"You were only bein' a friend. And I overreacted."

"I'm still worried about you."

"I know. But I swear, I'm not…" She swallowed. "I'm not sittin' all alone in the dark every night, gettin' hammered. If that's what you're worried about."

Jo's eyes went wide. "Is *that* what you thought I meant? Oh, God, honey…" She laid a hand on her wrist, shaking her head. "No way." Then, when Karleen nodded in acknowledgment, Joanna's eyes went all big again. This time, at the sight of Karleen's cart.

"Wow. Are you shopping for someone else?"

"No…what makes you say that?"

Jo picked up the rubber-banded bunch of asparagus. "You? Asparagus?"

"It looked good, what can I say?"

But Jo didn't stop there. "Broccoli? Apples? *Spinach?*" Her brow puckered, she lifted her eyes to Karleen. "Okay, spill. What's going on?"

Karleen ripped open the package of multi-grain bread in her cart and broke off a hunk, started to nibble on it. "Nothing's going on. Well, except that I've put on a few pounds so it occurred to me maybe I should start eating food with more nutrition and less calories. Only, you know what's weird? The past few days I've been *constantly* hungry. And yet most cooking smells make me feel icky."

She tore off another hunk of bread and stuffed it into her mouth, mumbling, "What?" around it as she chewed.

Jo was giving her the same weird look her mother had earlier. "Are you peeing like every five minutes?"

"Yeah, now that you mention it. Why?"

One eyebrow lifted.

A second later, Karleen sucked in a breath so hard she nearly choked on her bite of bread. "Oh, cra...er, crud. You don't think...?"

"I've been through it three times, Kar. Add swollen you-know-whats to the mix and I think you got yourself a real *bingo* there."

Feeling the blood drain from her face, Karleen clutched the handle of her cart before her knees gave way. "I can't...I couldn't... That's impossible, we, we used..." Another glance at the kid. "Something."

Joanna gave a short, dry laugh. "You know those twins that live at my house?" While Karleen stood there in total and complete shock, Joanna said gently, "It's been, what? Three weeks?"

"Closer to a month, actually."

"So you're late?"

"You know me, I've never been regular in my life.... Oh, Jo..." She turned what she knew were horrified eyes to her friend. "Do you really think I'm...?" The word lodged in her throat, like a dog not wanting its bath.

"The pharmacy's right over there, honey—"

"*Karleeeeeeen!*"

Karleen spun around to see Scott and Grady pinballing around the other customers, straight toward her.

Oh, Lord, not now...

Four little arms wrapped around her hips, nearly knocking her off balance. And she could decipher their mixed scents with the unerring accuracy of a parfumier's "nose," a blend of warm little boy and earth and baby shampoo and fabric softener and Play-Doh and Kool-Aid and—oh, yes—their father.

Who, wearing that expression of half-panicked relief common to all parents whose kids have disappeared for more than two seconds, was bearing down on the lot of them, his own cart piled high.

Oh, no. He'd been through this before. Would he be able to tell from her face that she was…you know? If she was, that is. Because maybe it was, well, something else. Some strange virus that made you ravenously hungry and gave you the nose of a bloodhound.

Troy's eyes met hers and panic sank its claws into the scruff of her neck.

"I'll see you later, guys," she said to the boys, peeling them off her legs. Then she took off, trusting Joanna to come up with something she wouldn't have to kill her for later.

Once home (after a quick side trip to Walgreens, since no way in hell was she gonna chance Troy's seeing her in the Smith's pharmacy), she lobbed the cold stuff into the refrigerator, then grabbed the pregnancy test and ran to the nearest bathroom. Her hands were shaking so badly she could hardly get the box open. No need to read the instructions, considering the number of "maybes" she'd had over the course of nine years and three marriages. All those years of *hoping,* of not doing anything to prevent getting pregnant and so much to make it happen. All those *Sorry, try agains*….

Lord, she was like Jell-O in a pair of mules.

She peed…. She held her breath…. She dared to look. *Congratulations!* the little pink line said. *You're a winner!* Karleen sank onto the toilet seat and burst into tears.

Chapter Six

Troy stared at the miserable woman perched on the edge of his sofa until the clanging in his head subsided enough to hear his own voice.

One slip. *One.* A single lousy (okay, not lousy) detour off the boringly straight, obsessively narrow track he'd followed for more than four years…

Why, God? WHY?

"You're sure?" he said. With remarkable calm, considering.

Not looking at him, Karleen smirked. "One test might lie, but I somehow doubt three would." She gave him what she probably thought was a brave smile. "You look like you could use a drink."

"I…no. Believe me, it wouldn't help."

He crossed to the window, although there was nothing to see in the pitch dark. The boys had been sound asleep for an hour. She'd called first to make sure, before she'd come over. And his gut had fisted then, at the tightness in her voice, as though she'd either been crying or was trying not to. The same way it had when she'd booked it out of the supermarket earlier.

"How long have you known?" His voice seemed to come from somewhere else, from some*one* else.

"Since about twenty minutes before I called you."

Troy faced her again, his heart breaking at her expression, even as it slammed against his ribs hard enough to bruise. Man, this sure wasn't anything like when Amy had told him she was pregnant. Not even remotely. He breathed deeply, trying to dilute the sick feeling. "So you didn't know in the store?"

That got a humorless laugh. "Not for sure. Although about a minute before you showed up I had a sudden inkling." Karleen's mouth flattened. It vaguely registered that she must have reapplied her lipstick before coming over. You had to hand it to a woman who had her priorities straight. "I'd been feeling strange for a few days, but I hadn't put two and two together until Jo…" She'd been leaning forward, completely still except for her incessant fidgeting with the stack of magazines on the coffee table in front of her. Now she tightly folded her arms over her middle. "Are you mad?"

He jerked. "*What?* No! Why would I be angry? And who with?"

"Me?"

"That's nuts, Karleen. Yeah, I'm a little poleaxed— okay, a *lot* poleaxed—but sleeping with you was my idea."

Her smile turned rueful. "Not entirely."

"Fine. Then either no one's to blame, or we both are. But getting mad isn't going to solve anything."

She gave him a brief, speculative look before her face disappeared into her palms and she mumbled, "This is freaking unbelievable."

"Guess the condom was faulty," he said, and she laughed again. Except it was about the saddest sound he'd ever heard. She dropped her hands, only to start messing with the magazines again, sorting them into new stacks based on no real method that Troy could see. Then she sighed.

"I tried and tried to get pregnant with each of my husbands," she said dully, "but it never happened. Something to do with my weird cycle. Every doctor I've gone to has said pretty much the same thing, that it wasn't impossible for me to get pregnant, only that it'd be harder for me than for most women. And that as I got older…" Another soft laugh. "Now I know what Sarah in the Bible must've felt like, finding herself pregnant at ninety after all those years of being barren."

Troy pocketed a stray Hot Wheels race car peeking out from the armchair cushion, willing the haze of shock—and extreme chagrin—to dissipate enough to start thinking in terms of *solution*. "Then you'd want to keep the baby?"

Silence jangled between them. "Is that a problem?"

"No. No, of course not."

"And if I didn't? Want to keep it, I mean?"

Troy took a deep breath. "How am I supposed to answer that? If I say it's up to you, it sounds like I don't care. If I say I'd have a hard time with…with the alternative, then you'll think I'm pressuring you into something you might not want."

"Oh, for God's sake, Troy…" Karleen sagged back into the cushions. "I'm here. I asked. Just tell me what you're thinking."

He looked at her steadily for a long moment. "I'm wondering if it's a boy or a girl," he said at last, surprising himself.

She nodded, then pushed herself up off the sofa. Now hugging herself, she walked aimlessly around the room, arranged nearly the way it had been in the old house, their old apartment, to give the boys a sense of continuity.

"Right now," she said, "the inside of my head feels like a tornado went through. To finally get my life to a place where I didn't feel like the rug was gonna get yanked out from underneath me…" Her fingers skimmed the pebbled base of a brass lamp. "I keep telling myself there's a baby growing inside me, and every time I say it the breath gets sucked out of me."

When she fell silent, Troy gently prodded, even though he already knew her answer, "You still haven't answered my question."

"I know." Her fingers hooked the edge of a bookshelf. "All those years I wanted to be a mama so bad I could hardly think about anything else…. You have no idea how long it took me to let go, to finally accept it wasn't meant to be." A smile flickered before she released a long, slow breath. "So, yeah, I want this baby. If it…" Worry shuddered across her features. "If it takes. Only…"

"What?"

"Figures, doesn't it? That I finally get my wish, only to be raising this kid on my own." She finally met his eyes. "Just like my mama and hers before her."

"Who says you have to raise this baby by yourself?"

She made a show of looking around the room before returning her gaze to his. "I sure don't see a husband anywhere around here, do you? And don't even think about going all noble on me by proposing, Troy, because if it wasn't gonna work between us before, it sure as heck isn't gonna work just because there's a baby thrown into the mix. God knows it didn't for my mother."

"I thought you said—"

"Oh, she was married. For about five minutes. My parents got hitched when Mama was six months along with me, but Daddy took off for parts unknown when I was a year old. She was barely nineteen, no education, no skills to speak off…" Her mouth tightened. "All I got out of the deal was his name. All she got was a broken heart and a whole lot of grief, from what I gather. So I sure wouldn't call that *working out*, would you?"

"I'm sorry."

"Why? It had nothing to do with you."

"I can't feel bad for you that you and your mother got screwed over?"

Karleen seemed to consider this for a moment, then shrugged. "Like I said, it's in the past. And I've worked my butt off to move on. But the irony's not sittin' real well, right at the moment."

"I can see that." Troy hesitated, then said, "I have no problem with marrying you, Karleen. And not because it's noble, because it's practical."

"For who?"

"The baby, for one thing. I'm not trying to back you into a corner, but if nothing else, you could go on my health insurance—"

"I don't need it, I've got my own. Look, I appreciate the offer, I really do. And I know I'm probably not makin' any sense, considering everything I just said. But I'm not in anything near the same position my mother was. I've got a house and a job and money put by. I'm feeling a little off balance right now, sure, but I suppose I'll figure it all out.

The same as you did," she added, her mouth curving slightly. "After Amy died. And from everything I can tell, you've done a pretty good job of it, too."

Before he had a chance to recover from the unexpected compliment, a soft, sleepy "Daddy?" caught his attention. Troy pivoted to see a yawning, wild-haired Scotty standing on very unsteady pins at the living-room entrance.

"Hey, squirt—whatcha doing awake?"

Trailing one of the half-shredded, and not particularly well-constructed, quilts Amy had painstakingly made for her babies while pregnant, the little boy trundled over to Troy and lifted his arms to be picked up. "You were talking too loud." He nestled against Troy's collarbone. "How come Karleen's here?"

Troy glanced over at the proud, troubled woman carrying his child, again trying to figure out the odd mixture of yearning and standoffishness in her face whenever she was around the boys. Then it hit him that Karleen was carrying the boys' brother or sister. A thought that had apparently occurred to her at the same moment, judging from her expression.

"Grown-up stuff, cutie," he said. "You need a drink of water or something?"

Scotty shook his head, then wadded up the quilt underneath his cheek and stuck his thumb in his mouth, his eyes already drifting shut again. Troy pointed one finger at Karleen.

"Don't even think about sneaking out while I'm gone."

God knows why she didn't. After all, what else was there to talk about? She'd said her piece, he'd said his, and that was that, far as she could tell.

And yet, here she still was, studying a large embroidered sampler on one wall, full of flowers and hearts and sappy sentiments about home and family.

She heard his footsteps on the stairs, felt him come up behind her. "My mother made that."

"For you and Amy?"

"Yeah," he said on a breath. "When we got married."

Karleen turned, one hand knotted against her unsteady stomach. The hunger had returned, a monster fish gnawing her insides. Her gaze swept the room. "No offense, but your house looks like something out of an L.L.Bean catalog."

"What can I tell you? I don't exactly walk on the wild side."

"So I see." She eyed the pillows on the plaid sofa, each one picking up one of the colors in the fabric. "My place must've given you hives."

"To be honest, I wasn't paying much attention to the decor."

The smile that tried to make an appearance died a quick death as the reality of the situation once again hit her like a blow. To her profound mortification, tears threatened to spill over her lower lashes; when she pressed a hand to her mouth, Troy pulled her into his arms, gently rocking her.

And heaven help her, she simply couldn't find the wherewithal to push him away.

"It's going to be okay, honey," he murmured, and she softly beat his chest.

"How do you figure that?"

Give the guy credit, he didn't have some glib answer in his back pocket. Instead, he simply held her, stroking her hair. Then, finally, he said, "I know you're shaky right now, but maybe you shouldn't reject my proposal out of hand. At least think about it."

As much as she was enjoying the moment, this would never do. Her hands planted on his chest, she reared back to look at him. "Please don't take this personally, Troy, but I do not want or need another husband. I've been down that road three times, and each time ended up in quicksand. So no more talk about marriage, okay?"

Uh-huh. One thing about not having been born yesterday was that she could read the look on a man's face better than she could the Bible. And with a lot less room for personal interpretation. So don't anybody tell her that wasn't relief she saw in those pretty green eyes. At least for a second or two, until that I'm-the-guy-it's-up-to-me-to-solve-the-problem look came back. Honestly.

"Okay," he said, in that tone of a man rethinking his battle plan on the fly, "consider the proposal off the table. But no way in hell are you raising this child *alone*. And I'm not only talking about money, although swear to God, if you even *think* of not letting me help financially—"

"No," she said quickly. What was she, nuts? "No, I don't mean that at all. As long as it's for the baby, fine. It's just the husband thing I have issues with."

Uh-oh. Narrowed eyes. "Well. As long as we're clear on that." Then his finger came up in her face. "But money aside, I'm here for this baby, and I'm here for you. In whatever way either of you need me. Is that understood?"

On a wave of emotional overload, a laugh burst from her throat. "I guess, if I had to get knocked up, at least I picked a decent man."

"Damn straight," Troy said without the slightest hesitation. "If I make a mess, I clean it up. If I screw up, I figure out how to fix it. As curveballs go," he said, his expression killing her, "this is a piker."

Her throat burning, Karleen pulled out of his arms,

digging into her pocket for a tissue. "Still and all, two total strangers, having a baby together…" She blew her nose. "How's that supposed to work?"

There went that look again. "It was never my idea to stay strangers, if you remember."

"I know. But it's probably smartest, in the long run."

"Says who?"

"The person havin' this baby."

"Well, the person who got you in that condition still doesn't agree. Especially now."

"You are one stubborn man, you know that?"

"Pot, meet kettle. Look, I get that we're different, okay? But where is it written we have to be clones of each other in order to get along? Hell, I work with people every day I have nothing in common with, and nobody's come to blows yet. So. When's your first doctor's appointment?"

Karleen actually squawked. "I have no idea, seeing as I found out I was pregnant about five minutes ago! And anyway, you don't have to go with me—"

He glared at her. She blew out a breath.

"Fine. I'll let you know. Can I go now?" she said, feeling like a cranky teenybopper.

Troy gestured toward the door. "Feel free."

She actually got all the way home before she threw up.

The next morning, after AIS's weekly teleconference with all the plant managers, Troy's only hope was to make it back to his office before Blake—who'd been shooting him *what's up?* looks the whole time—got to him.

No such luck. Blake snagged him before he'd barely passed through the conference-room door. He did, at least, wait until assorted VPs and such had dispersed before saying, "Wanna tell me why you look like somebody took apart your brain and then had no clue how to put it back together again? You hardly said two words during the meeting."

Troy glanced up and down the hall before focusing on a spot on the wall behind Blake's shoulder. "Sorry. I was a little…distracted."

"Ya think?" His partner steered Troy toward the elevator. "Let's go. Coffee's on me." When the brushed-steel doors glided open and Troy didn't follow, Blake braced his hand against the open door and glowered. "*Now*, Lindquist. And don't even think about giving me some crap about it being personal. When *personal* infringes on *business*, it becomes my business, too. So move your butt. Time's a wastin'."

Troy got into the elevator, leaning heavily against the paneled interior as it descended, his hands jammed into his chino pockets. "When did you turn into such a big pain in the can?"

"Consider this *payback* for peeling me off that bar stool a million years ago and talkin' me into this gig. You look like crap, man."

The elevator gently bumped to a stop on the ground floor. "And here I thought I was hiding it so well."

"Uh, no."

At ten in the morning, the Wendy's across the street was virtually deserted. Good thing. Not until they'd slid into a booth with their coffees, however, did Troy finally come clean. "You remember that conversation we had a few weeks ago, where you'd asked me if I'd done anything about Karleen?"

Blake's head shot up. "Yeah?"

"I may have left out a detail or two about what exactly happened."

"I thought you said *nothing* happened."

"I lied." Troy sipped his coffee, lifted his eyes to Blake's. Whose brows shot up.

"You *slept* with her?"

"Once. One of those brainless, it's-never-going-to-happen-again things. Going in, we both knew nothing was going to come of it, so there was nothing to talk *about*. Except…" He blew out a long breath. Blake immediately caught on.

"Oh, hell…she's not?"

"Oh, hell, she is. And yes, we took precautions. Such as they weren't."

Blake sagged back in his seat, shaking his head. "And I thought I was having a sucky day when the dog yakked up half a dead bird on the kitchen floor this morning. Hell, in your shoes, I'd be brain-dead, too."

Although Troy hadn't been all that hot on telling anyone—at least not yet—now that Blake knew, his lungs no longer felt as though they'd been sprayed with liquid nitrogen. "This wasn't exactly slotted into my schedule. Or Karleen's, obviously. Although she said she'd always wanted kids, so I don't think she's all that upset about the baby. The circumstances are something else again."

"I can imagine. And you?"

Troy felt his lips stretch into something resembling a smile. "Other than feeling like I'm hanging by two fingers off a cliff?"

Sympathy swam in Blake's deep brown eyes. "You've come through a lot worse."

"I know," he said on a sigh. "And at least this is fixable. If Karleen will ever stop being hardheaded enough to let me fix it."

"Meaning?"

"Meaning, at least I'm in the position to take care of both Karleen and this baby. But she's not having any of it."

"As in, marriage?"

"Well, yes. Except she's insisting we didn't know each other well enough or have enough in common to make a marriage work."

"Not that she has a valid point or anything."

"Especially since she's been married three times already."

"Dude."

"Yeah. And apparently there's some stuff about her mother... I'm still fuzzy on the details, but I'm gathering Karleen's got a real thing about trying to stand on her own two feet."

"There's a lot of that going around these days," Blake said dryly, referring, Troy supposed, to his own wife, Cass, who—despite being broke and, as it happened, also pregnant—had given Blake a similar song-and-dance before finally agreeing to remarry him last year. "In any case," the other man continued, "shotgun weddings went out of style with eight-track players."

"I know, I know. But this just feels so...shaky."

"To you. Obviously not to her."

"But that's what doesn't make sense. The whole thing about being a single mother's got her far more discom- bobulated than the pregnancy. And yet the more I tried to get across that she doesn't *have* to do this alone, the more she freaked."

"Because you're pressuring her, you numbskull."

"You don't even know her, Blake."

"No. But I know you. And I seriously doubt if this woman even comes close to you in the hardheaded department."

Troy frowned. "How can you say that? If anyone's learned to roll with the punches, it's me."

"Yeah, as long as you can choose which direction to roll. Nobody can ever accuse you of becoming paralyzed when stuff happens, that's for sure. But you do have this thing about taking charge. Being in control."

"And if I hadn't taken charge after Amy's death—"

"Not the same thing," Blake said gently. "You had two babies *depending* on you to take charge. And there's not a person who knows you who doesn't admire you for that. However, even you have to admit you used to be a lot more laid back about, well, everything than you are now. We never used to lock horns over stupid stuff the way we have in the past few years. But anymore…" He scrubbed a hand over his jaw, clearly weighing his words. "If things don't go your way, there is hell to pay."

Troy looked at him, stunned. "That's nuts."

"Unfortunately, it's not." Blake shrugged. "Doesn't bother me, partly because I know how to play you, partly because I understand what's causing it. But the word *micromanage* has come up among the staff, more than once."

"You're not serious."

"Yeah. I am."

When the fizzing inside his head stopped, Troy said, "I had no idea…. Why the hell didn't you say something?"

"Because I kept hoping it would blow over. That the old Troy would eventually kick to the curb this control freak who's taken over your body and we could get back to normal." His mouth thinned. "Unfortunately, it hasn't happened."

"Gee. Thanks for letting me act like a butt-head for four years."

Blake smiled. "It's not that bad. The staff doesn't hate you. They're just…wary of you."

"Yeah, that makes me feel better." Troy took a sip of his

coffee, but it tasted like crap. "Still. What's this got to do with Karleen?"

That apparently merited another several seconds of soul searching, or introspection, or something before Blake leaned forward again and said, "I'd kill for you, you know that. Nobody knows more than me what you've been through, or admired you more for the way you've handled it. Or understands how much of a monkey wrench this is, finding out some woman you barely know is having your kid. The thing is, though…it's not your problem to fix."

"And how exactly do you figure that?"

"Well, obviously you're partially responsible, I'm not saying that. But here's a news flash, buddy—women don't much like being given ultimatums. And they especially don't like feeling like somebody's threatening their autonomy. Doesn't matter what the motive is, or that you're only doing whatever it is 'for their own good.' That doesn't wash anymore. Trust me," he said with a wry smile, "I know whereof I speak."

Troy grunted. Blake downed the rest of his coffee, then said, "You want to regain control of the situation? Then like it or not you're gonna have to cede a lot of that control to her. Otherwise, you're gonna be majorly SOL." He checked his watch, then slid out of the booth. "We need to get back. I've got a conference call coming in from Denver at eleven."

When they got outside, though, Troy nodded toward their building as they headed back. "You think some damage control's in order?"

"Apologizing, you mean?" Blake shook his head. "Nah. Okay, so maybe your selective deafness has put a couple people's noses out of joint from time to time, but I don't think imminent mutiny's an issue. As long as you remember, a lot of these folks have been with us since the beginning. All they want is to be heard. And trusted. To know their opinion counts for something. The way it used to be before."

"Before everything went to hell in a handbasket?"

Blake swung open the heavy glass door leading to the lobby, striding to the elevator and punching the button. "And no matter hard you try, you can't stop those side trips from happening. None of us can."

"You do realize you're preaching to the choir?"

One side of Blake's mouth pulled up as the elevator door slid open. "You and Amy had a great marriage," Blake said as they entered. "I can't see you in some marriage of convenience, buddy, I just can't. Whatever the solution is, I seriously doubt that's it."

As Blake sauntered back to his office and that conference call, and Troy morosely trudged to his, he had to admit he couldn't see himself in some marriage of convenience, either. Which meant that Blake was right.

He hated when that happened.

Chapter Seven

Karleen could feel Troy's glare hot on her back as she handed over the clipboard to the gal behind the reception desk. The middle-aged woman scanned sheet after sheet of Karleen's medical history, then nodded.

"Okay, everything looks fine. How far along do you think you are?"

"Eight weeks and two days." Her face heated. "Exactly."

The woman made a notation on one of the papers. "And…this is your first pregnancy, right?"

"Yes."

"Any problems? Spotting? Nausea? Dizziness?"

"No spotting. I was sick some for a couple of weeks, but nothing too serious. Basically I feel fine. Except for wanting to eat every twenty minutes."

The woman chuckled. "That's about par for the course. And how will you be paying?"

"Oh, just a sec…" Karleen rummaged inside her purse for her wallet, then pulled out her insurance card. The woman entered her information into her computer, then told her to have a seat, they were running a little behind today but one of the midwives would see her shortly.

Karleen turned on her acrylic platform mules and clacked back to Troy. Who was easily the best-looking man in the room. Probably in the whole darn hospital. Any other guy in a sage-green polo and khakis would probably induce a serious yawn-fest. This guy, however…

What a mess, she thought, plopping back into the slightly worn padded chair beside him and shoving her hair behind her ear. *She* was such a mess, no less torn up inside about this—about him—than she'd been when all those sticks had turned pink a few weeks ago. How she could want to bop somebody upside the head who at the same time made her feel all tingly and warm inside, she had no idea. She just knew it wasn't good. Because she'd known plenty of men over the years who'd made her feel all tingly and warm (not to mention want to clobber them one), and it had never turned out well for either party.

Troy was leaning forward, his hands clasped between his knees, intently watching a young couple on the other side of the waiting room. They were giggling softly, the man's hand on the girl's enormous belly. Ohmigosh, she could see their baby kicking from way over here! Then the young man leaned over to kiss the woman on her cheek, and Karleen averted her gaze, embarrassed. Troy cleared his throat, like maybe he was embarrassed, too.

"Did the receptionist say how long it would be before they called you?"

"She didn't know. I got the feeling they were backed up, though, so it might be a bit of a wait."

Her eyes drifted to the couple again. The young man was apparently having an intense conversation with his unborn child. Karleen couldn't decide if it was sweet or silly. She glanced over at Troy, who had shifted his attention to another couple who'd just come in. They were holding hands, too, although the expectant mother didn't look to be any farther along than Karleen. Before she could stop it, a mixture of envy and irritation fisted in the pit of her stomach, at all these couples in love and so thrilled about their baby coming, that for all Troy insisted on being here with her today he might as well have been some stray she'd hauled in off the street.

It was perfectly obvious how uncomfortable he was. He'd insisted on picking her up—even though they could have easily met at the hospital, for heaven's sake—but they'd barely spoken on the way here. Considering the way her life had gone up to that point, didn't it just figure she'd now be sharing the most important event of her life with a virtual stranger?

Because despite getting together for dinner occasionally, or working with the boys in the garden, she couldn't say she felt any closer to him. Of course, having the twins around kinda killed any chance of real conversation. Then again, maybe Troy was doing that on purpose. Maybe, deep down, he wanted to keep his distance as much as she did, no matter what he'd said before. But since he'd clearly put out his own eye rather than go back on his word, here they were. With nothing really to say to each other.

She rearranged her long, ruffly skirt around her thighs, then slammed her purse on top of her lap. "If you need to get back to work, it's okay, I'll understand."

He gave her a funny look, his eyebrows dipped in that way men did when you might as well be speaking a foreign language. "Somehow, I think this takes precedence. And besides, how would you get home if I left?"

"They do have taxis in Albuquerque, you know."

He turned away, shaking his head. Karleen concentrated on breathing in and out, in and out, trying to steady her nerves. Then she crossed her legs, shaking her foot so hard her mule nearly fell off. Another coochie-coo couple came in. Great. She looked at her watch. Hard to believe they'd only been there fifteen minutes.

"They've got magazines," she said.

"Yeah. I see." Troy leaned over, picked up a battered *People* off the pile. Offered it to her. She shook her head.

He started flipping through the pages, still half turned away. Karleen glanced unseeing at the blur of photos, which all seemed to be of pregnant celebrities. She briefly entertained the idea of snatching the mag out of his hands and ripping it into shreds, instead deciding to search for something to talk about that would take their minds off why they were here.

"So. Whatever happened to getting the boys a puppy?"

He tossed the magazine back on the pile, picked up an old *Time* instead. "Turns out I'm getting them a baby brother or sister instead."

So much for steering the conversation into safer waters. "I'm not sure the boys'll be thrilled with the substitution."

To her relief, Troy smiled. A little. "Actually, I thought I'd hold off for a while. Until things settled down."

"And when might that be? When this one's outta college?"

"Good point." He got up, jingling change in his pocket. "I saw a soda machine down the hall. Want something?"

Karleen shook her head again, feeling like they had some game board between them, only one was playing checkers while the other was playing chess.

Two minutes later, he returned, Sprite in hand. He sat, popped off the top. Took a swallow. "So will you come with us? To pick one out?"

"One what?"

"A dog."

She blinked. "Why?"

"Because I thought it would be fun," he said wearily. "And I'm not sure I can handle a pair of excited four-year-olds and a puppy at the same time."

She fingered her purse strap. "Heck, I can't figure out how you handle the twins on your own. How come you don't have a nanny?"

"I did when they were younger. I'd have never survived juggling the business and two babies without help. But the woman I had didn't want to relocate to Albuquerque, and I thought, since the boys were older, anyway, they'd be fine in preschool. And I try to work at least one day a week at home. Still…" He tapped the can against his knee. Someone came out and called the very pregnant lady in for her check-up. Her S.O. helped haul her out of the chair; they both laughed. "I'm thinking seriously of looking for someone again. A housekeeper, at least."

"That makes sense."

Troy took a sip of his soda, then stared at the can like there was a secret code buried in the ingredients list. "Maybe we could work something out."

"About what?"

"To share whoever I end up hiring. You know, maybe you could leave the baby over at my house when you had to be out. Or the whoever could stay at your place while the boys were in preschool. And don't tell me you won't need anyone, not if you expect to keep working after the baby comes. I love my sons, but they definitely wore me to a frazzle during those first few months."

"Of *course* I expect to keep working! I love my job. And my clients count on me. I'd die if I had to give it up."

Although, truth be told, she had wondered how, exactly, she was going to handle that particular situation. How she'd be able to cart a baby and all the baby's stuff around with her when she was working, she had no idea. But neither was she thrilled with the idea of putting a newborn in day care.

"We could split the cost," she said.

She caught the head shake. And the smile. "Whatever."

"In any case, we don't have to make a decision this very minute."

Naturally, he frowned at her. Something he did way too much, far as she was concerned. "You don't want to put it off too long, either."

Somehow, Karleen held in her sigh. And the tears. Sometimes she felt like she was going to go under from all the pressure, to the point where it was beginning to seriously annoy her that she'd hardly had five minutes to even enjoy being pregnant. But the last thing she wanted was for Troy to think she was one of those moody, emotional preggos—never mind that she'd start blubbering these days over absolutely nothing—especially if she was supposed to be convincing him how strong she was. And she *was* strong. She was doing fine. She just cried a lot, was all.

Karleen also couldn't help feeling bad that this pregnancy was obviously contributing to *his* stress. She wouldn't dream of saying that to him, though. He'd jump right down her throat.

She picked up an *American Baby* off the pile on the

table beside her and started doing some aimless leafing of her own, trying to relax. Trying desperately not to dwell on everything that might be wrong, could go wrong still. Or to let her anxiety show. Because she didn't want Troy to think she was a worrywort, either. But she'd sure be a lot happier right now if it was Joanna sitting next to her instead of this man who for sure had to feel trapped.

A pair of midwives started a conversation on the other side of the room. Karleen caught Troy's mild glare. Well, maybe *glare* was too strong a word. A look of skepticism, maybe. Another bone of contention.

"You still mad because I decided to use midwives instead of a doctor?" she said, pretending to be more interested in some article on getting your baby to sleep through the night than his answer.

"I was never mad, Karleen. Just uncomfortable."

"And I told you, it's not like I'm goin' out in the woods by myself to birth this baby. I'm having it right here in the hospital, it's perfectly safe—"

Too late, she heard the words come out of her mouth. Her face on fire, she turned away. "I can't believe I said that, I am *so* sorry."

Troy reached over and took her hand, startling the daylights out of her. Because other than when they'd made this baby, and his holding her when she'd told him *about* the baby, they never touched. Which was fine with her. Things were complicated enough without letting those old hormones loose all over again.

But when his hand tightened around hers, all warm and strong, it suddenly hit her how scared *he* must be. Even more than her, probably. Not for her, she didn't think, since there wasn't any real attachment between them. And anyway, the odds of lightning striking twice were slim to none, which she was sure he knew. Still, it was like flying, she imagined—no matter what people said, the fact was that occasionally planes crashed.

Sympathy rushed through her, so strong she had to resist the impulse to bring their linked hands to her cheek, to kiss his knuckles in a way meant to reassure him that they were in this together. But she didn't, because there would have been no way to explain her actions that would have made sense to anybody. Given their situation, it wouldn't have been appropriate. So all she did was briefly squeeze his hand before extricating her own.

Because sitting around holding hands like they were a real couple wasn't appropriate, either.

Troy glanced over at Karleen as they walked back to his car after the appointment, still undecided about her outfit—a long, gauzy skirt that sat slightly below her waist and a low-cut, stretchy top that ended somewhat above it, both embellished with lots of sparkly stuff. A silver clip held back her hair, all the more to show off the flashing water-falls of silver and copper disks dangling from her ears.

Give the woman a crystal ball and the image would be complete.

"So," he said, opening her door for her, ignoring the eye-roll in response. "That went well, don't you think?"

Karleen gathered up her skirt and slid inside, rearranging everything around her knees. "I guess."

Troy shut the door, went around to his side. Marshaled what few forces he had left. Their conversations reminded him of his first car—the old Chevy would chug along okay for a while, only to give out without warning and at the most inopportune times. He slid in behind the wheel. "Is something wrong?"

She stopped fussing with her skirt and frowned at him. "What are you talking about?"

"You've hardly said a dozen words since we left the clinic."

Over her rhinestone-studded sunglasses, her brows lifted. "Like you've been such a chatterbox."

"I was only taking my cue from you."

Her lips smushed together, she faced forward, plopping her huge coppery purse on her lap. "So maybe I don't feel like talking right now. Don't take it personally."

He put the car in gear and backed out of the parking space. "I'm not sure how else to take it."

"Well, don't. I've just got some stuff to work through in my own head about all of this, that's all. It's got nothing to do with you."

"And if it weren't for me, you wouldn't have 'all of this' to work *through*." He cut his eyes over in time to see one side of her mouth tick. "Right?"

They pulled out into traffic. She cracked open her window. "You decided when you might tell the boys?"

"Is that what's worrying you?"

"Nothing's *worrying* me, Troy, honestly. But no, that's not what I was thinking about. It just occurred to me, is all."

"I haven't decided yet. Probably not until it's a lot closer to…to the due date. Or at least until you're showing. Two weeks is like two years to a four-year-old. Seven months would be incomprehensible." He hesitated. "I will have to tell my parents, though, when they come next month."

"At least that's one thing I don't have to deal with," she said on a sigh. "Only relative I've got is my aunt Inky, and frankly I don't much care what she thinks one way or the other about anything I do."

"Inky?"

"Ingrid. I couldn't say it when I was little and Inky stuck. She's my mother's younger sister. We don't communicate all that often except for when she needs to hit me up for a 'loan.'" She frowned when he went east instead of west. "Where are we going?"

"Shopping. When was the last time you saw your aunt?"

"I don't know," she said irritably, "a few years ago. And what do you mean, shopping? For what?"

"Nursery stuff."

"No, we're not."

"Dammit, Karleen, if this is another one of your I'm-paying-my-own-way deals—"

"No, it's not that." Then he caught her cocking her head. "You're still pissed about me taking care of my own medical bills, aren't you?"

She had him there. Oddly enough, Troy would have thought that four years of butt-, nose- and tear-wiping, of singing tiny boys to sleep or assuaging their fears would be more than sufficient to send Macho Man packing. And yet, damned if watching Karleen make all her own financial arrangements with the hospital didn't send the old male ego into a tailspin.

"I'm The Guy," he said. "I'm supposed to take care of this stuff."

"Says who?"

"Says my DNA encoding."

"Well, tell your DNA encoding to get over it. It's like I told you, I've been paying for health insurance for years. They owe me. And anyway, if this was appendicitis or somethin', you wouldn't be offering to pay, would you?"

"The next time I give someone *else* appendicitis, I'll let

you know. But what if you *hadn't* had insurance? What then?"

A pause. "I suppose that would've been different."

"Why?"

"It just would've, okay? Oh, for heaven's sake—I'm not going to risk my baby's safety for my own pride, if that's what you're worried about. But why should I accept your help if I don't need it...oh, shoot."

The tinny, upbeat tune got louder—and more familiar—when she wrenched open her purse and dug out her cell phone. Troy chuckled. "I don't believe it. 'Hard Headed Woman'?"

"Let me guess," she said, flipping open the phone. "You've got somethin' against Elvis, too.... Hello?"

"Nope. I'm crazy about Elvis."

He caught the brief, shocked look before her whole face lit up. "Hey, Flo! How are you?..." Then her forehead crimped. "Oh, I'm so sorry.... What'd the doctor say? Uh-huh... Well, that doesn't sound too bad. You're taking your meds like he told you?... Good. Of course I can do that.... No, honey, it's no problem at all.... Hold on."

Karleen rummaged in her purse again, pulling out a small pad and a fat red pen. "What do you need? Uh-huh, uh-huh..." She alternately scribbled and "uh-huhed" for another few seconds, then checked her watch. "I'm not sure, I'm not too far away, but somebody else is driving, I'd have to get back to my house first, to get my car.... What?" she said, frowning, when Troy poked her. "Hold on a sec, sugar," she said, then lobbed another "What?" to Troy.

"Emergency?"

She did an "eh" waggle with her free hand. "Flo used to be my neighbor, she's in her eighties, I sometimes run errands for her when her arthritis acts up—"

"Tell her we'll be there soon."

"I can't ask you—"

"Karleen. For God's sake."

She stared at him for a second or two, then said into her phone, "We'll stop by the store, then, and I guess we'll see you in about a half hour?...I swear, it's no problem. You sit tight, honey, and I'll be there in two shakes."

Two (or maybe three) shakes later, they drove up in front of a drab little box of a house—flat roof, chalky stucco, black ornamental shutters—in a neighborhood a half inch away from seedy. Still, early roses bloomed profusely on a handful of hardy bushes standing sentry under a front window, while clusters of happy-faced pansies crowded whiskey-barrel planters bordering the cracked driveway.

"Flo?" Karleen called when they reached the entrance, shifting several Albertsons bags to one hand to rap on the curlicued metal screen door. "It's me, sugar."

"I'm comin', I'm comin'," Troy heard from the other side, seconds before the door swung open to an explosion of vibrant tropical flowers on a loose dress, from which rose a gleaming, beaming face the color of bittersweet chocolate. Even leaning on a four-pronged cane, the thin woman gave Karleen a long, fierce hug, before letting go to smile even more broadly at Troy. "And who is this *fine*-looking young man?"

Karleen did the honors—not surprisingly, Troy was introduced as "my neighbor"—then they carted Flo's groceries inside and back to her bright yellow, excessively tidy kitchen. Cats of all colors, shapes and sizes milled about, watching the proceedings with a detached curiosity.

"Can I offer you folks something to drink? All I have is ice water, I'm afraid."

"Thanks, Flo, but we can't stay—"

"Water would be fine, Mrs. Johnson," Troy said. "But you sit. Just tell me where the glasses are and I'll get them."

"My, my…good-lookin' and a gentleman to boot," the old woman said on a laugh. Her eyes shifted to Karleen, who was busy unloading the groceries and putting them away. "Child, you can leave all that, I'll get aroun' to it eventually. Just bring me my pocketbook from the living room so I can pay you. You got the receipt? And what's that you got in your hand? Now you know I didn't ask for any ice cream."

"No, you didn't," Karleen said, holding out the pint of premium AIS Nutter-Butter Brickle. "But I know this is your favorite flavor, so it's my treat. You want some right now?"

A pleased, little-girl smile stretched the old woman's mouth. "Well, I don't suppose I'd turn it down if it was here in front of me."

Grinning himself, Troy pulled down an ice-cream dish from beside the glasses and handed it to Karleen, who'd already gotten a spoon from the drawer. A big ginger tom hopped up on a vacant kitchen chair, mewing nonstop. Her dish of ice cream clutched protectively to her sunken chest, Flo chuckled, low in her throat. "This isn't for you, you big beggar, and you know it."

Except she held out the ice cream-coated spoon to the cat, anyway.

For the better part of the next twenty minutes, Troy hung back, leaning against the counter as he watched the mutually affectionate exchanges between the two women. From their conversation, he pieced together the essentials, mainly that Flo had been there for Karleen off and on during her teenaged years, and that Karleen clearly adored her for it.

Eventually, though, Karleen stood, making noises about needing to get going. "But if you need me to take you to the doctor or anything…?"

"No, lamb, thank you, I'm fine."

"And what about your swamp cooler? You got it goin' yet?"

Flo chuckled. "You worry too much, you know that? The man across the street said he'd come over on Sunday and turn it on for me, so I'm covered."

Finally satisfied that Flo's needs were all met, at least for the moment, Karleen gave her another big hug—Flo not missing the chance to tell Troy to stop by again, anytime—and then they were back in the car, heading home, and it occurred to Troy that Karleen never had brought the old woman her purse so she could reimburse her.

"I didn't forget," she said. Then, after a couple of beats, she added, "Considering the number of times Flo fed me when my mother 'forgot,' the least I can do is buy the old gal groceries, now and again."

Troy waited out the flush of shame, for his initial—and less than complimentary—snap judgment of the woman sitting beside him. Because maybe Karleen's nails were glued on and her hair was bleached (this, he knew first-hand) and her breasts not really a C-cup, but there was nothing even remotely fake about her heart.

"…But since it about kills her to let me do stuff for her," she was saying, "I have to pull fast ones from time to time." When he chuckled, she squeezed shut her eyes and let her head fall back against the rest. "Don't say it."

"What? That it's okay for you to hoodwink an old woman into letting you help her, but it's not okay for me to help you?"

NO POSTAGE
NECESSARY
IF MAILED
IN THE
UNITED STATES

BUSINESS REPLY MAIL

FIRST-CLASS MAIL   PERMIT NO. 717-003   BUFFALO, NY

POSTAGE WILL BE PAID BY ADDRESSEE

SILHOUETTE READER SERVICE
3010 WALDEN AVE
PO BOX 1867
BUFFALO NY 14240-9952

Play the Lucky Hearts Game

and get...

2 FREE BOOKS and
2 FREE MYSTERY GIFTS...
YES! YOURS to KEEP!

yes! I have scratched off the silver card. Please send me my *2 FREE BOOKS* and *2 FREE mystery GIFTS*. I understand that I am under no obligation to purchase any books as explained on the back of this card.

Scratch Here!
then look below to see what your cards get you...
2 Free Books & 2 Free Mystery Gifts!

335 SDL ELVG   335 SDL EL2S

FIRST NAME	LAST NAME

ADDRESS

APT.#   CITY

STATE/PROV.   ZIP/POSTAL CODE   (S-SE-04/07)

Twenty-one gets you
2 FREE BOOKS and
2 FREE MYSTERY GIFTS!

Twenty gets you
2 FREE BOOKS!

Nineteen gets you
1 FREE BOOK!

TRY AGAIN!

"It's not the same thing."

Troy released a sigh. "Look, Karleen, I know this whole situation is crazy, but I'm getting really tired of being shut out."

Her chin snapped down. "I am not shutting you out!"

"Then what would you call it?"

"Saving my skin."

"From *what,* for God's sake?"

She faced front again. "You wouldn't understand."

Troy scratched his eyebrow, then dropped his hand back on the steering wheel. "Here's the thing, honey—I can't help being protective, anymore than you can help wanting to help Flo. That's just who I am. That doesn't mean I think you're weak or helpless or incapable of making your own decisions. Obviously you got along fine before you met me, so—"

"See, that's where you're wrong," she said. When he frowned at her, she added, "Yeah, for the past few years, I've been doing okay, but…" She leaned her head in her hand. "It wasn't always like that. *I* wasn't always like that."

"At the risk of being shot down again…care to explain?"

"It's a long, boring story."

"We've got a long, boring ride ahead of us."

Two, three blocks passed before she finally said, "None of the guys I married were bad men. Although the first wasn't a man at all, seeing as he wasn't but nineteen when we drove to Vegas and got married. I was eighteen, Mama had just died, and frankly, I felt like I'd been tossed out of an airplane with no parachute. And Ross caught me. Barely. Hung on for all of six months, too, until we both realized what a dumb thing we'd done.

"Fast forward a couple of years, a few dead-end jobs, a few dead-end relationships, to Jasper. I was twenty-one by then. He was older. A lot older, actually. He was one of the regulars at the restaurant where I was waitressing at the time. His wife had left him a year or so before, and he was lookin' for somebody he could take care of." Her shoulders bumped. "Since I was looking for somebody to take care of me, it looked like a good thing. Except he'd neglected to tell me *why* his wife had left him. And unfortunately, I'm not real big on sharin' my underwear."

"Ouch."

"Not that I'm judgmental or anything—each to his own, I always say—but once you see a guy wearing the Victoria's Secret thong he gave *you* for Valentine's Day…" Karleen shook her head as Troy thought, *Yeah, thanks for the image.* "Anyway, then I met Nate. And I thought, okay, third time's the charm, right? A fellow Texan, owns a couple of restaurants here and up in Santa Fe, not exactly hurting financially. And I tried, I really did, to be a good wife. But there again, it didn't work. We just…I don't know. Got bored with each other or something. I was certainly far better off than I'd ever had before, but something crucial was still missing. Long story short…I couldn't make him happy."

Troy frowned. "Why do you assume it was up to you to make *him* happy?"

"Well, I suppose that's the point, isn't it? That we were askin' something of each other that wasn't fair to ask. However, when *that* marriage failed, I finally took a long, hard look at myself, and I realized that'd been the problem all along, that I'd been looking for fulfillment or whatever you want to call it outside of myself. So I set out to correct that little fault. And here I am, seven years later, an independent woman with a career and a retirement account and my own house—or will be, soon as I finish payin' off Nate—and yes, my own insurance, and at long last I'm proud of who I am." She looked at him. "And that's a *real* good feeling."

Troy remembered the first time the accountant had shown them a P&L statement that showed them in the black, and he smiled. "Yeah. It is." A pause. "You keep in touch with your exes?"

"I still see Nate on occasion. We stayed friends, which is nice. I even went to his wedding a few years back. He got the right woman, this time. The others? No. Don't see much point."

"Did you love any of them?"

"You know, I ask myself that a lot. And the answer is…I don't know. I suppose I thought I did, at the time. I certainly *wanted* to. But looking back, I'm not sure I really knew what my feelings were. Although I will say, when each of my marriages ended? I felt a lot more disappointed than hurt. At the same time, I felt like I'd been sprung from prison. A prison of my own making, to be sure, but a prison all the same.

"It's like…I lose my sense of balance whenever I'm in a relationship. Just like my mama did. Instead of standing on our own two feet, we lean. And then when things go bad, we fall. And things always go bad, Troy. Always."

"Is that a warning?" he said quietly.

"No. It's an explanation. So now you know."

What he knew was that she was shortchanging herself. What he *knew* was that this was a big-hearted woman who'd forgotten to include herself on her to-do list. In the way that most mattered, at least.

"I'm buying the nursery furniture, honey," he said

quietly, earning him a frown. "You can pick out anything you like, but it's gonna be my signature on the credit-card slip."

"Boy, you really do have this thing about being in charge, don't you?"

"I have this thing about carrying my share of the load. Which I can't seem to do with you without bullying you into it. So we're going to do some role playing. I'm you. You're Flo. I'm being the good guy whether you like it or not."

That actually got a little laugh. "I never said you couldn't buy the nursery furniture, Troy." She looked back out the windshield. "Just not today."

Her sudden acquiescence threw him for a second, until his brain caught up to the last three words. "What's wrong with today?"

A long moment of silence preceded "It's bad luck to get everything ready too early."

Yo, her fear said. *Recognize me?*

All too well. Especially considering how close it had come to overwhelming him in the waiting room. Not that he should have been surprised. After all, it had taken nearly two years before he could even watch a movie or TV show about a woman giving birth, another year after that before the sight of a heavily pregnant woman didn't short out his brain. The last thing Karleen needed, however, was to pick up on his residual anxiety.

"Okay, we won't buy anything until you're ready. But…" He smiled over at her. "Is it bad luck to go looking?"

"It's very tempting," she said softly. "Thank you. But I'm not ready yet. Looking at cribs and changing tables and such… It makes it all so *real.*"

"And the sonogram didn't?"

"The peach pit with the heartbeat, you mean?" she said, .

but her hand went to her still-flat belly. He got a sudden flash of the kind of clothes she'd wear as the pregnancy progressed. Somehow, he doubted he'd be seeing a bunch of cute little dresses that tied in the back.

Like Amy had worn.

"Could we just go on home?" she asked.

"Sure," he said, nudging aside the slight disappointment at not being able to spend a little more time with her. Especially now that they were actually talking to each other. Like a showy flower, the more she opened up, the richer the color inside and the sweeter the fragrance. "You care if we pick up the boys first?"

"No, of course not. And by the way, bubba... It didn't escape my attention that you didn't let on to Flo that the ice cream was yours."

"I know," he said, and she shook her head.

They rode the rest of the way in silence, Karleen fiddling with one of the stones on her skirt as she stared straight ahead, and it occurred to Troy how dull and staid he was, next to her. How ordinary. Like bologna on white bread.

He picked up the boys, who were beside themselves at being sprung early. After they'd scrambled into their car seats and Troy had buckled them in, he slid behind the wheel, then glanced in the rearview mirror and said, "How'd you guys like to go looking for a dog this weekend?"

"Jeez, *finally,*" Grady said, but Scotty said, "C'n Karleen come, too?"

Troy looked over, one eyebrow crooked. She laughed. "I've got a couple of appointments on Saturday morning, but I suppose I could go in the afternoon. Or Sunday. Oh, my God... What landed in your driveway?"

Troy looked up, blinking in the glare of afternoon sun on

the unbelievably vast expanse of white obliterating his house.

"Good Lord," he said, pulling up behind the RV. "It's bigger than my first apartment. What on earth—?"

The door to the thing swung open and out popped his mother, arms outstretched.

"Gramma!" both boys cried, as his mother yelled, "Surprise!"

Indeed.

Chapter Eight

For the most part, Karleen was a big believer in the theory that, if you took the time to scratch beneath the surface, there was more to most folks than was often apparent when you first met them. Like Joanna's mother Glynnie, for instance, who didn't have nearly the rod up her butt you might think.

Troy's mother, however...

The woman had clearly taken one look at Karleen and thought, *I don't think so.* Something about the way the light had gone out of those bright blue eyes, how her smile had gone all hard-edged when Troy had introduced them. Like she knew it wasn't right to judge, but she was doing it anyway.

And under other, normal circumstances, Karleen probably wouldn't have cared one way or the other what some midwestern matron thought of her, having long since accepted the simple fact that, sometimes, people just didn't click. But seeing as how Karleen was carrying the woman's grandchild, it wasn't looking too good for their never having to lay eyes on each other again. So Karleen was willing to do her best to make things work between them.

But honestly. It was everything Karleen could do not to park her hands on her hips and say, "Do I look like a slut, or what?" since clearly Eleanor Lindquist, with her khaki camp shirt neatly tucked into her white cotton pants, her short beige hair and dull coral lipstick and little white Keds, had decided exactly that. Karleen could only imagine what her reaction would be when she discovered the truth. Which, God willing, wouldn't be until after Karleen was safely back in her own house, but she wasn't banking on that.

Naturally, Troy had apologized to Karleen up one side and down the other, as soon as they'd pinched out ten seconds alone when the boys had dragged Gramma and Gampa off to see their room. Karleen's guess was that he was fit to be tied, having his parents show up a month early, without warning, before he'd figured out how to tell them about their new grandchild. Which, she pointed out, wasn't exactly their fault, only then he got miffed at *her,* which she did not take personally. After all, she wasn't the one who'd gone and knocked up a gal from the wrong rung of the ladder.

And anyway, Karleen couldn't really blame Troy's mother for her attitude. In the other woman's shoes, she'd probably assume Karleen was a gold digger, too. In her *own* shoes, she imagined she was going to be every bit as bad with her own child. Maybe even worse, considering some of the boneheaded stunts Karleen herself had pulled over the years.

It wasn't that Eleanor had been rude to her or anything—

in fact, she was the one who'd insisted Karleen stay for dinner, which Karleen figured she'd probably better do, considering the situation. Still, *awkward* didn't even begin to describe the evening. If it hadn't been for the twins being beside themselves with excitement and thus remaining the center of attention all through the meal, Karleen wasn't sure how she—or Troy—would have survived.

So thank God for Troy's daddy—Gus—a gentle soul with a slow grin and kind gray eyes. Eleanor having shooed everybody—except Troy—out of the kitchen, Karleen and Gus now sat out on Troy's back deck, watching the boys playing hide-and-seek with a pair of flashlights in the dying light, like a couple of lightning bugs with Darth Vader complexes. Karleen had kicked off her shoes to sit barefoot on the steps, her back propped against the deck railing; Gus had commandeered a large wooden rocker, nursing a can of diet root beer from the case the Lindquists had brought with them. Not that she'd ever feel like she belonged, or could be a real part of Troy's family, but if it hadn't been for the baby business Karleen might've actually felt comfortable in the tall, slender man's company.

"So. You a native of Albuquerque?" he asked in his broad, flat accent.

"No, sir. I'm from Texas, originally."

"Ah. That would account for the accent."

Gentleness and humor laced the older man's words. Much like his son's, Karleen realized. "I guess, even though I've lived here for nearly twenty-five years. But you know what they say—you can take the tumbleweed out of Texas, but you can't take Texas out of the tumbleweed."

"Karleen, Gampa!" Grady called, his grin barely visible in the waning light. "Look what I can do!"

His cartwheel was executed with a lot more enthusiasm than skill, but Karleen laughed and clapped, anyway. Naturally, Scotty had to try, too, with even more bent elbows and knees than his brother. And Karleen laughed again, which of course spurred the boys to show off their new trick, over and over, tumbling like puppies in the patch of cool, soft grass. For weeks, she'd fought not to let them into her heart, at least not all the way. But this afternoon, when they'd scrambled into the car and thrown their arms around her neck, and it had finally, truly struck her that they were going to be her baby's big brothers, no matter what, she'd taken a deep breath and let go.

Too bad she didn't dare do the same thing with their father.

Gus chuckled softly when the twins cartwheeled right smack into each other, resulting in a tangle of little boys and a chorus of "Ows!" and much head rubbing.

"Y'all okay?" Karleen called out, and Scotty came over to her for a hug, palming his head. She kissed the boo-boo and gave him a squeeze, which she felt all the way to her own heart. Grady, however, was not about to cry, no matter how much his lower lip trembled. So she got up and went over to him, giving him a hug, anyway. Which he duly returned.

"The boys certainly seem to have taken to you," Troy's father said when she returned to the deck. "And you to them."

Seated again, she shrugged, hugging her knees. "I like little boys. It's when they get big that's the problem."

Gus laughed softly. "It's hard on them, not having a mother."

Karleen frowned. "I thought they never knew Amy?"

"I don't mean Amy, specifically. Oh, Troy had that housekeeper for a while, and she was okay, but it's not the same thing."

After a long, somewhat jittery pause, Karleen said,

"Please tell me you're not one of those people hell-bent on fixing up your son for the sake of your grandkids."

A grin preceded "Not just for the sake of the boys, no. Although from what I've seen I think you'd be good for them." He paused. "Troy, too."

Karleen felt her face heat. "Because I like his kids?" she said, playing dumb.

Even in the near dark, she could feel the older man's eyes calmly assessing her. Then he took a swallow of his root beer. None of the family drank, from what she could tell. Well, heck, what was one more nail in the coffin?

"Whoever you think you're fooling about your relationship with my son," he said, "it sure as hell isn't me."

"Sorry to disappoint you," Karleen said. With remarkable calm, she thought, considering how badly her stomach was churning. "But Troy and I are a non-item." Her mouth twisted. "And I think it's pretty safe to assume your wife would blow a gasket if we *weren't.*"

Another chuckle. "Amazing, the way that woman can make her opinions known without saying a single word. But don't let her get to you. Her bark's a lot worse than her bite."

"It's not her bark I'm worried about, it's her growl."

"And the way the hair raises on the back of her neck?"

"That, too."

"So. You don't like Troy?"

Karleen shot a mildly annoyed glance in the older man's direction. "Of course I *like* Troy. What's not to like? But the idea of us together is downright laughable."

"Why? Because you're nothing like his first wife?"

"No, because I'm nothing like *him.* Or any of you, for that matter."

There. She'd said it. Let 'em deal.

"I may not say much," Gus said after a moment, "but I

consider myself a keen observer of my fellow man." He tapped the outer corner of one eye. "You're right, you're not a thing like the twins' mother. Or us, maybe. But Troy looks at you as though he'd happily flatten anyone who dared to hurt you." Gus smiled. "Including his own mother, if necessary."

Now her face positively flamed. "No offense, Gus, but I think maybe you're seein' what you want to see. Not what's really there."

"No offense right back, young lady," Gus said mildly, "but there's not a damn thing wrong with my eyesight. Not these days, at least—"

"Karleen! Karleen!" Flashlight beams darting drunkenly over the lawn as they ran, the boys barreled across the yard, Scotty throwing himself across her thighs. She ruffled his blond waves, releasing the little boy perfume of grass and dirt and the slightest hint of watermelon shampoo. "There's all these little green things in the garden, you c'n see 'em real good with the flashlights! Come look!" he said, pulling her to her feet.

"Gampa, too!" Grady put in, stomping up onto the deck to pull his grandfather out of the chair. "Our punkins are coming up!"

Gus huffed and puffed, pretending to have great difficulty in getting out of the chair, only to then stand so quickly in response to the boys' tugging that they both landed on their butts, and Karleen laughed and her hand went automatically to her tummy, only by the time she realized it she caught Gus's lifted eyebrow.

Oh, hell.

"Why do I get the feeling," Troy's father said in a low voice as they walked across the yard, "that you're growing something this summer besides pumpkins?" When she didn't say anything, he put his arm around her shoulder and gave her a brief hug, and she very nearly dissolved into tears right there and then.

Although he couldn't hear his father's and Karleen's conversation for his mother's virtually nonstop prattle, Troy had been watching Karleen with his children through the kitchen window as he'd loaded the dishwasher, and the thought had come, *You do not want to lose this woman.*

"She's pregnant, isn't she?"

Dishwasher soap squirted everywhere as Troy's head jerked around to his mother. Or rather, his mother's back, since she was shoving leftovers into the refrigerator. Between the boys and Eleanor, Karleen had had virtually no choice about staying for dinner, although she'd looked as though she'd rather trek across Siberia in January— naked—than make small talk with his parents.

Right now, he'd join her. In Siberia, naked, whatever.

"Why on earth would you think that?" he said, stalling.

"Troy. Please. She was in the bathroom constantly, she ate as though she didn't know where her next meal was coming from and her breasts are positively *enormous.* Call it an educated guess."

Neatly dodging the breast comment, Troy shut the dishwasher door and started the cycle, then turned to face the music. And his mother's far-too-astute gaze. Her demeanor wasn't severe, exactly. Just no-nonsense. After everything she'd been through, he couldn't blame her. "Yes. She is."

"Is it yours?"

He tried a smile. "Got it in one."

Her entire body seemed to sag. "Oh, Troy, honey… What were you *thinking?*"

"What I was thinking is frankly none of your business. Which is pretty much what I'm thinking now, actually."

His mother's mouth tightened. "There's no need to be insolent."

"Then how about not acting like I'm a teenager who knocked up his sixteen-year-old girlfriend?"

"Troy. Honestly." She blew out a breath. "Are you…going to marry her?"

"Not that you're judging her or anything."

Twin coins of color bloomed on his mother's cheeks. "She's nice enough, I'm sure. She's just not…" She waved one hand.

"Amy?"

"Oh, honey." Tears shone in Eleanor's eyes. "Amy was so perfect for you, you know your father and I both loved her from the moment we met her. What on earth could you possibly have in common with this woman?"

"It's okay, Mom. We're not getting married."

"Oh, thank God," his mother said on a gush of air.

"Don't thank God, thank Karleen. Since she turned me down."

Relief turned to renewed horror. "You're not serious. You actually asked her to be your wife?"

"Considering she's carrying my child, it seemed the polite thing to do."

His mother gawked at him. "Don't tell me this pregnancy was actually *planned?*"

"No," Troy said quietly. "It wasn't. And since neither one of us is quite used to the idea yet, either, I'd appreciate it if you'd back off for a minute."

"I'm sorry," his mother said curtly. "I mean, really,

forgive me for being concerned. You lay this bombshell on me and then don't expect me to react? Especially after everything we went through with your father—"

"Mom," he said wearily. "Enough."

She turned back to the island, yanking off a length of plastic wrap to cover the leftover sautéed vegetables. "So when were you planning on telling us?"

"When we were ready. Not my fault you guys got bitten by the RV bug and showed up early."

His mother tossed him a glance over her shoulder, the corners of her mouth barely turned up. "And ruined the surprise?"

"Something like that, yeah."

Once the vegetables had been put away, she said, "I'm surprised Karleen didn't…you know. Take care of things. Nobody has to have a baby they don't want these days."

Troy crossed his arms. "Who says nobody wants this baby?"

After several seconds of locked gazes, his mother looked away. "I can't believe I'm hearing this."

"Well, believe it. And besides, Karleen went through three marriages without getting pregnant—"

"Did you say *three* marriages? Oh, dear God."

"It's okay, I'm thinking the boy right out of high school and the cross-dresser didn't count."

"Oh, dear *God.*"

"Mom, I know this is a shock. It was for me, too. And Karleen. But what can I say? Stuff happens. You either cope, or go under. So maybe the situation isn't exactly ideal—"

"Ideal?" his mother practically shrieked. "For God's sake, Troy, this is nothing but some, some romantic *fantasy!* You cannot possibly make a *life* with that woman—!"

"Oh…sorry," Karleen said behind them, and Troy spun around. Her face pale, she glanced from him to his mother and back again. "I was about to ask if you wanted me to get the boys ready for bed. But I can see I'm not needed so I'll just be getting on back to my place—"

"Karleen—"

"It's okay, Troy," she said, backing out of the kitchen, her smile breaking his heart. "She's not sayin' anything I haven't already said. Seems your mother and I are actually on the same side. Right, Mrs. Lindquist?"

"Where are you going?" his mother called after him as he strode to the door.

Troy wheeled on her, his throat working overtime. "Dammit, Mom, I love you, you know that. But right now I don't like you very much. Whether it makes any sense to you or not, I'd like nothing more than to make a life with *that woman!* So if you don't mind, I'm going to see if I can apologize for my mother's brain having apparently fallen out of the RV somewhere along I-25!"

Karleen had barely shut her front door behind her when she heard Troy knocking on it like some kind of fool, calling her name over and over, banging and banging and banging until she feared for his hand.

She yanked the door open, fending off his next blow. "In case you missed it, I had the doorbell fixed weeks ago."

"I'm sorry," he said.

"For putting dents in my door?"

"Better your door than my mother. Which probably isn't the best way to treat someone who was in labor with you for twenty-six hours." When Karleen winced, he said, "I weighed eleven pounds at birth."

"Get *out*."

"No, actually, I'd like to come in."

"I'm really tired, Troy—"

"Just for a minute."

She backed up and let him pass, remaining by her door as he walked into her living room, sinking onto the edge of her sofa. "I apologize," he said.

"For what?"

"My mother being an ass?"

"That's a horrible thing for a son to say about his mama."

"Be that as it may." He shoved his hand through his hair. "There's a reason I went out of state for college. And never went back."

"Don't apologize for your mother. She's only lookin' out for your best interests, like any other mother would. Well, almost any other mother. Mine never quite caught on to that concept. So count your blessings."

Troy blew air through his nose, then said, "She guessed, by the way. That you're pregnant."

"Yeah, I figured that's what must've brought all of that on. I gather she didn't exactly take the news well."

"You could say."

"She's right, Troy. About us. Like I said, she and I are on the same side in this. As opposed to your father," she said on a sigh. "Who guessed, too, by the way. Don't ask me how. No, actually, I take that back—he probably figured there was only one reason why you and I would have anything to do with each other."

Troy frowned up at her. "That's a little harsh, don't you think?"

"Maybe. But it's true. I like your daddy, by the way. You take after him."

"Thank you. But let's get something straight right now—my wanting to hang out with you has a lot less to do with this baby than you might think."

"I wasn't talking about the baby. I was talkin' about sex."

"I know you were," he said. "But it's more than that, too. Which I think would be perfectly clear considering that we only *had* sex once."

"Oh, but what a once it was," she said lightly, only to feel everything freeze inside when his eyes bore into hers.

"News flash, honey—I've moved past *like*. In fact, at the rate I'm going, I'll have zipped right past *have strong feelings for* by next week."

Her ears ringing, Karleen watched Troy intently for several seconds, then pointed toward the kitchen. "I'm about to die of thirst," she said, walking away. "You want anything?"

Even though he said, "No," he followed her to the kitchen, then through to the patio doors looking out over the backyard as she pulled a chilled bottle of fruit juice out of the fridge. She twisted off the bottle cap, taking a sip as she cast a glance at those strong, go-ahead-and-burden-me shoulders.

"That's some dangerous road you're lookin' to go down, buddy," she said to his back. "Which I think your mother just made crystal clear."

She saw one corner of his mouth lift. "My mother wanted me to be a lawyer, but she didn't get her way with that one, either. I think I was in middle school the last time she had a say in who I associated with."

"Or got pregnant?" she said with a small smile.

"That, either." He nodded toward the outside. "Why do you keep the pool lights on if it's covered?"

Karleen frowned at his subject switch, but shrugged. "I feel better with them on, that's all. Somehow knowing there's a great big hole in the ground…" She shuddered.

"Did you ever use it?"

"Oh, all the time. I love to swim. But like I said, it got to be too much of a hassle to keep it up."

"Because you can't afford it."

She stiffened. "That's not—"

"True?" He looked at her, a mixture of annoyance and kindness in his eyes. "Karleen. I'm not blind. Your car is ancient, your stucco's flaking off in places, you don't use your pool. Why won't you just admit that money's an issue?"

Over in her corner, Britney came to; a second later, her wheel started whirring. Karleen took another swallow of her juice, then went over to give the hamster her nightly snack. "Okay, so I'm not rolling in it like *some* people I know. And I know the house needs to be re-stuccoed, I'm workin' up to it. But the pool's a luxury. And the car's still running, so…" Hamster nuggets rained onto the cedar shavings; Britney scurried over to play Stuff the Pouch. "So I'm careful with my money. Since when is that a crime? I could get a new car, or fix the pool…or sock money away for my old age. I choose plan B."

Several beats passed before Troy said, "I'm calling a pool service tomorrow." When she pivoted, her mouth open, he held up a hand, traffic-cop fashion. "It'll be good exercise while you're pregnant, so no argument. And the service will handle all the maintenance so you won't even have to think about it."

Pride warred with gratitude inside her head. Gratitude won out. "Thank you," she said.

"You're welcome. Of course, this means the boys and I will be over here to swim regularly."

"How did I know there'd be a catch?"

"Ah, but there'll also be a pool boy."

Karleen clipped shut the hamster food bag, then brushed the crumbs from her fingers. "Your mother will have a cow."

"This has nothing to do with my mother. A small but crucial point that seems to be eluding you."

"I bet she loved Amy to bits, though, huh?"

Troy looked at her steadily for a long moment. "Let's just say Amy came along at a time when Mom would have been thrilled with anyone who wasn't complicated, or threatened her sense of the Way Things Should Be. It wasn't Amy she loved, I don't think, as much as what Amy represented."

"Looks to me like she hasn't changed her mind on that score."

"And I repeat, what my mother thinks has no bearing on my decisions."

"And if you think I'm fool enough to get involved with a man whose mother hates me, think again. Besides, I thought we'd cleared this up, that nothin' was going to happen between us."

"Something is *already* happening between us, Karleen. And I dare you to look me in the eye and tell me my feelings are one-sided."

It felt like a hot little firecracker went off inside her chest, exciting and painful at the same time. Karleen opened her mouth to do just that—deny it—but the words got all wadded up in her throat. What man had ever looked at her like that, declared his intentions so earnestly? Nobody, that's who. None of her husbands, none of her boyfriends…

Oh, Lord…did this suck or what?

"You're not supposed to have feelings for me, Troy."

"Too bad."

"Too bad is right," she said, trying desperately to keep the shakes at bay, "because spending the evening with your family only confirms what I already knew, which is that I don't fit in with them, or who you are. Anymore than I'd expect you to feel like a part of what's left of my mother's family, back in Texas."

His brows dipped. "I thought you said there wasn't anybody besides your aunt?"

"Not close, true. There's cousins out the wazoo, though, each one more of a hick than the next." She pressed a hand to her heart. "I can be honest about who I am, and what I come from. I don't always like it, and I've worked to change the parts of that legacy, I suppose you'd call it, that don't do me any good. Still and all, I am who I am. And your mama's right, Troy—there's no sense getting all romantic about this."

Troy narrowed his eyes slightly, then unfolded his arms and walked over to her, sliding one hand around the back of her neck and lowering his mouth to hers. She might have made a tiny *mmmph* of protest, only it turned so quickly into a purr of need it hardly counted. The kiss went on and on and on, until everything inside her went all soft and puddly, until hot tears stabbed at her eyes and her heart felt like it would break from the sweetness, the stupidness, of it.

At long last Troy came up for air, even though he kept that hand on her neck, his cheek firmly pressed against her temple. "Still think there's nothing going on here?"

Karleen forced herself to look up at him, into those sweet, foolish eyes. "Since I don't see any magic wands around here, I don't see much point in answering that question, do you?"

Their gazes battled for several seconds before he let her go and walked off, slamming the door shut behind him.

She told herself hormones were the reason she cried for nearly ten minutes afterward.

Chapter Nine

By late June, most days were hot and dry, like a good desert is supposed to be. Karleen was careful, though, to only water her garden in the early morning or after the sun went down, and between that and Troy's biggest cottonwood shading the garden during the hottest part of the day, her tomatoes and cucumbers and cantaloupes—and the pumpkins—were coming along just fine.

So was the baby, praise be.

"Disgustingly healthy," was how the midwife had, with a broad smile, pronounced both Karleen and her little passenger. And now that the first trimester was past, both the exhaustion and barf-fests had eased up. She was still emotional as all get out, but at least the sight of raw chicken no longer sent her racing to the john.

"When c'n we pick the punkins?" Scotty asked, interrupting her thoughts. He was crouched so close she could practically *feel* his breathing as she kneeled in the cool, early morning dirt, yanking out weeds with roots to China. On the other side of the fence, Grady—whose interest in horticulture wasn't anywhere near as pronounced as his twin's—romped with Elmo, the Irish setter/poodle mix (they were guessing) puppy that, in the end, the boys' grandparents, not Karleen, had helped choose from the pound.

The grandparents who had decided to stay for nearly a month, much to Troy's chagrin and Karleen's immense relief, although you would have thought it would've been the other way around. But since their presence put a decided damper on Troy's trying any more funny business—and since Gus had been in hog heaven, what with Troy's house needing so many repairs—their hanging around had truly been a blessing in disguise. However, judging from the worker-ant routine back and forth between the house and the RV over the last day or so, Karleen guessed Troy's parents would be hitting the road fairly soon.

She happened to glance up as Troy came out of his house, dressed in a navy-blue knit shirt and Dockers, looking all handsome and solid and, God bless him, normal, and he looked over and their eyes met, and Karleen—who had gone from feeling perpetually exhausted to feeling perpetually ready to rumble—mused as how a little funny business might not be remiss, right about now.

She let out a mighty sigh.

Small fingers tapped her arm. "Karleen? Whatsa matter?"

"Oh, nothing, sugar," she said, yanking at the next weed.

"So when c'n we pick the punkins?"

The dog stuck his nose through the chicken wire Troy'd nailed along the post-and-rail to keep the mutt in the right yard, then woofed at Scotty, who giggled. Karleen smiled. "Not until they turn orange. It'll be weeks and weeks yet before that happens."

"Will they get real big?"

"Hopefully. We'll have to wait and see."

"Scotty!" their grandmother called, her hand shading her eyes as she stood on the deck. When she noticed he was with Karleen, her mouth tightened. Still, she nodded and said, "Good morning, Karleen."

"Mornin', ma'am. That's a real nice color on you," she said, nodding at Eleanor's crinkly, coral two-piece dress. Karleen had to give the woman points for coming over to apologize, the morning after the Lindquists' arrival. And once reassured that Karleen was, indeed, not out to ensnare her son, Eleanor had relaxed enough that they could at least be cordial with one another, even if Karleen wasn't exactly seeing a huge potential for their ever being bosom buddies.

"Thank you," Eleanor said, a breeze ruffling the hem of her skirt. If not her hair. "It's a lovely day, isn't it?"

"It is that. Gonna be hot, though."

"I imagine so. Still, it's a dry heat."

"Yes, ma'am," Karleen said, although she mentally rolled her eyes. Hot was hot, far as she was concerned. Although there was something to be said for being able to take a shower, dry off and *stay* dry. As opposed to the one time she'd gone back to Texas for a family reunion and basically had dripped the entire three days she'd been there. That had not been fun. But then, neither had the reunion.

Anyway, that was apparently as far as her conversation with Troy's mother was going to go, since Eleanor then said, "Come on, Scotty—you need to eat breakfast and get cleaned up, or we're going to be late for church!"

The little boy made a face, stabbing his kiddie trowel into the dirt. "I don't wanna go to church," he muttered for Karleen's ears only. "I'd rather stay here with you and Elmo."

At least she got first billing over the dog. She looked up to see Troy walking toward them, and all those hormones started panting and wriggling like the stupid dog. Honestly. "Go on, now," she said, giving the boy a hug. "You don't want to keep your grandma waitin'. And anyway, you and Grady are gonna come over and swim later, remember?"

The little boy nodded, then swiveled his head to look up at his father. "You coming, too?"

"Sure am," Troy said, his low voice coursing through her the way it always did. Yep, the man was definitely the full package. In more ways than one, a thought which did nothing to calm down those panting hormones. Troy hauled Scotty up and over the fence, lightly swatting the four-year-old's backside before pushing him toward the house. "So scoot—Grandma made pancakes."

"Grandma always makes pancakes," Scotty grumbled as he trundled off. "I'm bored of pancakes."

Karleen got to her feet, dusting off her knees. As usual, Troy's eyes went straight to her belly, pooching out quite nicely now underneath her stretchy tank top. She supposed she was going to have to do something about maternity clothes before she started to look like a sausage in too-tight casing.

"We're gonna have to tell 'em soon," Karleen said softly, watching the boys troop up onto the deck, the pup tripping them the entire way. "Grady asked me yesterday why I was getting fat."

Troy's eyes shot to hers. "I'm sorry—"

"It's okay, I am." She made a face. "I've already put on

ten pounds, and the midwife said most women only gained around five the first three months."

"So the appointment went okay?"

Some unexpected business thing had prevented his going with her for her last check-up. For all her certainty that she'd wanted it that way, she'd been surprised by how much she'd missed him. Which wasn't how it was supposed to be, not at all.

"Yes, fine. More than fine. But anyway, I was thinkin'…the boys might like to be part of this, you know? Helping me to get the baby's room ready, maybe?" She flushed. "When the time comes, I mean."

"I think that's a great idea," Troy said, obviously pleased. "But that means we either tell them tonight, or not until they come back in August."

"Come back? From where?"

A shadow crossed his features. "My parents offered to take the boys with them for the rest of the summer. They're going to do some sightseeing, then return to Wisconsin for several weeks before driving back down here."

Her jaw dropped. As did her stomach. "And you're actually letting them?"

"I didn't exactly jump at the offer, to be honest. Not at first. But they haven't seen the boys much since they were born. It was hard for me to get away, and my father really hasn't been up to traveling before now. It'll be good for all of them, I think."

"I'm sorry—has Gus been sick?"

Troy looked slightly startled, then smiled. "He's fine now."

Karleen's gaze drifted over to Troy's deck, where his mother was setting out plates of food for the boys. Gus came through the door, Scotty perched high on his shoulders, and Karleen's eyes misted.

"Funny he never mentioned it. We chatted over the fence a lot, late at night," she said in answer to Troy's slight frown. "Your mother and I might have issues, but your daddy's a real sweetheart. I hate to think of him suffering. Still," she said on a rush of air, "I can't believe you're lettin' the boys go for... how long? Six weeks?"

"Closer to seven."

"Wow. And they just got the dog, too."

"Believe it or not, they're taking the dog with them."

"You have got to be kidding."

"It was the only way they could convince the boys to go."

"Well, I'll be," Karleen said softly, crossing her arms. "Hard enough to imagine your mother with a pair of four-year-old boys 24/7—in an RV, no less—let alone a half-grown dog."

"She raised three boys, I suppose she'll survive my sons and a dog for a couple of months."

"Be that as it may, I still don't know how it's not killing you to let them go. It's killing me, and they're not even mine."

His expression softened. "You really mean that?"

She frowned. "That I'll miss the little buggers like crazy? Heck, yeah, I mean it. I love your kids, Troy."

"It's just the concept of loving me you have trouble with, then?"

"Oh, no, you don't—"

"Oh, yes, I do. Karleen…" He reached over the fence and snagged her hand. "I've never been separated from the boys for more than a night since they were born. So, yes, letting them go for this long is the hardest thing I've ever done. I know they'll be fine, and I'm sure we'll talk every day, but how I'm going to get through the summer without them, I have no idea. I only agreed because it will give us more time to get to know each other."

She sucked in a breath. "No."

"Yes."

She sucked in another breath, then let it out saying, "You think there's room for one more person in that RV? I'll sleep with the dog, I don't care—"

Troy's laugh cut her off. "You're not going anywhere, you're staying right here where I can keep an eye on you and our baby." He let go of her hand and backed away. "And we will get to know each other better, honey," he said. "Count on it."

Over the phone to Joanna later that night, Karleen recounted most of the conversation with Troy, ending with "And here I thought I'd be relieved when his folks left!"

"Just goes to show," Joanna said. Only then she didn't say anything more, and Karleen's antennae shot straight up. "What?"

"Oh, nothing. Nothing you want to hear, anyway."

"You think I'm being an idiot, don't you?"

"*Idiot* might be a little strong, but…yeah, basically. I haven't decided if you keep pushing this guy away because you're afraid you'll find out you really don't have anything in common, or because you'll discover you do."

"You're right, that definitely wasn't anything I wanted to hear. And what in tarnation is that supposed to mean, anyway?"

"Okay, think back. To after Bobby's and my divorce, and how you kept after me to put myself out there, start dating again, even though I made it more than clear I'd rather gargle with antifreeze. Finally, I knuckled under, and I hated it with a purple passion. Then Dale came along, and I wasn't interested, but you kept pushing and shoving and trying to shake me awake, because that's what you do. And thank God for it, because eventually all that pushing and shaking opened my eyes and I realized what a good thing I very nearly missed.

"Dale and I aren't a perfect fit, Karleen," Jo said, more gently. "We weren't raised the same way, don't have the same background. But none of that matters. Well, okay, it matters, but we work through it because *we* matter. You forget, Troy's twins and Chance play together at least a couple of times a week, so I've gotten to know Troy over the past couple of months. He's a keeper, Kar. So pardon me if I find your resistance a bit hard to swallow."

"You don't understand, Jo, I—" Wiping tears off her cheeks, Karleen jumped slightly when her doorbell rang. "Somebody's at the door, I've gotta go. I'll talk to you tomorrow, okay?"

Unless she could somehow avoid it, she thought, jumping again when she opened her door to find Troy's mother standing there, in all her permanent-pressed glory.

"Not who you expected, I know," Eleanor said. "May I come in? I won't take up much of your time."

"Oh, um…sure." Karleen stepped aside to let the woman in, remembering her manners enough to ask if she'd like something to drink.

"No. Thank you. The guys think I've gone out for a walk." Her gaze swept the living room, landing for a couple of very telling seconds on the fake leopard throw covering up the worn spot on the couch. Then Britney's personal playground, which Karleen had recently relo-cated in here. One thing Eleanor couldn't accuse her of, however, Karleen thought smugly, was slovenliness, since Karleen could not abide a messy house. Still, Eleanor shook her head slightly, then met Karleen's eyes.

"I take it everything's okay with the baby?"

Karleen felt a slight frown pinch her forehead. In the entire month Eleanor had been here, she'd never once asked about the pregnancy. "So far, so good."

"And you're feeling well?"

"Fine, thank you."

A brief smile flashed over the older woman's mouth. "Taking your vitamins?"

"Yes, ma'am."

"Well. As long as you and the baby are okay, that's the important thing." She walked over to the hamster's cage; Britney hopped off her wheel and scurried over, sitting up on her haunches and begging. Little hoochie. "I lost track of the number of hamsters, gerbils and guinea pigs the boys went through," Eleanor said. "Troy named his Fred."

"Which one?"

Eleanor chuckled softly. "All of them." She turned, her hands stuffed in the pockets of her wraparound skirt; Britney resumed her race to nowhere. "I suppose you're wondering why Gus and I are taking the boys for the summer?"

Karleen perched against the sofa arm, surreptitiously covering up the spot where she'd practically rubbed the fabric bald trying to remove a nacho-cheese stain. "Actually, I hadn't given it a whole lot of thought. Well, other than thinking that you and Gus must be a whole lot braver than you look." At Eleanor's funny expression, she blushed, then added quickly, "Although Troy said you haven't had much chance to spend a lot of time with them…oh." Her blush deepened. "You're taking them to keep 'em away from me?"

"The thought had occurred to me—at least, it did a few weeks ago—but no. That's not why. I knew, however, if we got the boys out of Troy's hair, he'd undoubtedly use the opportunity to…woo you."

Heavens. When was the last time she'd heard anybody use that expression?

"And don't pretend you don't know what I'm talking about," his mother continued. "I know Troy's smitten with you. And he's always been remarkably single-minded about going after—and getting—what he wants."

"Then he's met his match with me, 'cause I don't lay down and roll over all that easily." At his mother's lifted brows, she gave a dry laugh. "That didn't come out exactly how I meant it. I know how this must look, especially to somebody like you. And I'm not gonna pretend I'm something I'm not. God knows, I've been around the block enough times to wear a groove in the sidewalk. But it had actually been a while for me, too, when your son and I made this baby."

To Eleanor's credit, she didn't flinch. "I believe you."

Karleen shrugged. "Doesn't make any difference to me whether you believe me or not. Just like the…circumstances leading up to this situation make no difference as to the outcome." She tilted her head, frowning slightly. "Troy's actually talked this over with you?"

"No, of course not." Eleanor's mouth quirked at the corners. "But I'm not an idiot."

"So what is it you're doin', exactly? Warnin' me off?"

One eyebrow lifted. "I was given the impression I didn't have to."

"You don't. Which is what I'm not getting. Why you're telling me this. I mean, yeah, you're doing a fair job of pretending you don't hate me—"

"I don't hate you, Karleen! That's just it! I—" To Karleen's shock, Eleanor's eyes got all sparkly before she blew out a breath. "I'll admit, my initial reaction to you was knee-jerk and small-minded. Then finding out you were pregnant, and you're so different from Amy…" She squeezed shut her eyes for a moment. "I'm sorry. That was horribly unfair."

"You got that right. Especially since it's not like I can help it."

"I know that. Which leads me to what I'm trying to say. The thing is…I've been watching you with the boys. They adore you, and with good reason. You're wonderful with them. And you've charmed my husband, too," she said with a fleeting smile. "As well as…as my son. I don't know that you and I could ever be friends, exactly, but I'm not the kind of woman who can't admit when she's wrong. And I was definitely wrong. Not about how different you and Troy are, I still have my reservations about how good you'd be for each other in the long run, but…" Her mouth pinched. "You're a good person, Karleen."

"Did it hurt to say that?"

His mother laughed softly. "More than you know."

Thoroughly confused, Karleen got up to twist closed the living-room verticals, then turned back around. "Then what's the problem?"

"I take it you still feel the same way about Troy? That you don't see this working out between you?"

Ignoring the twinge to her heart—not to mention to other, more intimate areas—Karleen nodded. "Yes."

"Then that's the problem."

"I don't—"

"As I said, Troy doesn't give up easily. *Dogged* doesn't even begin to cover it. He's also responsible to a fault. He's infatuated with you, Karleen. And you're having his baby. Heaven knows, he had plenty of girls after him in high school and college, but he's only been really in love once before in his life and…"

Eleanor hauled in a breath. "It's funny…you hold your baby for the first time, and you think you only have to protect them for so long. Until they finish high school, perhaps. Or college, at the very latest. That there has to be some sort of statute of limitations on wanting to keep them safe. I mean, really," she said on a tight laugh, "Troy's going to be forty next year. He's a hugely successful businessman. He hasn't needed, or wanted, my protection in years. But knowing that doesn't stop a mother from hurting when her child hurts. And after Amy…"

Her hand pressed to her mouth, Eleanor glanced away, then returned her gaze to Karleen, tears sheening her eyes. "If you're as determined that this won't work as he is to *make* it work…I just can't see any good come of this."

Her own eyes burning, Karleen waited for several beats before saying, "I don't want to hurt anybody, Eleanor. Least of all Troy. But I'm not sure what you're asking. Or what you expect me to do."

"I don't know," Troy's mother said on a rush of air. "But I guess…I just thought if I was the obstacle to, you know, you and Troy getting together…"

Karleen's eyes went wide. "You *want* me to marry him?"

"I want him to be happy. And because of that, I won't stand in your way."

"All your *reservations* notwithstanding?" After his mother's curt nod, Karleen breathed out, "Whoa—didn't see that one coming. Still and all…this isn't about you. Going through the motions simply because I'm pregnant might've made sense years ago, but not anymore."

"Then you don't have feelings for my son?"

Karleen waited out the stab of pain. "It's because I do have feelings for him that I'm not taking up his offer. I'm no good at marriage, Eleanor. And your son deserves..." She swallowed. "He deserves somebody who *is*. Like you said, for the long run. So why put all that energy into something that in all likelihood is only going to fall apart, anyway?"

Troy's mother regarded her for several seconds, then released a breath. "That's that, then, I suppose."

"Yes, it is." She paused. "So you can leave the boys here."

"Not on your life."

Karleen laughed, then crossed her arms. "Can I say something?"

A wry smile pulled at the older woman's lips. "As if I could stop you?"

Karleen smiled, too, then said, "If I can be half the mother you are, I'll be doing okay."

Eleanor's brows lifted. "Even though I'm meddling and annoying as hell?"

"If that's what it takes to show you actually give a damn about your kids, then yes, ma'am. You're a good person, too, Eleanor. And I'm a lot less put off by the idea of you being this baby's grandma than I was when I first met you."

Troy's mother laughed, but it didn't escape Karleen's attention that she didn't make any move to hug her or show any sign of affection. "I suppose that's progress, then. Well...I won't keep you any longer," she said, heading toward Karleen's door, only to turn when she got there.

"You don't have to answer this question—I don't expect you to—but assuming you were telling the truth about it having been a long time since you'd...been with somebody else before you and Troy, you know..." She cocked her head. "Why did you? And why him? You don't want his money, you don't obviously want his name or protection. So what *did* you want?"

Then she was gone, giving Karleen something to chew over for the rest of the night.

She was still chewing a week later, on the evening of the Fourth, as she breast-stroked the length of the pool. Guilt, gratitude and sun-warmed water rippled over her as she swam, careful to keep her bleached hair out of the chlorinated water.

Joanna had invited Karleen to a barbecue at her place, but she hadn't felt up to going. Used to be, she never minded being odd man out at one of Jo's shindigs. But today the thought of being around that many happy people in one spot made her want to hurl.

The water sloshed up over her face for a second; when her vision cleared, she saw Troy come out on his deck, dressed in cargo shorts and a loose T-shirt, holding a flat, bright, cellophane-wrapped box under one arm.

Fireworks.

Karleen turned, pushed off the side, headed toward the deep end of the pool.

She'd barely seen him in the week since the boys had left. He'd gone away on business for a couple of days; after his return, his car was gone in the mornings when she got up, the lights in the house rarely on until ten or eleven at night. He'd called a couple of times, to check up on her, but the conversations had been short and almost imper-sonal, leaving her to wonder if his mother had been over-stating a thing or two. If she'd imagined Troy's words, the look in his eyes.

Leaving her to wonder what in the hell was wrong with her that she should find this possibility anything but a profound relief.

From what she could tell in the light spilling across the

deck from inside his kitchen, he seemed to be surveying the yard. After a bit, though, he carried the box back inside, shutting the French doors behind him. Karleen wondered why he hadn't gone to Blake's house or someplace for the holiday—she knew he and his partner were close—but then, she didn't suppose it was any of her business.

She climbed out of the pool, wrapping a Betty Boop beach towel around herself as she trekked back into her house, barefoot and dripping, just in time to hear the telltale *whoosh*-CRACKLE-*pop-pop-pop,* see the disco-esque strobing in her living room. She peered out the front window; Troy stood at the foot of his driveway, his hands in his pockets as the fountain spewed its pyrotechnic confetti ten feet in the air, blindingly bright wisps of red…blue…white…gold.

Still barefoot, Karleen let herself outside, grateful for the blanket of smoke and darkness. Troy pulled another fountain from the box, carried it out to the middle of the road, set it down, lit it, got back. After a second's sizzle, she sucked in her breath when a thousand coppery spiders lit up the night, each airborne for only a moment before plummeting to their graceful, glorious deaths.

"You like fireworks?" Troy asked, startling her. His gaze was fixed on the petering display; she'd had no idea he'd seen her.

She chuckled despite the sudden, tingly sensation in the pit of her stomach. "If it sparkles, glitters or flashes, you know I'm there."

"Right." He tossed the dead fountain into a bucket of water. "I'd bought these for the boys. Before I knew they wouldn't be here." A flashlight beam speared the darkness as he selected another one from the pack, checking for the fuse. "It would have been their first year."

Karleen palmed the mound cushioning the tiny life growing inside her. In the history of humankind, had a father ever missed his children more? She swallowed past the knot in her throat and said, meaning to cheer him up, "It's okay, they'll enjoy 'em just as much next year. Maybe even more."

Troy set the next fountain in place, waiting out a sudden breeze. "Funny how I don't put as much stock in 'next year' as I used to."

He lit the fuse and backed away, but the firey display wasn't anywhere near bright enough to dispel the thick, oily loneliness suddenly swamping the moment. And them, Karleen realized with a sort of grim acceptance. So she tucked the damp towel more tightly around her breasts and crossed the yard, climbing over the low fence to stand beside him. To stand with him, a pair of battered souls against the night and the memories and the loneliness.

"I'm perfectly okay with you staying over there," he said, not watching her.

"I know," she said, not watching him back. "Just don't get any ideas."

"Wouldn't dream of it."

But when she dared to glance over at him, she thought maybe he didn't look quite as miserable as before.

Even if the moment, like the fireworks, was destined to go right up in smoke.

Chapter Ten

"An' we're sleepin' in your room, Daddy!" Grady chirped in Troy's ear. "I got the bed by the window last night, but Scotty gets it tonight. It's so cool! Grandma said we c'n play wif all your cars 'n' trucks, too, if we're real careful."

With a tired chuckle, Troy tugged off the tie Blake had needled him into wearing for the video conference that day as he let himself into his stuffy, silent house. Despite Grady's happy babbling, Troy felt equally as airless and empty, a sensation only heightened whenever he'd talked to his boys over the past four weeks. He was no more used to their absence now than he had been those first few absolutely horrendous days when he'd felt as though his chest would cave in from missing them so much. The only positive was not having to feel guilty about business trips or bringing work home. But, then, he only brought work home as a lame attempt to stanch the seemingly bottomless hole in his heart.

Troy opened the freshly stripped and stained French doors to let out some of the stuffiness. Although in June the temperature always sank with the sun, by late July, even after 8:00 p.m., the heat often clung stubbornly to the day, leaving plants and psyches limp and enervated.

The grinding squawk of an extension ladder pulled him out onto his deck. He looked over in time to see Karleen brace the ladder against the gutter, then scamper up it and onto her flat roof like a squirrel with a Daisy Duke complex, a Lowe's bag dangling from one wrist. Not her typical jewelry choice.

"Hold on a sec," he muttered into the phone, muting it before he yelled, "And just what the hell do you think you're doing?"

One panel of her swamp cooler already detached, she whirled around. Peachy rays from the setting sun licked at her bare legs, set the glittery fabric stretched over her rounded belly ablaze.

"The pump blew," she said. "Had to wait until it cooled off some before I could get up here and fix it."

"You've done this before, I take it?"

"Yes, Troy, I have done this before. You go on with your phone call, I'll be down in a sec."

After the Fourth, they'd reached what he could only call an uneasy truce: They occasionally had dinner, and sometimes she even forgot to look like the heroine tied to the train tracks, hearing the chugga-chugga-CHOO-CHOO! right around the bend.

Didn't stop Troy from wanting to play Dudley Do-Right, however.

"I'm back," he said to his son, keeping an eagle eye on

the daredevil wielding a screwdriver and pliers on the roof next door. "How's Elmo?"

"Fine," Grady said. "He *finally* stopped throwing up so much. Last time it was a mouse or somethin', you shoulda seen it. We could even see the bones, it was really cool! Grandma said it was a good thing, else she was gonna leave 'im on the road somewhere. But I could tell she was only joking…."

"Lemme talk, it's my turn!"

"Uh-uh, I'm not done yet!"

"Yes, you are. Grandma says. Gimme the phone—"

"I said, I'm not finished!"

"Grandma! Grady won't let me talk to Daddy!"

"Let Scotty have a turn, honey," Troy heard his mother say in the background. "Then it's time for your baths."

Both boys went, "Awww…" then Grady said, "I gotta go. Love you."

"Love you back, squirt. Big hug—"

"S'me, Daddy," came Scotty's more gravelly voice. "Do we hafta take a bath every single *night?*"

Karleen hefted the cooler panel back into place, secured it, then gathered up her tools, the box, the bag and started back toward the edge of the roof.

"You have to do whatever Grandma says, buddy."

She turned backward, hooking one foot on the first rung. Troy held his breath.

"That sucks," Scotty said.

"Yeah, I kinda thought so, too, when I was your age."

Delicately gripping the ladder's sides, Karleen shimmied down nearly as quickly as she'd gone up. When she reached terra firma, Troy's breath left his lungs in a *whoosh*. "But the good news is, bathing every night cuts way back on the belly-button lint population."

Scotty giggled, then said, "Whatsa nanny?"

Troy sank into one of the deck chairs. Having shucked her sneakers, Karleen grabbed the hose snaked in the grass to water her garden. Every time she moved, those fake stone rings on her hands flashed in the sun. Oddly, he was getting used to them. "A lady who helps take care of children. Sort of like Mrs. Jensen. You remember her?"

"Uh-huh." Scotty's words kept fading in and out, probably because he was wiggling around. "She made me and Grady take naps when we didn't wanna. Will the new nanny make us take naps?"

Troy snapped his attention back to the conversation. "What new nanny?"

"The one Grandma says we might get when we get back. 'Cause you're gonna have your hands full. Full of what?"

Thank you, Mom.

"Oh, you know. You guys. Work. Taking care of this house. So I'm thinking about hiring somebody to help out."

"Why?"

"Because it would make life easier. We'll talk more when you get home."

"'Kay. S'Karleen there?"

A question posed every night. If Troy had expected their crushes to evaporate within a few days, he'd been sorely mistaken.

"She's over in her yard, watering the pumpkins."

"Are they big yet?"

"Getting there."

"Cool! C'n I talk to her?"

"Well, let's see…" Troy hauled himself out of the chair and headed toward the fence, calling her name. She ignored him. What the—?

Then he noticed the tiny wire running from her ear to the pack-of-gum-sized MP3 player hooked onto the waist-band of her jersey shorts. So he moved into her line of sight, waving the phone until she noticed him.

"It's Scotty!" he said when she unplugged herself.

With a huge smile, she dropped the running hose and tromped across the grass to take the phone. "Hey, sugar! Whatcha up to?"

Not everybody could keep up a phone conversation with a four-year-old, let alone sound as though she actually enjoyed it. But Karleen wasn't faking the way her whole face lit up whenever she talked to the boys.

Or whatever had prompted her to keep him company on the Fourth.

Or still worried his mother enough to sneak over to Karleen's "for a little talk" the day before they'd left. A conversation that Karleen had point-blank told him was between her and his mother and to keep his nose out of it.

Except she hadn't once looked him in the eye.

"...Oh, no!" she now said on a strangled gasp. "He ate a *mouse?*...I bet it was. What a dumb cluck!" She looked over at Troy with laughing eyes, shaking her head. Then she froze, the laughter dying on her lips. "Oh, sugar, that's real sweet of you to ask, but I can't be your nanny.... Well, because I already have a job, for one thing." Then she pressed her fingers against her lips. "I can't do that, either. Of course I love you, honey, I love you and Grady to bits, you know that. But friends can love each other, too.... Okay, I hear your grandma calling you, so you better go on.... I miss you, too, sugar. You be good, okay? And I'll see you real soon."

She handed over the phone, then tramped back to the hose and resumed her watering, and Troy remembered what Blake had said, about ceding control, about not pressuring her. But *damn,* he wanted her so much he thought his brain would melt. Standing beside her on the Fourth without touching her had damn near killed him.

"I asked Karleen if she could be our nanny," Scotty said in his ear, which did nothing to assuage the potential meltdown. Only then—thank God—Troy heard his mother going on about Scotty's needing to come on before the water got cold, and he breathed the sigh of the reprieved.

"Go take your bath, cutie. We'll talk tomorrow, okay?"

"'Kay. Love you."

"Love you, too."

Troy clapped shut the phone and slipped it into his pants pocket, then leaned one hip against the top fence rail. Karleen glanced over, then back, aiming her hose at another part of the garden. Overhead, a cicada began to drone so loudly Troy's skull vibrated.

"Don't even think about giving me grief for gettin' up on the roof," she said.

"Why would I do that? After all, it's not like you're pregnant or anything."

She blew out a sigh, pushing her bangs out of her face with her wrist, and Troy's hormones started humming. In four-part harmony. "The pump needed fixin'. And plumbers charge you a hundred bucks just to set foot on your property."

Troy shook his head, then said, "Garden's looking good."

"It is, isn't it?" she said, radiating pride. "It's been rainin' a bit more'n usual. That always helps. This hard stuff from the aquifer—" she wagged the hose, making the stream do a loop-de-loop "—is the pits."

"Maybe. But you definitely have the touch."

When she didn't say anything, he wondered if he'd

somehow insulted her. Only then she said, "There's something about a garden…I don't know how to explain it." She bent over to pick something off a tomato plant. "It's about putting down roots, I suppose. Not just the plants', but your own as well. That you'll actually be around to see the fruits—or vegetables, in this case—of your labor. Does that make sense?"

"Completely," Troy said softly, feeling a tug. Then he added: "I hear Scotty asked if you'd be their nanny."

Karleen snorted. "It gets worse. He also asked if I could be their mama."

"Did he now?"

Her eyes narrowed. "You put him up to it, didn't you?"

"Nope, he came up with that all on his own. Not that this would be a problem from my end, you understand."

"All too well."

"But just so you know, I'd still get someone else to help out around the house. And with the kids. Although, now that I say this, I'm getting quite an image of you in one of those cute little maid uniforms."

"Lord, you are one sick puppy," she muttered, moving on to the melons. Which were approaching basketball size. Scary. "You're home late. Again."

"You've been keeping track? I'm touched."

"You live next door. It's summer. It's kinda hard not to notice when you come home."

Troy chuckled. "I suppose you already had dinner?"

"I did. At dinnertime, strangely enough."

After a brief pause, he said, "We still on for tomorrow?"

He saw her back tense before she aimed the water farther over. "You know, there's no guarantee they'll be able to tell, if the baby's not turned right—"

"Karleen."

"Fine," she said on a rush of air. "Yes, the appointment's at four-thirty."

"And we really do need to discuss the nanny thing. But you keep putting it off. Or is it me you're putting off?"

Her eyes lifted. "Hallelujah, Lord, he's catching on. However, in the interest of being neighborly and all…how was your day?"

Troy shrugged, even as he noted that these conversations stretched a little further every day, that she opened up a tiny bit more. Not enough yet for him to see completely inside, but he'd take what he could get. "Put out a fire or two, increased my net worth…the usual. You?"

"Pretty good. Talked to Flo, she's going out to California to visit her daughter. With any luck, they'll keep her, she shouldn't be living on her own anymore. Oh, and one of the gals in Glynnie's office is getting married in October, a big shindig at the Country Club, and half the ladies in the firm are beggin' me to help 'em. Why are you looking at me like that?"

"I'm not looking at you—well, okay, I am looking at you, obviously—but I don't get it. Why all these women need help finding something to wear."

"The same reason they *need* ice cream, I s'pose," she said with a is-he-dense-or-what? eyeroll. "And anyway, if they didn't—" Karleen walked over to turn off the hose "—I'd be out of a job." She dumped the trickling hose into the grass. "Out of curiosity, when was the last time you set foot in a department store?"

"Willingly? 1973. And only because Santa was there," he added at her raised brows. Karleen laughed. "Hey, I'm a guy," he said. "I can't go into a mall without shots."

"Well, here's a news flash—lots of women feel the same way. Especially the busy ones. And that's where I come in. Because what you—and they—see as a jungle, I see as Six Flags." She grinned, *really* grinned, lighting up every bit of the darkness inside him. "So it's definitely a win-win situation. Just don't tell anybody I do most of my own shopping at the flea market, Target or off eBay."

"Your secret's safe with me."

"Hey, I learned my lesson, after watching my mama and her sister blow everything they made—which wasn't any great shakes, believe me—on booze and clothes and stupid stuff they didn't need, never setting anything aside for a rainy day. Of which there were more than I want to think about. So it's bills, then savings, then if there's anything left over, I treat myself. I may be wearing last year's designer knockoffs on my feet today, but at least I know I'll still have a roof over my head when I'm eighty."

"You're a very wise woman, Karleen Almquist."

"Aside from being accidentally pregnant at thirty-seven, you mean."

Their gazes wrestled for a long moment before Troy said, "Come over here."

"Why?"

"Just get over here, dammit."

Amazingly enough, she did, although with a look in her eyes like a dog ready to bolt at the slightest provocation.

"Give me your hand."

After a second or two, she did that, too. And Troy didn't betray her trust by trying to draw her closer, no matter how much he ached to do exactly that. Instead he simply kept her fingers gently, but securely, wrapped in his and said, "Like I said. You're one smart cookie. Smarter than probably ninety percent of the human population, frankly. Yes, you are," he added when she pulled a face. "And if you can impart half that wisdom to our son or daughter, he or she is going to be one very lucky kid."

Color exploded in her cheeks; she glanced around, as though not sure where to put the compliment. Finally she met his eyes again, her mouth pulled to one side. "Laying it on a little thick, aren'tcha?"

"Only calling it as I see it."

A little snort preceded her snatching her hand from his. "I'll see you tomorrow," she said, then walked away, leaving the air perfumed with her fear.

Monsoon season was in full swing, thick gray clouds clogging the late afternoon sky like blobs of wet cement. Like her mood, Karleen thought as she locked her car in the hospital parking lot and her cell rang, and it was Troy, and her tummy did a series of backflips, and she told her tummy to *cut it out.*

Like that was gonna happen.

"Hey," she said over the wind, "where are you?"

"Stuck in freeway traffic," he grumbled, sounding like the thunder beginning to crank up in the distance. Yeah, they made quite a pair. "Huge backup. On this side, anyway, the other side's moving fine. Short of the car's morphing into a helicopter, I seriously doubt I'm going to make it in time. Are you okay?"

Weaving through the parking lot, she rolled her eyes, even as she pointlessly tried to keep her wind-whipped hair out of them. "Yes, Troy, I'm fine. Maybe you should forget it—"

"Nothing doing. I think we're starting to move, anyway. Don't leave until I get there. And if I miss it, get pictures!"

Oh, for heaven's sake, she thought, silencing her phone before she went inside. It was only another check-up, for goodness' sake.

A delusion she actually held onto until the sonogram technician pointed to the screen and said, "Looks like she's cooperating today," and Karleen—who clearly wasn't firing on all cylinders, said, "She?" and the technician laughed and said, "Your daughter, sweetheart—you're having a little girl," and Karleen stopped breathing. At least, that's what it felt like.

Hands trembling, heart racing, Karleen put her clothes back on in a blur. A thrill of terror spiked through her as she drifted back out into the waiting room, the sonogram photo clutched in her hand.

A baby girl.

A *daughter.*

A chance to get it right, this time.

Or die trying, she thought, touching the tiny image, tasting this and that name on her tongue. Emily, Sarah, Meredith… Strong names. Proud names. The most un-hick names she could think of.

"I'm gonna do right by you, sugar," she whispered, her eyes all prickly. "Swear to God, I'm not gonna let you down."

She sensed Troy sliding into the seat beside her. He gently pried the photo from her fingers; after a moment, he chuckled.

"No pee-pee?" he said, and she choked on her laugh.

"No pee-pee," she affirmed, then leaned against his shoulder, and he wrapped his arm around her and held her close, and Karleen shut her eyes and forgot, for the moment, what, exactly, she was supposed to be fighting.

By the time they left the hospital, giant spears of sunlight pierced the slate-blue clouds, studding everything in tiny amber globes and leaving the air fresh, chilled, invigorating. In a definite what-the-hell mood, Troy took Karleen's hand as they crossed the parking lot to her car, entwining their fingers. She glanced up at him, smiling slightly. Trembling, not so slightly.

"I see rumba ruffles in our immediate future," he said, and she laughed.

And leaned against him. Again. His heart rate spiked. From that, from the news, from pretty much everything, even as terror peeked from behind the euphoria, laughing its nasty, nasal little laugh. *Not now,* Troy thought, and it receded. For the moment, at least.

Oh, dear God—a little girl was going to call him Daddy.

Instantly, images of frilly baby outfits and long, shimmery blond hair and pink doll houses and prom dresses and *wedding* dresses and beating the boys off with sticks flashed through Troy's thoughts. His boys were his buddies, his comrades, his future partners-in-arms. But a daughter…

He sucked in a breath. And smiled.

"You goin' back to work?" Karleen asked when they got to her car.

"Nope." Troy bent slightly at the knees to look into her eyes. Wide. Amazed. Slightly unfocused. "You sure you're okay to drive?"

"Would you *stop* that?" she said, ramming her key into the lock. "I'm fine."

"Liar."

Her mouth twisted. "Okay, I'm not fine. But I'm not in any danger of drivin' off the road, either." She flapped at him. "So go away."

Still, he tailed the 4Runner all the way back to their houses. And when he pulled into his driveway, he noticed she was still sitting in hers, hands clamped on her steering wheel, staring out the windshield.

Troy got out, hopped the fence, walked over. Motioned for her to lower her window.

"Problem?"

"Uh-uh," she said, and burst into tears.

Troy yanked open her car door and hauled her into his arms, and she clung to him, sobbing her heart out, and then she was pleading with him to hold her, to not let her go.

"I can do that," he said, telling himself not to get his hopes—or anything else—up.

Then she lifted her tear-streaked face to his and he kissed her, and she moaned and kissed him back, still clinging, their daughter bumping a little foot or something against his stomach, and hope set all those fenced-in hormones free, and he was a goner. And she looked into his eyes and said, "I need—" and he said, "I know," and led her inside her house, that insanely, wonderfully bizarre house, and slowly, slowly undressed her, peeling away her clothes, her fears, her resistance.

By the time he'd shed his own clothes, sunlight shot through the crystals dangling in her bedroom window, littering her bed, her naked body, with a hundred rainbows. Troy placed a soft, lingering kiss on each one in turn, sometimes forgetting which ones he'd already kissed so he had to start over, which made her laugh through the remnants of her tears.

"I'm sorry," she whispered, her brow knotted, her eyes closed. "So sorry—"

"I'm not," he said. "Roll over."

"I can't, my stomach—"

"Not on your stomach. Trust me," he added, stroking her hip when she frowned up at him.

She got on all fours and Troy curled himself to her spine, shielding her, their unborn child. One hand braced on the mattress, the other weighed first one breast, then the other, before slowly, slowly sliding over her bump, and on down...to tease, and spread, and dip inside, one finger, then two...gently, firmly, gently again, smiling as her breathing went more and more shallow.

She arched back, whimpering, pleading...and he kissed the nape of her neck, tasting her, before carefully, tenderly, filling her.

Claiming her.

She cried out, and he was lost.

And he never, ever wanted to find his way back.

Afterward, they lay spooned together, facing her window, her skin warm under his hand as he stroked her stomach. She hadn't said a single word, but Troy could practically hear her *I can't believe I did it again*. He tugged her closer.

"So tell me about the crystals," he murmured.

"What?"

"The crystals." He reached around to fold his hand over hers. "Why you've got such a thing for sparkly stuff."

"You makin' fun of me?"

The words were teasing, but the vulnerability underlying them pierced his heart. He cupped her shoulder, easing her around to face him. "Hey. You're the most exasperating woman I've ever known. But I would never, ever make fun of you."

Karleen lay on her back, her eyes one with his, for several seconds before pushing herself up and out of the bed and putting on a cotton robe. Then she walked over to the window, palming one of the figurines before coming back to sit cross-legged on the bed.

"This is Kitty," she said, reverently handing him the

piece of cheap glass. "My first. She used to sit on the corner of my second third-grade teacher's desk—"

"Your *second* third-grade teacher?"

"We moved three times that year. Anyway, Kitty'd sat right where the morning sun'd catch her and throw rainbows all over the blackboard. She's not real crystal, just cut glass, but to an eight-year-old, she was magic. When I left, four months after I got there, Mrs. Moon gave her to me. Said that way, I could take my rainbows with me wherever I went."

With a crooked smile, she took the piece of cut glass back from him. "And it was true. Whenever things got rough, I'd look at Miss Kitty and she'd be all shiny and bright and glittery, and she'd make me feel that way inside, even when I didn't want to. And somewhere along the way I decided I wanted to surround myself with glittery things, things that would catch the light and bounce it back to me. Things that make me smile."

"Like the birdhouses?"

She laughed. "And all the junk in the yard. It's crazy, I know." The little figurine flashed as she turned it over and over in her hand. "It's all cheap stuff, collected little by little over nearly thirty years. I know you think it's pretty tacky—"

"As it happens, I'm learning to like tacky."

Karleen twisted to look at him, one eyebrow arched, and Troy groaned, and she laughed. Then he pulled her down beside him, wrapping her in his arms and kissing her for a long, long time.

"As it happens," he murmured, eventually, "I like surrounding myself with things that make me smile, too. That make me feel good. That—what was it you said?—catch the light and bounce it back? Like a certain sassy blonde

I know." When she didn't say anything, he said through a shaky smile, "Of course, if the feeling's not mutual, if you think I'm too staid or predictable or boring or—"

"No!" she said, covering his mouth with her fingers. "Oh, God, no. There is nothing even remotely boring about you, Troy Lindquist. But rainbows aren't real, sugar." Tears crested on her lower lashes. "They're just illusions. And momentary ones, at that."

He gathered her to his chest, his chin in her hair, willing her to relax. To trust. "You're *real*, honey. *This* is real. Whether it lasts for one night or a lifetime. And that's good enough for me."

She didn't reply. No argument, no apology, nothing. Instead she sagged against him, eventually falling asleep. In his arms.

A small victory, Troy thought, but a victory nevertheless.

Crrrrrack *ka-BOOM!*

Troy bolted upright in the bed next to Karleen, willing his brain to process the storm, the hour, his presence in Karleen's bed at the hour. Rain slashed at the windows, pummeled overhead; outside, a waterfall sloshed over a faulty gutter. Another lightning flash seared his retinas, accompanied by more skull-rattling thunder.

And somehow, Karleen—on her side, facing him, the sheet barely grazing her ribs—snoozed through the whole thing.

Resisting the temptation to wake her, Troy got up to relieve himself, only to realize they never had gotten around to dinner and that he was subsequently starved. As Karleen would be, once the storm penetrated her consciousness enough for her stomach—and the baby—to send out "take care of me" signals.

Troy silently pulled on his clothes, then tiptoed out of the bedroom to make sure the rain wasn't coming in any of the windows. In the living room, Britney was doing her best to trim her pudgy little butt on her wheel. Troy clicked on the lamp by the sofa; clearly taking Troy's presence in stride, the hamster waddled down from the wheel to look up hopefully at him, her whiskers twitching. He obliged her by dropping into her cage a few hamster goodies, which she promptly shoved into her cheek pouch. Would that he could feed the humans in the house so efficiently.

As Britney stuffed and munched, Troy took a good look at Karleen's living room, for the first time noticing not only the amazing quantity of dog-eared paperbacks—romances, mysteries, celeb tell-alls—crammed inside the white laminate bookcases, but that they were all in alphabetical order by author. That the cheap prints on the walls were hung perfectly straight. That there wasn't a stray magazine or newspaper anywhere.

That clearly she craved order every bit as much as he did.

"You goose," he whispered, smiling, then headed back to the kitchen, where he flipped the nearest switch, illuminating the god-awful Versailles-wannabe chandelier over the breakfast nook. *Okay, food,* he thought, opening the fridge. A minute into the serious contemplation of the relative merits of eggs over grilled cheese, he thought he heard a bell or something over the storm.

He pulled his head out and listened, frowning.

"What are you doing?" Karleen said from the kitchen door, and he nearly had a heart attack.

"Looking for food. You scared the crap out of me—"

"Shh—was that the doorbell?"

Carton of eggs in hand, Troy looked at Karleen. Who,

he duly noted, looked pretty damned good, even with bed-head and no makeup and cheeks that were looking more and more like Britney's every day.

"You generally have callers at ten at night?"

"Uh-uh," she said, yawning and starting for the door, and Troy said, puffing up, "Like hell. I'll answer it."

"You know," she said to his back as he stomped down the hall, "if you hadn't've been here, I would've answered it, anyway."

Ignoring her, he opened the door to an older, cheaper version of Karleen, like a two-bit drag queen doing Dolly Parton. One long-nailed hand caressed the extended handle of a bruised and battered wheeled suitcase, the other balanced a smoldering cigarette.

"My, my, my," the blonde said, giving Troy a bold once-over. Grinning broadly, she flicked ash onto Karleen's porch. "And who might *you* be, honey?"

Behind him, Karleen muttered the mother of all swear words.

Chapter Eleven

If it hadn' it been for the baby, no way would Karleen have been able to eat. But Troy wasn't taking no for an answer, watching every bite of scrambled eggs disappear into her mouth even as he dispatched his own like he hadn't eaten in a week.

She couldn't imagine a sleeping nightmare worse than the one she was living for real, right now, in her own kitchen. Bad enough she'd slept with Troy again, but then to have her aunt show up, out of the blue…

Well, okay, not so out of the blue. This was Inky, after all. And it wasn't like the signs hadn't been there all along—the phone calls, the pleas for money, the increasingly helpless whinings. But between the pregnancy and Troy, there'd been nothing left over for worrying about what her aunt might be up to.

Yet another example of how ignoring something doesn't make it go away.

Karleen glanced over at Troy, refilling their milk glasses before sitting back down and resuming his meal, and squelched a very heavy sigh. If their earlier hanky-panky had only been about sex, that would've been one thing. Trouble was, she'd already started her free fall long before that; nothing to be done now except wait for the inevitable *thud* when she hit bottom. So at the moment she was far too much of an emotional wreck to play nice. With anybody.

Why was it, she mused as she forced down another bite of eggs, that the more she tried to take charge of her life, the more things seemed determined to spiral out of her control?

"I still can't believe you didn't tell me you were *pregnant*," Inky more or less squealed, her makeup a little desperate-looking in the overhead light. With a slight somebody-walking-over-your-grave shudder, Karleen lifted a hand to her own tangled, mangled hair.

"I didn't figure it was any of your business."

Hurt flooded her aunt's tired blue eyes, weighted with too much mascara, dulled by too many forgotten nights, too many hung-over mornings.

"But I'm this baby's great-aunt, Leenie," she said with a twitching smile in Troy's direction. A scrawny hand reached over to cling like a greedy insect to Karleen's wrist. "And I know how long you've waited for this, how much you always wanted to be a mother!"

"Which is precisely why you can't stay."

Unnaturally thin brows shot up, followed by a breathy, nervous laugh. "Oh, now, I'm only talkin' about a few days, not forever. Just until I pull myself together again."

"You know, it is truly amazing, how after all these years you can still sound so sincere."

Apparently deciding to drum up support from whatever camp she could, Inky now turned to Troy. "It's the pregnancy makin' her talk like this. Maybe you could—"

"Oh, no," he said, holding up one hand. "Whatever's going on here is between you and Karleen. I'm just here for the food."

Inky gawked at him for several beats, then seamlessly started in again with Karleen. "I don't have anyplace else to go, sugar." Ah, yes. Cue the crocodile tears. "I told you, I lost my last job, and there were slim pickings back in Lubbock. So I figured, maybe there'd be something here in Albuquerque. And you and I—well, and this baby," she said, smiling at Karleen's bump, "we're all we've got."

"You are not part of that equation, Inky."

Instantly, all the sweetness and light drained from her aunt's voice. "You can't throw me out, Karleen. We promised your mama that we'd look out for each other."

Karleen nearly laughed out loud. "When did you ever look out for me?" she said, pushing away the uneaten eggs. "It's always been me sending *you* money, making sure *you* were okay."

"Then how is it I can count on the fingers of one hand the number of times you've called me in the last ten years? We used to be so close, baby. Then suddenly it was like you didn't want to have anything to do with me."

"Maybe because I finally got tired of trying to help someone who doesn't really want to be helped." Vaguely, she was aware that Troy had stopped eating to listen intently to every word. "How many times have you sworn you were gonna stop drinking and pull yourself together, stay with one job for longer than a month or two? Ever since I was a child, Inky, it's been one broken promise after another. So excuse me for not wanting to be dragged down anymore. And don't even *think* about smoking in here," she said when her aunt pulled a pack of cigarettes out of her purse.

Inky actually had the nerve to look taken aback, but she tossed a saccharine smile at Troy, then slipped the cigarettes back in her purse. Anybody else would have been too humiliated—or at least ticked off—to stay after Karleen's outburst in front of a total stranger. But not Inky. Oh, not Inky, who had spent so much of her life being humiliated, she'd become immune to it.

And in that moment, Karleen knew she'd lost the battle, a thought that curdled the eggs in her stomach. Because short of calling the cops to physically remove her aunt— and on what charge? Mooching?—she was stuck. With Inky, in her house, until her aunt decided to leave of her own accord.

One trembling hand curved around the baby as a sick feeling of helplessness, of doom, washed over her, that despite all her hard work she'd never be completely free of the genetic taint of bad booze, bad men, bad decisions.

"It's only for a couple of days," Inky said, ever hopeful. Ever delusional. Then she smiled. "I promise."

Regrets tingeing the cool, rain-sweetened air, Troy watched Karleen's face in the light spilling from the open front door as they stood on her porch. Her arms crossed over her belly, Karleen kept her gaze averted, even though her rock-solid jaw said it all.

"You sure you don't want me to stay?"

"Positive."

Still, Troy propped himself against the railing bordering the porch, one leg stretched in front of him. At his back, water dripped steadily from the eaves, splattering around Karleen's plastic roses. "I don't like the idea of your having to handle this all on your own—"

"I can handle Inky. God knows I've been doing it all my life."

God also knew that this was familiar enough territory for Troy to recognize denial when he heard it. "I'm sure you have. But you don't need the stress right now."

"Then please don't add to it," she said quietly, just as Inky yelled her name

from inside the house, only to then appear in the doorway.

"Is it okay to use the towels already hangin' up in the hall bath? And you shouldn't leave the door open like that, honey, there's like a thousand moths in here…. Oh, I'm sorry, Troy!" Flashing him a smile, she pulled her flimsy, floral robe more tightly around her doughy figure. Fingers decorated with chipped red polish clutched a wineglass, clearly filled with her own stash, since he knew Karleen didn't have anything in the house. "I didn't realize you were still here, darlin'. I won't be a sec—far be it from me to be a third wheel! The towels, Leenie?" she redirected to Karleen.

"Yes, those towels are fine," she said, and off her aunt went, humming loudly. Karleen stared after her for a tellingly long moment, then finally returned her gaze to Troy.

"Call me Leenie and you're dead."

"Wouldn't dream of it."

"The crazy thing is," Karleen said softly, almost more to herself than to him, "she's not a bad person. She's just—"

"High maintenance?"

A tiny smile flitted over her mouth. "That's one way of putting it." She paused, then said, "But she's never going to change, anymore than Mama did." Her gaze speared his. "Do you get what I'm saying, Troy?"

He folded his arms over his chest. "You're not your aunt, Karleen."

"No. But she's part of who I am. And nothing's gonna change *that*."

"If you got your act together," he said, "why couldn't Inky?"

"Because I *wanted* something better for myself. Maybe I wasn't an alcoholic, but I could still see the dead-end road in front of me." She shook her head. "Inky can't. Just like Mama couldn't. And even if…" She paused, as though unable to bring herself to say the words. "Even if we did give this a shot, how're you gonna feel the first time she passes out at Thanksgiving, or comes on to one of your relatives? What would your *mother* think?"

Even if we did give this a shot…

Troy stuck his hand underneath the dripping water, relishing the cool against his heated skin. "My father's a recovering alcoholic, Karleen," he said, not looking at her. "Believe me, I've lived through my share of uncomfortable holiday dinners."

Several long moments passed before she said, "Gus? That sweet man?"

"That *sweet man* put us all through holy hell for years. Until my mother left him, about ten years ago. Told him if he didn't get help, they were through."

"Oh my God, Troy…I had no idea."

"Not many people do. So count yourself among the elite few who know the great Lindquist family secret."

"So that was his 'sickness'?"

"Yeah." He twisted to look at her, flicking water from his hand before crossing his arms over his chest. "He's been dry for six or seven years. It wasn't easy, Kar. It still isn't. The temptation never completely goes away. But he was about the same age as your aunt when he finally realized what he stood to lose if he didn't get a handle on his addiction. So it's not too late. It's never too late."

Karleen walked to the other side of the porch, heavily bracing her hands on the railing to look out into her yard. Troy followed her gaze, half watching several of the twirly things spinning slowly in the leftover breeze, gleaming dully. "Then maybe your daddy had a stronger motivation than my aunt's ever had. Because heaven knows, I'm sure not it. I've done everything, said everything I know how, but…" She straightened up again, poking at a wind chime. "You're right, Inky's the last thing I need to be dealing with right now. And I know I gave lip service to throwing her out…" Her arms strangling her middle, she looked at him, anguish—and shame—contorting her features. "But I can't."

"I know, honey. Believe me, I know how hard this is on you. My brothers and I all thought Mom had a screw loose when she walked out on Dad. That's why it kills me to think of you going through this alone."

Her jaw hardened again. "And I'm not about to inflict this mess—*my* mess—on you. Or the boys. Oh, God, especially the boys…" She looked away for a second, then returned her gaze to his. "Thanks, Troy, but I don't need your help."

Troy swallowed back the hot, bitter taste of frustration and said, as gently as he could manage, "You know, there's nothing wrong with being proud of who you are or what you've accomplished. But sometimes there's not much difference between pride and stubbornness."

As he expected, her eyes flashed to his, her brows drawn together. Then she spun on her heel and headed back inside.

"Funny," he said before she reached the door, "the woman I fell in love with would rather put out her right eye than back down from a challenge."

Karleen whipped around. "And you call *me* stubborn? Don't you get it, Troy? The woman you fell in love with doesn't exist!"

"Bull."

Her saw her eyes squeeze shut, her chest rise and fall as she tried to steady her breathing. "This isn't backing down from a challenge, Troy," she said at last, her voice shaking, and he felt like a jerk. "This is refusing to listen to somebody tell me that everything I've fought for is, what? Wrong? Stupid? That I've got no right to determine my own destiny?"

"Dammit, Karleen—I'm not trying to interfere with your choices! Hard as this may be to believe, wanting to help you get where you need to go isn't some kind of threat to your autonomy."

Her hand, and her gaze, flew to her tummy when the baby apparently kicked. After several seconds, she finally lifted her eyes. And in them, past the adamancy, and the determination, Troy saw a yearning that broke his heart.

"My pride is all I've got, Troy. The only thing I can count on. And I spent too many years clawing my way up out of hell to let anybody—not you, not even this baby—take it away from me. I know this doesn't make sense, and I don't expect you to understand…but I simply can't cope with you and Inky at the same time. And anyway, this is family business. So if you care about me, and our child, you'll do whatever makes life easier for me right now. And right now, I need you to go."

Once again shouldering aside his annoyance, Troy stood and walked over to Karleen, palming her belly. The baby stirred, a flutter against his hand. "*This* is family business, too. And if you think I'm going to simply walk away and put you out of my mind, then you don't know what *family* is nearly as well as you think you do."

As he crossed the wet grass, he heard Inky say from the porch, "Oh, Lord, sugar...I hope you two didn't have a fight on my account...."

"You do realize, don't you," Joanna said from the other side of the picnic table in her backyard, "that Karleen would take both of us out without a second's thought if she knew we were talking?"

Troy allowed a tight smile, keeping an eagle eye on Joanna's youngest as he scampered like a curly-headed bug over the enormous wooden fort and swing set on the other side of the yard.

"It's okay, my life insurance policy's up to date."

Joanna chuckled and refilled his lemonade glass, then hugged one knee as she, too, let her gaze drift over to her son. The still-high, late afternoon sun tangled with all those crazy red curls for a moment until she looked back at him, concern swimming in her big gray-green eyes. Naturally, when he'd finally broken down and called her, she'd already known about Inky's return, ten or so days before. Nor did she seem terribly surprised when he'd asked if they could meet after he got off work. But frankly, he was at his wit's end. Wanting to fix the situation and having a clue how to go about that were two different things. From where he was sitting, Joanna was his best, and possibly last, hope.

"I get that she's scared," he said. "I get that she doesn't want to slip back into old destructive patterns. What I don't get is what that has to do with me."

"No," Joanna said, smiling. "You wouldn't."

"What's that supposed to mean?"

She shrugged. "That you're not a woman, mostly. That you're not *that* woman, specifically." She stuck a finger in her lemonade, swirling the ice cubes around. "I know this is a cliché, but Kar's like an abused dog. She could be starving, but the thought of trusting a stranger—even one with food in his hand—is even more terrifying than the possibility of starving to death." When Troy frowned, Joanna blew out a breath.

"I don't know how much Karleen's told you about her life. Knowing her, not a whole lot. But I practically lived it with her. Not that she ever got comfortable with the idea of me coming over to her house when we were kids, but I did anyway. Partly because I was curious, I admit, but mostly because I could tell her home life embarrassed her. And I made it my mission to get her to understand that it didn't matter. Not to me. And anyway," she said, smiling, "my mother was hardly ever around, so I thought any mother at home was better than no mother at home." The ice cubes clinked when she took a sip. "I was wrong."

"Was Karleen abused?"

"Mmm, no," she said, swallowing. "More like neglected. Left to raise herself, for the most part. From what little I saw, I think her mother really did love her. And at least she'd stopped the constant moving by then. But she still had her priorities skewed."

"She was an alcoholic?"

"Yeah."

"Did you ever meet Inky?"

"A few times. She was in and out. I'm not sure how Emmajean—Karleen's mother—managed to keep a roof over their heads, but she did. Which was more than you could say for Inky, who was always out of work, kicked out of her house, whatever. And the men…God. Each one a bigger loser than the next. I know it all sounds very afternoon talk show, but I'm not making any of this up. It's a testament to Kar's character that she came out of it as unscarred as she did."

"Except she didn't. Come out unscarred."

Joanna lifted a hand to fluff her hair off her neck. "Apparently not." A soft, humorless laugh fell from her lips. "And typically, she kept looking for acceptance in all the wrong ways. Not that I have much room to talk—I married too young, and for the wrong reasons, just like she did. The difference is, she *kept* marrying for the wrong reasons. And each time the marriage dissolved, she felt like more of a loser herself."

"She blamed herself for the breakups?"

"Not entirely. But a failed marriage is a failed marriage. She might have never fallen victim to the alcohol, but it took her a lot longer to figure out how to stand on her own two feet."

"So she sees falling in love as a weakness,"

"I think it goes even deeper than that."

"Meaning?"

Her gaze met his, a tiny frown dissecting the space between her brows. "As close as Karleen and I have been all these years, through all the crazy things we did together as kids, all the crying jags we shared when we got older…I always suspected she was holding a piece of herself back. That she never completely felt as though she fit in. As if she was straddling two worlds—the one she grew up in, which she hated, and the one she wanted but never quite felt she deserved." Her mouth flattened. "Not surprising considering how often she'd been let down."

"Like the starving dog."

"Exactly. That's not to say she's not proud of how far she's come. But it's as though she's imposed some sort of personal glass ceiling on herself."

"And now she sees her aunt's return as a threat to whatever progress she's made."

"I wouldn't doubt it." Joanna took a sip of her drink. "I take it you're in love with her?"

Troy stared at his lemonade glass for a long moment. "Hopelessly."

"Oooh, that was more than I'd hoped for." Joanna laughed softly. "Although I don't envy you."

"At the moment, I don't envy me, either."

"You can't let her think you pity her, you know."

"Why would I pity someone who's overcome as much as she has?"

Joanna gave a regal little nod. "Right answer."

"So do I have your blessing?"

That got a loud laugh. "Oh, you had my *blessing* from the first time we met. What you have now is my deepest sympathy." At Troy's grunt, she smiled and asked, "Did this help?"

Troy unfolded himself from the table, downing the rest of his drink. "Actually, it did. Although at this point, this isn't about me, not really. It's about Karleen. And our child. I want more, but…" He shook his head. "Sometimes, I guess the hurt simply goes too deep."

"No hurt goes that deep, Troy. Don't you get it? She wants *more,* too, but nobody's ever given it to her. All Karleen's *ever* wanted is to be won over, by a man more stubborn than she is. Someone willing to actually fight for her instead of shrugging and walking away." Shielding her eyes from the sun, Joanna looked up at him with an enigmatic smile.

"You've gotten this far," she said gently. "Don't give up now."

A towel twisted over her swimsuit after her morning swim, Karleen padded barefoot into her kitchen…where she immediately spotted a filled ashtray on the counter that hadn't been there when she'd gone outside a half hour before.

She picked up the disgusting thing with two fingers and carried it into the living room, holding it out as far from her body as possible.

"You're dripping all over the floor, sugar," Inky said from the sofa, where she sat in her shortie nightgown and robe, her bare feet crossed on Karleen's glass coffee table, watching the *Today Show* while she did her nails.

"And how many times have I told you in the past two weeks—" Karleen set the ashtray on the table in front of her aunt "—that I don't want you smoking in the house?"

Her aunt flicked her a glance. "Sorry, honey. But it was rainin' last night again, and I didn't want to go outside."

"This isn't from last night, it's from this morning. It's bad for the baby, and I won't have it."

"Oh, now, don't go gettin' all high and mighty on me, Karleen. Your mama and I both smoked when she was carryin' you, and you turned out just fine."

"Other than the near constant colds and crap I had all through elementary school? I'm serious, Inky. No. Smoking. Inside. The house."

"Party pooper," her aunt called after Karleen as she stomped back to the kitchen for a glass of orange juice. And maybe a couple pieces of raisin toast while she was at it. In the midst of pouring herself a glass of juice, Inky appeared in her line of vision.

"You want me to fix you some eggs or pancakes or something?"

"No. Thank you." To be fair, her aunt hadn't expected Karleen to wait on her, and often had dinner ready and waiting when Karleen got home from a late appointment. True, Inky was usually already halfway to wasted by then, and true, regularly consumptions of chicken-fried steak and breaded okra and corn bread was wreaking serious havoc on what was left of her figure, but the woman meant well, even so. "I'm fine with toast."

"Now you know that's no kind of breakfast for a pregnant woman," Inky said, clip-clopping in her pink satin Frederick's of Hollywood mules to the fridge. "Sit down, it won't take me but a second to fix you a real break-fast. You enjoy your swim?"

"Mmm," Karleen said, giving up the fight. She felt the bottom of her bikini, making sure it was dry before she sat down. She looked positively ridiculous in the thing with her big old belly front and center, but if all those Hollywood types could let everything hang out—in public, no less!—she supposed she could get away with it in her own backyard.

"Yeah," Inky said, setting Karleen's skillet on the stove and giving it a squirt of PAM, "it's real nice, you having a pool. Although the pool boy leaves a lot be desired. He was here yesterday, did I tell you?" She cracked three eggs into a bowl, then took a whisk to them. "He was sixty if he was a day, with a gut on him that might as well had Bud-weiser stamped right across it."

"That's just...wrong," Karleen said, trying to keep a straight face as she flicked open the morning paper.

"You're telling me. Got myself all fixed up for nothing."

Inky adjusted the heat under the pan, which sizzled when she poured the eggs into it. "Say what you will about that ex of yours, he did okay by you in the end. Leaving you this great big house and all."

"Nate didn't *leave* me the house. I'm buying it from him."

Inky whipped around, spatula raised. "You are not."

"I am."

"You can afford to do that?"

"He gave me good terms, but yeah. I can afford to do that."

Shaking her head, her aunt turned back to the stove. Neither said anything until Inky set their breakfast in front of them and sat down, at which point Karleen not-so-subtly pushed the classified section across the table.

Inky looked up. "You tryin' to tell me somethin'?"

"It's been two weeks, Inky. Not a couple of days. You can stay as long as you need to, but you've got to get a job. Any job, I don't care. Where are you getting the money for the booze and cigarettes, anyway?"

Her aunt bristled. "I don't suppose that's any of your business."

"Since you're living in my house and eating my food, I suppose it is."

"Food *I* cooked, if I may remind you."

"Inky. Please."

"Okay," her aunt said on a huff, "if you must know, I hocked some of the jewelry Sammy gave me. Not for near as much as I thought I'd get—cheap SOB—but I got enough to tide me over for a while. So—" she waved her fork at the paper "—I have no intention of taking the first job that comes along. And anyway, what are you worried about money for? Isn't Troy supporting you and the baby?"

Karleen's gaze snapped to her aunt's. "*What?* No, he's not supporting me! Why on earth would you think that?"

"But I thought he was one of those rich entre...entre-preters...oh, you know what I mean."

"Entrepreneurs. Yes, he is. But that has nothing to do with me. Of course he'll help support his child, but I'm not part of the package."

Her aunt put down her fork. "Not for want of him trying, if my hunch is correct." When Karleen didn't respond, Inky huffed. "And here I always thought you were the intelligent one in the family. He asked you to marry him, didn't he? And you turned him down."

Karleen met her aunt's gaze dead-on. "I had my reasons."

"What possible reason could there be for you not marrying a good-looking, wealthy man who's obviously crazy about you? And whose child you're carrying, to boot? Have you lost your mind?"

"No, actually for once I'm being completely level-headed about things. Troy and I just aren't a good fit."

One over-plucked brow lifted. "You obviously were at least once."

Karleen stood abruptly, carrying her dishes to the sink. "Being good together in bed isn't enough to sustain a relationship, Inky. Which you of all people should know."

"Oh, now, don't be like this, honey...you know I've only got your best interest at heart—"

"You have never had my best interest at heart!" Karleen said, wheeling on her aunt. "It was always about living for the moment, for both you and Mama! The next drink, the next man, the next night out on the town. I love you, Inky, and I know you love me, in your own strange way. But if you really gave a damn about me, you'd sit down and come up with a plan to sort out your life. Starting with doing something about your drinking problem."

"I do not have a drinking *problem*," Inky said stiffly.

"Yes, I'll admit I like my wine in the evenings, but I never touch a drop before lunch. And I gave up the hard stuff a long time ago. So there's no need to go gettin' your panties in a wad." She smirked. "Or are you worried that'll somehow hurt the baby, too? That she can somehow smell the wine fumes from all the way inside your belly?"

All the old feelings of rage and frustration rose up, stinging Karleen like a thousand jellyfish tentacles. Dammit—she'd turned her back on this life, on everything that had tried so hard to suck her down into the depths with her mother, her aunt, any number of her other family members who, like Inky, would die—literally—before they'd admit they had a problem. But while her back was turned, her life had been waiting for exactly the right moment to find her again.

Except…

Except *now,* she realized, she wasn't the scared little girl, or the confused teenager, or the clueless young woman still waiting for something or somebody to come along and rescue her. So she parked her hands on her rapidly expanding hips and said, "Here's how it's gonna be, Inky—either you pull yourself together, or find someplace else to live. I will change the locks on the doors when you're out, if it comes to that. Because I refuse to raise *my* little girl in a house filled with broken promises and unrealized dreams. You wanna self-destruct, you go do it someplace else."

Horror exploded in her aunt's eyes. "You giving me an ultimatum, Karleen?"

"All tied up in a bow," she said, then stomped down the hall to get dressed for her morning appointment.

Chapter Twelve

"Oh, you didn't have to do that!" Karleen's aunt trilled, taking the white bakery box from Troy. Wearing black shorts and a tank top that revealed far too much wrinkled cleavage and over-tanned leathery skin, she flipped the box open, gasping at the triple chocolate cake inside. "Shoot, boy…if that gal doesn't marry you, I'll marry you myself!" She nodded at a second box, still in his hand. "And what's that?"

"For Karleen."

Plucked brows shifted north, but all she said was, "Well, come on in, make yourself comfortable while I finish up in the kitchen. I talked to Karleen a little bit ago, she sounded like she'd be home in a few minutes."

Troy followed Inky back to the kitchen, where the scents of garlic, basil and tomato sauce blessedly overpowered the woman's perfume. Heaven. Which it would not be once Karleen got home and found him there, he was sure.

As fired up as he'd been after his talk with Joanna to *do something*, what that something might have been had yet to present itself. Not good for a man more inclined to take action than mull over a thousand possibilities. He'd checked up on Karleen nearly every day—much to her obvious consternation—but this would be his first opportunity in two weeks to actually get more out of her than a perfunctory "I'm fine."

Should be interesting.

He set the box in the center of the already-set table, chuckling at the gold lamé place mats underneath the Corelle. "I take it she has no idea you invited me over for dinner?"

"Are you kidding? There are a few brain cells left underneath all this," Inky said, pointing to her froth of stiff, pale blond hair. "Those that aren't pickled yet, anyway. You want something to drink?"

Troy lifted an eyebrow, but Inky shook her head.

"I know what you're thinking, but even though a good red Chianti would be perfect with this…" She let out a truly regretful sigh. "I'm watchin' my Ps and Qs these days. So. Water, soda, juice…?"

"Water's fine. Thanks."

Inky pulled a bottle out of the refrigerator, pouring it with great fanfare into a plastic goblet decorated with cartoony tropical fish. Her silvery-blue eye shadow glistening, she handed the glass to him, then opened the oven door to peek inside. "I hope you like chicken parmesan, it's this recipe I got off this Eye-talyan woman who lived in the apartment above me the one winter I lived in Nashville. It's all made from scratch, none of that processed chicken or bottled sauce. Takes the better part of the afternoon, but it's worth it."

Smiling, Troy eased himself up onto a bar stool. "So you like to cook?"

"I sure do. And I'm pretty good at it, if I say so myself. Don't get much opportunity to show off for strangers, though, so this is a treat for me."

"As I'm sure it'll be for me, too. It smells great."

She beamed. "You're a real sweetheart, aren't you? But then, I could tell that right off. Why my niece can't see it is beyond me."

Troy took a sip of his water, meeting the blonde's gaze. "Maybe that's the problem. Being too nice, I mean. I'm seriously considering getting a Harley and not shaving for three days."

Inky laughed. "Don't forget the tattoos. The scarier, the better. Oh, and you gotta work on your sneer. Like this," she said, curling one side of her bright red mouth.

His smile fading, Troy glanced down at the crazy water glass, then back up at Karleen's aunt. "You do realize my being here isn't likely to change her mind?"

"You *not* being here isn't going to change her mind, either. So I figure it couldn't hurt, right?" She reached up to fiddle with one large gold hoop in her ear, her brows pulled together. "Maybe I haven't exactly been a shining example, but I'd do anything to see that gal happy. Which is more than she's clearly willing to do for herself. Oh!" she said at the sound of the garage door opening. "That's her now. Act natural!"

Troy stood just as Karleen came through the door leading from the garage into the kitchen. Her hair was more or less up, her body more or less covered in a leopard-print sundress held in place, as far as he could tell, solely by her breasts and a pair of skinny ties around her neck. An assortment of beads, feathers and metal disks dangled from earlobes to shoulders. And on her feet, matching leopard-print shoes with wedged heels that brought to mind ancient Inca temples.

A look only she could pull off.

She looked from Troy to her aunt, then let out something like a laugh.

"Now, sugar," Inky said, rustling through a bunch of plastic bags on the counter, "don't go making more of this than it is. I just figured it'd probably been a while since Troy'd had a good home-cooked meal. So would you mind fixing the salad while I make the... Oh, come on, I know it's in here somewhere."

"What?" Karleen asked, desultorily pulling out a head of lettuce from the vegetable bin.

"The bread. I know I bought some...." More rummaging, followed by a Look of Extreme Consternation. "Damn. I must've left it at the store."

Karleen dropped the lettuce like it was hot. "I'll go get some—"

"You will do no such thing, missy." Inky grabbed a set of keys and a purse off the end of the counter. "It won't take but two seconds, you stay here and get that salad going."

Karleen stared at the space where her aunt had been a moment before, then started tearing up the lettuce. "Lord, she's even more devious when she's sober."

Troy rubbed his mouth. "So...on a scale of one to ten, how pissed are you?"

Several pieces of shredded iceberg flew into a glass bowl. "About an eight."

"Could be worse."

"Not much."

After what he figured was an appropriate pause, he said, "Any chance of you're looking at me anytime soon?"

"Not if I can help it."

Not being a complete fool, Troy decided against pointing out that her taking out her annoyance with her aunt on him was perhaps a tad irrational. In fact, most other men would have given up by now, got out while the gettin' was good. But since the whole point was to prove to her that he *wasn't* like most men, he dug out his cell phone and flipped it open, clicking the display for several seconds before coming up behind Karleen and holding the phone in front of her. On a soft "Ohhh," she took the phone from him for a closer look.

"Lord, the dog is *huge*. And the boys…" She shook her head, and he could practically see a layer or two of resistance slough off. "I can't wait to see them again."

"Only one more week," he said, clapping shut the phone and slipping it back into his pocket. "I've got something else for you, too."

Clearly intrigued in spite of herself, she looked up at him. "What?"

Troy retrieved the gift-wrapped box from the table and held it out. Karleen's gaze flicked to his as she flushed with obvious pleasure; then she wiped her hands on a dish towel and snatched it from his hands, the box top clattering to the floor in her haste to get it open. The tissue paper batted back, she let out a squeak of laughter.

"I don't believe it," she said as she lifted the tiny pink Onesie with Diva-in-Training written on the front in a flowery, glittery script. "And the *shoes*…" She let out one of those totally female, isn't-this-too-cute-for-words? sounds at the miniature lace-trimmed, satin shoes…and another one for the prissy little headband.

Then she stilled. "You actually went into a department store to buy these, didn't you?"

"I did. And look—" he lifted his arms "—I didn't even get hives."

Laughing softly, Karleen set the box on the counter, neatly tucking everything back into the tissue paper. "Thank you," she said, again not looking at him. She pulled a plump, shiny tomato out of a bowl on the counter, briskly rinsing it off before plunking it onto the cutting board. "They're all adorable."

Troy leaned against the counter, watching her swiftly dice the juicy, glistening fruit. "I've got a couple of possible nannies lined up to interview. Let me know what's good for you and I'll set up the appointments."

She shoved a stray hair behind her ear. "Doesn't matter, just tell me when and I'll be there."

He shifted, watching her earrings tremble as she worked. "So now that we've broken the ice, how about a kiss?"

As he hoped, her head swung around, her mouth open, and Troy swooped down for a nice, long, sweet smooch.

"*Why* do you keep doing that?" she asked the moment he pulled away.

He grinned. "Why do you keep letting me?"

"I don't *let* you," she said, returning her attention to the tomato. "You just go ahead and take what you want. And why are you laughing?"

"So if some guy, say, you never saw before came up and tried to plant one on you, you'd simply let him?"

"No! I'd—" She clamped shut her mouth.

"You'd what?" Troy said, toying with a strand of her hair by her shoulder, making her shiver. When she didn't answer, he chuckled. "Oh, come on, Kar—you like kissing me as much as I like kissing you. Why don't you simply admit it and make life easier for everybody?"

Whack, whack, whack went the knife before she finally said, "Easier for you, maybe. Not for me. Now can we please change the subject?"

"No problem." Still leaning against the counter, Troy let go of her hair, folding his arms. "So how's it going with your aunt?"

Karleen shrugged, scraping the tomato into the bowl. "I told her if she wanted to be around the baby she had to clean up her act."

"Really?"

"Really. And I guess it worked. To some extent, at least. She's definitely cut back on the drinking. And she swears she's looking for a job."

"You don't sound too hopeful."

Karleen went hunting in one of the bags for a cucumber. "Considering how many times she's sworn to change her stripes, only to fall right back into her old habits? And then pulling this little number—" she waved the paring knife between them "—didn't exactly rack her up any points, either."

"Or me?"

"Or you. You could've said no, you know."

"And why would I have done that?" When Karleen snorted softly, Troy pilfered one of the cucumber slices and popped it into his mouth. "You really think she'll still be here when the baby comes?" he said, chewing.

"Who knows?" Karleen said wearily, and Troy took the knife from her.

"Go sit down. You look beat."

"I'm fine—"

"Go," he said, pointing the knife at her, then the kitchen table. "Sit."

"You are *such* a bully."

"That's me, Troy the Terrible."

However, he heard her sigh behind him as she sank onto the chair. "I shouldn't be this tired at five months along."

"Not that you're stressed or anything."

"Says a major contributing factor to that stress."

Troy plunked the knife onto the cutting board and turned around. "Do you want me to leave?"

"God, yes."

"Think of your aunt."

"Believe me," she said with an edge to her voice that warranted taking seriously, "I am."

He wiped his hands on a paper towel and approached her. "You need to keep these up," he said, gently clasping her ankles to set her feet on a second chair. Then he crouched in front of her. "And maybe you should think about ditching the high heels. You could break your neck in those things."

Her eyes met his, glistening with tears. "Lord, if we did live together, one of us would be dead within the week."

"I'll take my chances."

Their gazes tangled for a second before she looked away. "Don't."

"Don't what?"

"I told you—"

"That you couldn't deal with me and your aunt at the same time. I got it. But even you've admitted she seems to be pulling herself together. So that just leaves me." He stroked her shins, refusing to take his eyes off her face. "Why am I so scary, Kar? I'm just a man. A man who's fallen in love—"

"Don't," she said again, the word barely more than a whisper. "Please."

Her apprehension wound around his heart even as he wrapped one hand around both of hers, laced tightly in her lap. Joanna's words shuffled through his brain, about how Karleen had never felt as though she really fit in anywhere, that, no matter how hard she'd worked to distance herself from her past, she still so often felt like an interloper in her present.

That he shouldn't give up.

"Do you have any idea how many days I feel like a total fraud?" he said.

Her eyes shot to his. "What?"

He smiled. "Blake and I worked our butts off to make Ain't It Sweet a success, but we had no idea it would take off the way it did. So I see my name listed as the CEO of a Fortune 500 company and I think, who the hell is this guy? Because deep down I'm the same middle-class schmo from Madison, Wisconsin, still the same chronically broke college kid riding around in the fifteen-year-old Chevy Nova that cost me a whopping two hundred bucks."

After a pause, he added, "Still the same kid who never knew from day to day if his father would be sober enough to even talk to him. So maybe we're not so different after all."

A long moment passed before Karleen said, "Go finish up the salad. If it's not done by the time Inky gets back we'll never hear the end of it."

When he'd been chopping for several seconds, though, she said, "Not one single woman on my mother's side of the family has ever had a relationship that lasted more'n a few years, Troy. Not *one*. We called it the Betsy Curse, in tribute to my great grandmother, who had seven children with four different men. The men in the family all married for life, but the women... Pathetic. We even used to take bets how long somebody or other's new beau or husband was gonna last."

The off-pitch note of her pain vibrated between them. "So you think your marriages were cursed?"

"What would you call it? And what does it matter? A curse, a run of really bad luck, a string of coincidences... The hurt's the same."

He dumped the sliced cucumber into the bowl, then turned. "And the fear?"

Her mouth twisted. "Fear's not a bad thing if it keeps you from making the same stupid mistakes. I don't know, maybe if I had a better handle on what had gone wrong before, I might feel more secure about trying again. But I don't. Yeah, I suppose I can chalk up my first two marriages going bad to being too young, or naïve, or both, to know what I was getting into. But I thought I'd had a few things figured out by my third, and that one didn't work, either. And the very thought of failing again, failing you..."

Ah.

"You won't fail me, Karleen."

Her eyes filled. "Oh, Lord, what *is* it with you? You don't know that! And what's more important, *I* don't know that. You want forever, Troy. And I have no clue how to do that! So you can shower me with pretty talk till the cows come home, but it doesn't change anything. I'm sorry, but this is one battle you're not gonna win."

Irritation spiked through him. "Pretty talk? Is that what you think this is?

When I tell you I love you, you think that's just *words?* Why would I do that, Karleen? Why would I keep putting myself in this position if I wasn't sincere?"

"Because I'm having your baby, for one thing!"

He stared at her, wondering how far he dared push, finally decided it wasn't like he had a whole lot to lose. "Is it so hard for you to believe that somebody could love you, just for you?"

Her eyes widened—*bull's eye.* And in them, he could see the starving dog, petrified to trust, but weakening all the same. Finally, though, she shook her head. "It really kills you not to be in control of the situation, doesn't it?"

"Not any more than it does you," he lobbed back.

He saw her chest rise with her breath as she rubbed her belly. "You are not the boss of me, Troy Lindquist," she said quietly, "and that's that. And why are you laughing?"

Because it was that or hit himself over the head with one of the cast-iron skillets hanging over the stove. But damned if he was going to run. If it was *more* she wanted, then by gum, *more* she would have.

"Because," he said, carting the salad to the table, "I'm getting this image of you going head-to-head with our teenaged daughter. Should be fun."

For the next several minutes at least, he savored the completely flummoxed look on her face.

A week later, Karleen was out back, picking still more tomatoes, when she heard a commotion out front that signaled Troy's parents'—and the twins'—return. She straightened, staring in the direction of all the shouts and laughter, a thick, sticky mixture of dread and anticipation clogging her throat. Not only because she and Troy had to finally come clean about the baby—she was beginning to look like she was trying to smuggle one of the pumpkins underneath her maternity T-shirt—but because the boys' being home again was bound to make things between her and Troy even messier than it already was.

And that was pretty damn messy.

Inky came out onto the back patio, flapping her hands to dry her nails. She'd found a clerical job with a small contractor, but since Inky was still in the stone age when it came to computers, it didn't pay much over minimum wage. So Karleen wasn't holding out much hope that this one would last longer than any of the others. She also had a hunch her aunt had started drinking again. No surprise there. When the inevitable you-know-what would hit the fan, Karleen couldn't predict, but the waiting was about to take her under.

"I take it that's them?" Inky asked. Karleen nodded. "Lord, couldn't you just eat those little boys *up?* His mama sure looks like she thinks she's God's gift, though. Sounds like it, too, bossin' everybody around."

"Oh, Eleanor's not so bad," Karleen said, twisting off another tomato from its caged vine. Since Troy's revelation about his father, Karleen had been inclined to see his mother in a more kindly light. "Bein' protective's not a crime. And she raised a good man. So I suppose she did at least something right."

Inky's gaze on her back was hotter than the mid-August sun, but she apparently decided to let Karleen off the hook this time.

"I'm goin' out tonight, did I tell you? A new guy, we met down at work. Who knows, maybe this'll be the one!"

Oh, Lord. Karleen watched as, still wagging her hands, her aunt clomped back inside, leaving Karleen to her tomatoes and her dread and an inner turmoil that only seemed to increase by the minute.

Troy was a good man, a kind man, a man who made her feel like she mattered, and her refusal to accept what he was offering hardly even made sense to her, at this point. Because the truth was she loved the man with everything she had in her. To have somebody like that actually love her back…

In some ways, she wanted nothing more than to simply let go, to let herself believe in something she hadn't believed in for a long, long time. But for too many years, she'd been the victim of false hope and unrealistic expectations. Men had said they'd loved her before, and changed their minds. They'd pursued her for the challenge, too—Troy's mother's words about his determination to get whatever he wanted never far from her thoughts—only to lose interest once she'd given in.

Add in her own justifiable—in her mind, anyway—fear of failure and the plain fact was she was tired. Tired of being disappointed, partly, but mostly of being that victim. So a big part of her taking charge of her life was learning what to avoid.

Including heartache.

Too bad heartache seemed to happen anyway. Like being It in a dodgeball game with cement blocks tied to your feet—no matter how hard you tried, you just couldn't get out of the way fast enough.

Karleen set another warm, ripe tomato in her basket, then stretched out her back. Damn thing had been giving her five fits, even though she had, in fact, given up wearing such high heels. Not because Troy had bugged her about it, though, but because she'd decided it probably wasn't safe, tromping around on stilts when she was beginning to have trouble seeing those stilts underneath her. Bad enough she had to ask Inky to polish her toenails for her these days.

The basket was getting heavy—how on earth three little plants could produce so many tomatoes was beyond her. She'd give some to Joanna, of course, whose talents did not expand to gardening. And, it occurred to her, some to

Troy's mother. Since the woman was bound to be part of Karleen's life for many years to come, she supposed a little sucking up wouldn't hurt.

Troy's patio door whooshed open; the boys and Elmo came roaring outside, and Karleen got that firecracker feeling in her chest again. Spotting her, the twins let out a whoop and tore across the yard, only to stop dead in their tracks ten or so feet from her fence. Mouth open, Scotty looked at Grady, then back at her.

"Are you gonna have a *baby?*"

Troy stepped out onto his deck, and their eyes met, and five thousand emotions roared through her, not the least of which was that she wished—oh, how she wished!—that she had the courage to take one more chance. That for the children's sake, at least, they could be a real family instead of whatever they'd manage to piece together.

Fixing a smile to her face, she set down the full basket and crossed to the fence, arms wide. "First things first— get over here and give me a hug!" The boys scrambled over the fence, and she plopped down cross-legged on the grass so she could hug them both, kissing first one, then the other, in their damp, messy curls.

"So are you?" Scotty asked.

By this time, Troy had climbed over the fence as well, to squat down beside them. He looked at her, and she nodded. Whatever was or wasn't going on between them, for the next few moments at least, this was about the boys.

"Karleen and I have a little surprise for you guys," he said. "You're going to have a baby sister, sometime around Christmas."

Grady gaped at his father. "No way," he said, so seriously that Karleen couldn't help but laugh. Then she took two grimy little hands and pressed them to her belly, where the baby had launched into her hip-hop number.

"Feel her kick?" she said, and Scotty leaned over to lay his ear against her tummy, and she tenderly stroked his curls, tears burning the backs of her eyes.

As thrilled as Troy was to have his sons home again, the sting of knowing that the woman he loved didn't trust him enough to share that love hadn't abated one whit. Not that he didn't understand her fear, because he did. In spades. After Amy, he'd certainly never figured on falling in love again. Marrying again—for companionship, for sex, for the boys—was one thing. Losing his heart a second time, however… He'd had no idea it was even possible.

Let alone to a woman who couldn't have been less like what he'd thought he was looking for. Falling in love with Karleen was like going to buy a minivan and ending up with a Corvette.

"Daddy?"

Remembering to smile, Troy sat on the edge of Grady's bed; the little boy immediately clambered onto his lap, pulling Troy's arms around him. Elmo flopped across Troy's feet, letting out a huge doggy sigh, as if *very* glad to be home, and Troy hung on tight to his son, reveling in the feel and smell of what he'd missed so terribly all those weeks. The boys were obviously having a hard time wrapping their brains around this new—to them—development. Not that they'd said much yet, but Troy could hear the gears grinding inside both blond heads as they desperately tried to make things add up.

"Yeah, squirt?"

"How do they know the baby's a girl?"

Relieved, he smoothed back his son's hair, as, like a

tropical snake, a skinny arm suddenly dangled from the upper bunk. Troy gently tugged at Scotty's fingers; a giggle floated down from overhead. "They used a special machine to take a picture of the baby inside Karleen. And they could see she's a girl."

Grady's brow puckered. "How? Is she wearing clothes?"

"No, dummy," Scotty put in, hanging over the safety bar. Half the time, both boys ended up in the bottom bunk, but they always started out the night separately. "Girls don't have *peenusses*."

Skeptical blue eyes shot to Troy for confirmation. "Yeah," he said, just waiting for the inevitable *But how does the baby come out?* query. "That's pretty much it."

Grady hugged an orange-haired Wild Thing stuffed toy to his chest. "What's her name?"

"Karleen and I haven't decided yet."

"Is she gonna live with us?" came from the peanut gallery.

Troy waited out the sting, then said, "She'll be here a lot. But mostly she'll live with Karleen. You'll be able to see her all you want, though."

"That's dumb," Grady said, hugging the toy harder. "Why can't we all live together?"

Troy briefly considered pointing out that once the baby became mobile—and insatiably curious about her big brother's things—their not all living in the same house wouldn't necessarily be a bad thing. Still, he'd gladly put up with the inevitable shrieks and bellows and "Why'd we have to have another baby, anyways?" if it meant putting up with Karleen, too.

"Because we can't," he said, thinking, *Yeah, that's smooth.* He maneuvered Grady back onto his pillow, tickling him for a second before tucking a racing car-patterned sheet and summer blanket around assorted skinny limbs. "You guys have had a long day," he said, kissing first Grady, then prodding the dog off his feet before reaching up to hug and kiss Scotty as well. "We'll talk more in the morning."

His father was settled into the sofa in the family room, watching some Civil War documentary on the History Channel. Having enough battles of his own to fight these days, Troy continued on to the kitchen, where his mother was washing out thermoses and things from their trip. Speaking of battles. He would've turned tail there, too, but he was thirsty.

Troy could feel her watching him as he crossed to the refrigerator for a soft drink. He pulled the can's tab and dropped into a kitchen chair, his feet crossed at the ankles.

"Don't start," he said.

Eleanor shook her hands and grabbed a dish towel, then joined him at the table, sinking her chin into her palm. "The boys talked nonstop about her the whole trip. They're completely in love."

"They're four," he pointed out.

"You're not."

Troy took a swallow of his soda, then leaned forward, averting his gaze. "I told her about Dad."

His mother straightened, her hand suspended in midair. "Why on earth did you do that?"

"Because she needed to know that somebody understood."

"Oh, no... She's not—?"

"No, her aunt. And her mother, apparently. Karleen's had it pretty rough." His eyes swung to his mother's. "And you know how it is—it's easier to beat yourself up for something that's not even your fault than to admit that maybe the problem's bigger than you are."

Understanding dawned in his mother's eyes. "She won't let you in."

"Not far enough to do any good. And don't you dare say it's probably for the best."

"Fine, I won't say it. But for goodness' sake, honey… sometimes, all a person can do is say *enough is enough* and move on."

"You didn't with Dad."

"The hell I didn't. When I walked out of that house I was fully aware that I was quite possibly walking out on my marriage, too. I still loved your father, but I'd had it with his refusal to admit he needed help."

"You're talking apples and oranges, Mom—"

"Not as much as you might think. Stubbornness is stubbornness, no matter what form it takes. Honey, Karleen has many good points—a lot more than I'll admit I gave her credit for in the beginning—but trust me, nothing hurts more than being shut out. Except, perhaps, realizing there's nothing you can do to *make* the other person open up. And the harder you try to force open the door," she said, her eyes littered with jagged shards of leftover pain, "the more determined the person on the other side becomes to keep it closed."

Much, much later, as Troy lay awake, listening to the grandfather clock in the living room chime every freaking hour on the hour, he had to admit his mother had a point. Still, he couldn't simply say "Oh, well," and walk away, leaving Karleen to rot inside that damned emotional foxhole she'd dug for herself. Whether that made him weak or strong, he had no idea. But that was who he was. So the world, and his mother, and Karleen, would just have to damn well deal.

Around six or so, he gave up sleep as a lost cause, pulling on jeans and a T-shirt to retrieve the Sunday paper from, natch, the middle of his front yard. He'd no sooner snagged the paper out of the wet grass, however, when a

moan from Karleen's yard stopped him in his tracks. He
looked over, doing a double take.

Because there, among the pinwheels and whirlygigs
and cast-stone fauna, Karleen's aunt lay flat on her back,
passed out cold.

Chapter Thirteen

Troy tossed the paper onto his porch and started toward the yard, a host of rancid memories leaking into his fresh, hot-off-the-grill fury. Out of the corner of his eye, he saw his father step outside in a white T-shirt and droopy cargoes, his fishing hat plopped on his head.

"Oh, no… Is that Karleen's aunt?"

But Troy didn't stop to answer, sensing the older man following him as he hopped the low fence and strode over to Inky. He loomed over her comatose form, his hands clenched, fighting off the combination of disgust and dismay washing over him.

"It's always worse, seeing it from the other side," his father said in a low voice beside him, then gently squeezed Troy's shoulder. "I know I've already apologized for what I put all of you through, but I'm so sorry, Troy. A thousand times over."

"I know. But right now," he said, considering his options, "I'm only worried about Karleen."

With a soft groan, Inky stirred, opening one eye. Except for her wrinkled dress, raccoon eyes and haystack hair, she didn't look any the worse for wear. A smeared, shaky smile stretched across her face.

"Hey there, sugar," she said, wiggling the fingers of one hand, then trying to sit up. "Guess I didn't quite make it to the front door…. Oh, hell." With another groan, she collapsed bonelessly back onto the grass.

"Inky!" Karleen squealed from the porch, yanking her shortie robe closed as she hustled barefoot down into the yard. Troy caught a glimpse of beet-red face as she skittered past to clumsily drop to her knees beside her aunt, snatching pieces of grass and such out of the woman's hair as she lit into her.

"You promised, dammit!" she said in a low, dangerous voice. "You *promised* we weren't gonna go through this again!"

"I'm sorry, baby," Inky murmured from her prone position, her eyes closed, then clamped limp fingers around her niece's wrist. "But would you mind if we dealt with this later? I don't feel so good."

"I'm sure you don't. But oddly enough, I'm not exactly experiencin' a wellspring of sympathy for you at the moment, either—"

"Karleen…" Troy began, but she shot him a look that froze the words in his throat. Beyond the mortification and the helpless anger—emotions he knew all too well— there was no mistaking the emotional and physical toll her aunt's addiction was taking on her. Especially at this hour. And without her makeup. Her eyes were bloodshot, her skin practically colorless, and exhaustion and worry had begun to seriously erode the early pregnancy plumpness in her cheeks.

That's it, he thought.

Not that he had any idea at the moment what *it* was supposed to be, but before the day was out there was going to be some serious man-action taken or his name wasn't Troy Lindquist.

Grasping her aunt under the arms, Karleen heaved the now-moaning woman into a sitting position. "It's okay, I've got it, you can go now," she grunted.

Right. As if Troy had any intention of letting a pregnant woman—especially this pregnant woman—singlehandedly haul her larger aunt to her feet.

Troy glanced at his father, then gently lifted Karleen out of the way. "We know the drill," he said, grabbing Inky's arms while his father got her feet.

"Even if I was usually the one playing the part of the drunk," his father said.

They started toward the house, Inky stretched out between them like a felled deer, until she suddenly came to enough to mutter, "I think I'm gonna be sick...."

Ten seconds later, after a cursory glance at her poor plastic roses, Karleen led everyone into the house, directing them to deposit her aunt in the hall bathtub (yes, fully clothed). It was clear, both from her tight-lipped expression and her take-charge attitude, that she, too, knew the drill. All too well.

Inky mumbled something incomprehensible and passed out again, snoring softly.

Karleen ushered both Troy and his father down the hall. "Thank you," she said as graciously as a woman can who's just had a drunken relative delivered to her bathtub, "but I'll take it from here."

When they reached her still-open front door, Troy's father took her by the shoulders. "If there's anything I can do—"

"Thanks, Gus." She stood on tiptoe to kiss him on the cheek. "But I'll be okay."

He gave her a quick hug and Troy a raised eyebrow, then went outside, where he located Karleen's hose and started to wash down her roses.

"Just shoot me now," she mumbled.

Troy stood as close as he dared behind her, haunted by his conversation with his mother. "You know, denial's not only a problem for the person with the addiction."

She pivoted, frowning. "My aunt just passed out in my front yard. I'm not *denyin'* anything, least of all that she needs help."

"No, you're just denying *you* do."

He saw tears gather in her eyes before she looked away, and Troy had to squelch the urge to shake her.

And yet, it wasn't like he didn't understand where she was coming from, didn't remember his own feelings of helplessness and humiliation as a kid. Or the staunch example his mother had set all those years. But then, the downside to pride was that it made you believe even an illusory sense of control was better than nothing. But if pride was all you had, he realized with a rush of tenderness for the woman in front of him, you hung onto it with everything you had in you.

How could he take that away from her?

Very, very carefully, he thought, as something sparked inside his head.

So when she said, quietly, "Please go, I'll be fine," all he said was "If you need anything—"

"I know," she said. "Thank you."

Over the Tetris-like sensation of ideas falling into place

in his brain, Troy heard the door shut behind him as he walked away. The boys were still asleep when he got back to his house, but his parents were both in the kitchen, which smelled of coffee and heated griddle, waiting for the sizzle of pancake batter. They both turned to him, their brows raised expectantly.

"Okay," he said. "Here's the plan…."

Her aunt's announcement left Karleen so stunned, it took her a good half minute to find her voice. "What do you mean, you're moving out?"

"Just what I said." Inky scooped all her underwear out of the top drawer of the bureau in Karleen's guest room and dumped it into her soft-sided bag. "Troy's payin' the deposit and first month's rent on an apartment, on two conditions—that I don't screw up on the job he's offerin' me, and that I stick with AA this time." A bunch of tops joined the underwear in the bag. "I've already been to my first meeting, Troy's daddy went with me before he and Eleanor went back to Wisconsin."

"How…? When…?"

"Troy and his daddy came over to talk to me on Sunday afternoon. Lord, I must've looked like death warmed over. God knows I felt like it. Anyway, you'd gone off with Troy's mama and his boys to the mall. From what I could piece together, that was part of the plan. To get you out of the way so they could deal with me without you gettin' all out of shape."

Karleen watched her aunt scurry around the room, tossing this, that and the next thing into her bag, trying to digest this unexpected—and borderline bizarre—turn of events. And where Troy got off playing God. The creep. And why his doing so was making her heart go pitty-pat in a way it had never done before. Still, being of a sound and realistic nature, she couldn't help but say, "And why is *this time* different from all the other times?"

Her aunt gave her a wounded-to-the-quick look. "You know, I wouldn't mind a little support. If Troy trusts me, why can't you? After all," she said, folding up the grass-stained dress from her little adventure and stuffing it into the bag, "it's not like he doesn't have firsthand experience with the subject. And if his daddy could make it…well, then, so can I."

"In theory, yes." Karleen lowered herself into the wicker chair by the bed. "But you can hardly blame me for being skeptical."

Inky regarded her for a second or two, then let out a rush of air before sitting on the edge of the mattress across from her. Her charm bracelet jingled when she reached for Karleen's hand. "I can't go on the way I have been, honey," she said. And Karleen had to admit, that was a new level of sincerity in her aunt's eyes. "And I can tell you're at the end of your rope with me. And frankly, so am I. Passing out on your lawn like that…" Her head wagged from side to side. "That's just not *right*."

Out of the corner of her mental eye, Karleen could see the angels, huddled in the wings, waiting for their cue to shout "Hallelujah!" But she wasn't ready to give it to them, not yet.

"…Especially since it's because of me you keep putting off Troy."

"Excuse me?"

"Oh, come on, honey—when you said you had your reasons for not accepting his marriage proposal, it doesn't take a genius to figure out I was one of those reasons."

"You weren't-" When her aunt lifted one brow, Karleen

sighed. "So what's this about a job?" she asked, pulling her hand out of her aunt's and leaning back in the chair. "Doing what?"

Inky got up again, this time to get her shoes from the closet. "Cooking, believe it or not. To start, anyway. Something about needing a lunchtime cook for their new cafeteria? But they also have these training classes I could take in the afternoons, using a computer and what-all." She looked at Karleen, her eyes actually sparkling. "And it doesn't pay stupid minimum wage, either."

Underneath Karleen's halter top, the baby shifted. The flutterings were beginning to feel more like real kicks now. She soothed a hand over her belly, then lifted her eyes again to her aunt. "It won't be easy."

"Tell me something I don't know."

"And if you backslide—"

"There will be holy hell to pay. From all sides. I know that, too. I also know it's high time I stop giving lip service to how much I love you and start proving it. And before you jump to any conclusions about Troy only doing this to get in *your* good graces…" She shook her head. "He's not. Said he knew that was a lost cause."

Karleen swallowed past the sudden knot in her throat. "He actually said that?"

"He did. Then again he also said nothing was more important to him than your welfare—and the baby's, of course—so make of that what you will." Inky laughed. "In fact, he said he was *this close* to bodily removing me from your house, he was that worried for you. Now did I get everything out of the bathroom…?"

"Inky, you don't have to leave. Really. You can stay as long as you want—"

"And deny myself the same opportunity to stand on my

own two feet as you? No way. Yes, I'm accepting the leg up Troy's offerin' me, but so what? All he's doing is giving me a chance. I'm the one who has to make something of it."

"But I still don't understand—"

"Why he's helping me? That one's easy. Because you won't let him help *you*. So he figured out how to get around that little obstacle. And let me tell you something else, missy—the day *I'm* too scared to take the chance on a good man like that is the day they'll be saying my eulogy."

"But—"

"And don't even start about *the curse*. That's a lot of hooey and you know it. Whatever curse there was, we all brought on ourselves. If you set your sights low, lowlifes is about all you can expect to attract. But the minute you started to believe you were capable of more than your mama, or me, or Granny, or any of the rest of 'em, you left all of us in the dust. Hell, girl—if you went to all that trouble to pull yourself up out of the mud, why not enjoy what's waitin' for you on the shore?"

As Karleen sat there, blinking at her aunt, Inky went on. "And you know, whether *I* 'make it' or not is beside the point. Not that I don't intend to. But Troy's wanting to protect you, to take care of you, to stand by you, *is*. How you can just throw that away is beyond me."

Inky zipped closed her bag, then hauled it off the bed before tippy-tapping over to kiss Karleen's cheek. "Well, I'm off to start my new life." She smiled. "Maybe you should think about taking the next step in yours?"

Two glasses of ice water in his hands, Troy walked over to Karleen, standing on his deck. Her gaze rested on his yard, deeply shadowed in the late afternoon light, even as her hand rested on her tummy. "So what did you think?"

he asked, handing her one of the glasses, which she took without meeting his eyes.

"The first one, definitely. Mrs. Brooks." She took a sip of the water, hugging herself with one arm. She'd dressed conservatively—for her—in a black tube top maternity pants outfit, her hair pulled back into a ponytail. She still wore at least a half-dozen rings, but she'd toned down the bling by a few thousand kilowatts. "I liked her smile. And her sense of humor."

Smiling himself, Troy took a seat on the glider. "Then I'll call her back, have her come over when the boys are here."

Karleen nodded, but made no move to leave.

Here it comes, he thought, bracing himself. Or rather, re-bracing himself, since for three days he'd been holding his breath, waiting for one pissed-off pregnant woman to land on his doorstep to read him the riot act. That she hadn't, even when he'd called to say he'd set up interviews with a few potential nannies, had rattled him more than he was about to let on.

Then again, perhaps she'd only been marshaling her forces before launching her attack. When she finally turned to him, however, her brows drawn, instead of anger he saw only genuine curiosity.

"The only thing I don't understand," she said, like they'd been having this conversation all along, "is why you'd take such a huge chance on somebody you don't even know."

"I take it we're talking about your aunt and not Mrs. Brooks?"

A smile tugged at her lips. "Sorry. Yes."

"Let's just say I decided to believe her when she said she was ready. Because I saw the same combination of defeat and determination in her eyes that I saw in my father's, when he finally realized what he stood to lose. You're all Inky has, honey. The last thing she wants is for you to hate her."

"If I'd been capable of hating her," Karleen said, "it would've happened long before this."

"I know."

"Still," she said on a breath, "she's stumbled so many times before…."

"So did my father. So do most alcoholics. It's a day-by-day battle, Karleen. But you can't give up. In fact, they're counting on you, to keep being strong when they aren't."

Karleen looked away again. "Inky said you told her it had nothing to do with me."

"No," he said quietly, "what I said was, I didn't step in because of anything I hoped to gain for myself. In fact, considering your oft-stated position on letting me help you, I figured you'd have my head on a platter. But it had everything to do with you."

When she faced him this time, the frown was deeper. "I don't—"

"I did it because I know how hard it is to be someone else's support when you're still trying to get your own act together. And because I love you."

"Why?" she choked out. "Why do you love me? I've been nothin' but a pain in the butt the whole time."

"Not the *whole* time," Troy said, smiling. "And when you weren't, I saw flashes of something that had been missing from my life for far too long."

"It can't be that simple."

"Sure it can. If you let it."

Her brow still crumpled, Karleen looked away again, holding her sweating glass to her throat; Labor Day was fast approaching, but fall weather wouldn't happen for a good six weeks yet. "I was mad as hell at you at first. For sticking your big old nose in. I might even be still, a little. But if this takes…" One ringed finger toyed with a thin gold chain resting against her collarbone. "It'd be pretty small of me to resent you for accomplishing something I never could…" Her mouth pressed tight, and, with a pang, Troy realized exactly how much she was laying herself on the line.

"Don't shortchange yourself, honey," he said. "If Inky hadn't been ready, nothing I'd said would have made any difference, either. And she was ready because of you. You'd had years to loosen the lid. All I did was pop it off."

Karleen let out a soft half laugh, then set her glass down on a nearby table, picking up her keys instead. Her flat sandals slapped against the wooden deck as she crossed to him, then leaned over to kiss him on the cheek. "Thank you," she whispered.

Troy grabbed her wrist, fingering her steady, rapid pulse. Her pupils bloomed in her eyes, dark and wary. And he smiled again, oddly at peace. "You deserve everything you want out of life, sweetheart. With someone who gets who you are. And appreciates it."

Then he dropped her hand, lacing his **own** across his stomach and squinting out over his yard. For several seconds, Karleen didn't move, until at last she whirled around and slip-slapped down the steps and across his yard, through the gate his father had inserted in the fence between their properties.

And Troy watched her, an old song playing in head. Something about wishing her cozy fires and bluebirds and lemonade. But especially, he thought as his heart splintered into a million pieces, he really did wish her love.

Even if it wasn't with him.

And then, on a long, shuddering breath, he set her free.

* * *

When the sun came up the next morning, Karleen was right there to witness it, seeing as she hadn't slept but maybe three hours the entire night. She unfolded herself from the chaise on her patio and went back inside, where Britney was still up, too, running her skinny little paws off on her exercise wheel. Karleen fixed herself a fresh buttered bagel and carried it out to the living room, where she pinched off a plain piece for Britney and dropped it into her cage.

All night long, she kept seeing that look in Troy's eyes. The look that said *he* was the one who "got" her.

Who loved her.

Really, truly loved her, the way no man on earth had ever loved her before. He looked at her like she was everything, made her feel like he'd do anything for her. In fact, he already had, hadn't he?

She chewed her bite of bagel for a while, thinking about that. Underneath her heart, the baby squirmed, like she was trying to get comfortable.

"The thing is, sweetie," she said, rubbing her tummy as she paced back and forth, "maybe I'm goin' about this all wrong. I know, I know…that's the last thing you expected me to say. But then, never let it be said that your mama can't admit her mistakes. Well, here's another one— maybe…maybe your daddy and I aren't so different, after all. I mean, I suppose I could learn to live with Early American. If I absolutely had to."

Her cheek pouch stuffed with fresh bagel, the hamster lifted sharp, beady eyes to Karleen, clearly astounded.

Figuring she may as well take advantage of her audience, Karleen plunked down into a chair close to the cage, twisting her feet around the chair legs the way she used to do when she was little. "So what do you think,

Brit? I mean, I've got a really crappy track record, right?" She pinched off another piece of the bagel, gave it to the hamster. "If I go for it, and it doesn't work... Oh!"

The baby kicked harder than she ever had before, and Karleen laughed. "You tryin' to tell me something, li'l bit?"

And as Karleen sat there, licking butter off her fingers, she thought...why *shouldn't* she have another shot at happiness? So she had a few broken marriages in her past. So what? Troy *wasn't* like the others. But more important, *she* wasn't the same person now she'd been then, either. Like Inky had said, she set her sights a lot higher these days. And if she believed she deserved better in every other aspect of her life, then why in the name of all that was holy shouldn't real, true love be part of that package?

She sucked in a breath. Lord, Inky was right. Everybody was right. Including Troy. She did deserve the best life had to offer.

Or, in this case, what the father of her child had to offer. Which was more than a name, or his protection, or even his money, but the chance to get it right.

"Britney, sugar," she said as she got up, giving the hamster the last little bite of bagel. "Don't take this the wrong way, but you are *not* enough."

Her cheeks stuffed with bagel, Britney waddled back to her sleeping tube. Somehow, Karleen didn't think she'd taken offense.

Suddenly overcome with exhaustion, Karleen lay down on the couch in the living room, almost immediately falling asleep. And when she awoke two hours later, the room was filled with rainbows.

Not illusions. *Promises.*

Hauling herself upright, she caught sight of one of the

child-care books Eleanor had insisted on buying for her when they'd been at the mall. As if pushed, she got up and riffled through the piles of God-knew-what on her desk in the corner of the room until she found the piece of paper she'd written the Lindquists' address and phone numbers on. Then, before she could talk herself out of it, she grabbed the portable phone from the coffee table.

The minute she heard that somewhat imperious voice on the other end of the line, she burst out with, "Eleanor, it's Karleen. Who, if I haven't completely screwed things up with your son, is gonna be your new daughter-in-law. No, you listen to me," she said when Troy's mother tried to interrupt. "I love Troy with everything I have in me, more than I've ever loved anybody in my life, and I know he loves me, too. More than anybody's ever loved *me*. And I know I may not be the classiest thing going, but I swear on the Bible that I will make him the best wife I know how, and your grandsons a good mama, and—"

"Karleen," Eleanor said, chuckling.

"What?"

"Why are you telling *me* all of this?" she said, then Troy's daddy was on the phone, saying, "Please tell me you finally got your head on straight," and she said, "I guess so," and he said, "Good. Now get off the damn phone and go put that poor boy out of his misery."

Since nobody had come up to Troy after the morning conference and given him a concerned, "Is everything okay?" he felt reasonably sure whatever had come out of his mouth had made sense. Once out of the meeting, however, he'd plopped into the chair behind his desk, staring out his window at the vista of city and mountains and sky, replaying a particular fantasy in his head, one where he was Errol Flynn and Karleen was one of those doe-eyed twenties actresses, and he'd swoop down in a manly manner and cart her off to some remote island where he'd lavish riches and attention on her all the rest of her life and she'd shut up and let him lavish, dammit.

Life, he thought, glowering, should be more like a silent movie.

"Troy?" came his secretary Mallory's voice through his intercom, startling him.

Especially, he thought, glowering some more, the silent part.

"There's a Karleen Almquist here to see you?"

He blinked at the phone for two or three seconds before stabbing the answer button. "Send her in. And for God's sake, keep everybody else out."

He came around his desk as she walked through the door. They both froze, he in the middle of the floor, she with one hand behind her, still on the doorknob. She was dressed all in white, some wrinkly, floaty thing that made her look like a pregnant angel, especially with her hair all piled up on top of her head, although the Frisbee-sized earrings and unapologetic cleavage kinda nixed the angel look.

Then she was in his arms, and they were kissing, and even though about five thousand *What the hell?* bells were clanging inside Troy's head, who was he to question having his favorite pair of lips in the world against his? Finally, though, the bells got so loud he had to pay attention to them—which was the annoying thing about bells— so he gently set his hands on her shoulders and put a good quarter inch between them.

"Not that this isn't far superior to your average coffee break…but is there a point to this? Or did you wake up this morning and think, *Let's go torture Troy?*"

Softly giggling, she lowered her head to his chest. And he wrapped her up in his arms, just because he could. And the baby kicked, just because *she* could. And Karleen whispered, "Ask me."

Troy stilled, it taking a minute to summon back enough brain cells from elsewhere to process her question. But when they got there, all out of breath from zipping to and fro like that, they started shouting, *What the hell do you think she's saying, fool?*

He held up one finger. "Hold that thought," he said, then did some zipping of his own, over to a small safe he kept in the office. A minute later, he was on one knee, holding out the small aqua box. Karleen's eyes got huge.

"Is that…?"

"Just a little something I picked up last time I went to Dallas," he said, then flipped it open, and she let out a soft "Oh, my God," and looked as though she'd faint, so he figured he'd done good.

"Will you marry me, Karleen?"

"Sugar, for that ring I'd marry Godzilla."

"Nice to know. Is that a yes?"

One hand clamped onto the edge of his desk, she awkwardly lowered herself to her knees, as well, threading her arms around his neck. "Yes," she said, her eyes watery, her mouth stretched into the brightest smile he'd ever seen. "Yes, yes, yes," she said, kissing him again. "I was only kidding about the Godzilla thing, though."

"I knew that," he said, then took the three-carat Tiffany out of the box, removed the ten-dollar glass monstrosity from her ring finger, tossed it over his shoulder where it clunked off the top of his desk, and slipped on the real deal. "But I know how much you love sparkly things."

She chuckled. Then she said, "I think we both need to get up now before we're stuck here forever."

"Good idea."

He hauled her to her feet, and they kissed some more, after which she went over to the window to watch the ring sparkle in the sunlight. And Troy waited for the penny to drop.

"Troy?"

"Hmm?"

"If I kept saying no…" She turned. "Why'd you have an engagement ring in your safe?"

Smiling, he crossed to her, taking her in his arms again. "I could let you go—I *had* let you go—but somehow, I couldn't give up on you. Not quite yet."

"I see. How long were you plannin' on waiting? Before you did give up?"

"Oh, I don't know." He shrugged. "Forty, fifty years, maybe?"

Her eyes teared again. "You really won't leave me, will you?"

"Not as long as there's breath in my body. Jeez," he said when the baby walloped him. He placed his hand on Karleen's belly, chuckling when Little Miss Diva kicked him again. "What are you doing in there, peanut?"

Laughing, Karleen covered his hand with her own. "A Snoopy dance. That her mama's finally come to her senses."

"You mean, like this?" Troy said, letting her go to launch into an old football victory dance from the dark ages, and Karleen shrieked with laughter, and Troy saw a lifetime of laughter, and tacky lawn ornaments, and making love underneath leopard-print throws, and a four-poster bed flanked by brothel-worthy lampshades.

And filled with their children.

And he danced all the harder.

Epilogue

"Is it time to get her up yet?"

Holding her satin robe closed, Karleen went into the baby's room, her breasts full inside the nursing bra, her feet already cramped inside her white satin bridal sandals. Still in his jeans and T-shirt, five-year-old Scotty stood beside the crib in the dimly lit room, his long fingers wrapped around the rails, peering at his sleeping baby sister. From the kitchen she could hear Inky and Eleanor—Troy's parents were staying in Karleen's old house, which she'd decided to keep for the time being as a guesthouse for relatives—arguing with the caterers. While the sound produced a bubble of contentment in the center of Karleen's embarrassingly full chest, no way in hell was she going anywhere near the kitchen until this wedding was *over*.

"It is," she said, cupping Scotty's head before reaching

in to stroke Meredith's tummy. While both boys adored their baby sister, Scotty still couldn't take his eyes off her, even after four months. And, as the fuzzy-headed baby's eyes fluttered open, her tiny pink mouth stretching into a huge, toothless grin, Karleen could relate. She scooped the baby out of the crib and carried her over to her changing table to change her soggy diaper. "I have to feed her before I get dressed."

Watching the procedure, as he always did, with a combination of fascination and disgust, Scotty said, "Mama?"

"Yes, honey?"

"Why are you and Daddy getting married again if you're *already* married?"

"Well," Karleen said, cuddling the dry baby to her chest and starting out of the room, Scotty trailing behind her, "the first time was about making things neat and tidy and legal. This time, it's about celebrating." Which she sure hadn't felt like doing those last months of the pregnancy when her belly would enter a room five minutes before the rest of her. And wouldn't you know, Little Miss Diva had come two weeks late, to boot.

"And besides that," Troy said, coming up behind them in the hallway and hauling Scotty into his arms, "no way was I going to miss out on seeing this woman in a pretty white dress. Come on, buddy—let's go bug your grandmother and let Mama feed your sister."

Her husband leaned over and gave her a kiss that was a lot longer than it needed to be, and not nearly long enough, then strode back down the hall as Karleen stood there, watching him, pleased to discover that somewhere along the way she'd stopped wondering when she was going to wake up and find out this had all been a dream.

She went back into their bedroom, with the four-poster

bed with its traditional hobnail bedspread, and lowered herself into the plaid wing chair in the corner, where Meredith could get a good look at the rainbows splashed across the wall from all the crystals dangling from the red damask lampshade by the bed, and let out the sigh of a truly contented woman.

An hour later, she walked down the aisle, out in their backyard under a bank of flowering cherry trees (dotted with brightly colored birdhouses), in a designer wedding dress more beautiful than she could have imagined. And Troy stood up there, waiting, his gaze true and sure and calm, and she knew, without a shadow of a doubt, that for the first time—and the last—this man would work at their marriage as much as she would.

Because he was her partner.

Her friend.

The only man who'd ever bothered to see past the surface.

"Hey, there," he whispered when she reached him, cracking everybody up by kissing her before the minister had even started his *We are gathered here todays*. "Yes, ma'am," he said, eyeing the low, crystal-trimmed neckline, "this was *definitely* worth the wait."

She laughed, and gave her bouquet to Joanna—who'd never had a chance to serve as her maid of honor before this—and took Meredith from her aunt, and the three of them stood up there before God and everybody and made promises that Karleen knew deep in her heart would be kept.

Then Troy surprised her with a new wedding ring, this one a ring of diamonds to match her engagement ring, which he slipped over her new acrylic with a wink. And another kiss.

The dress, the ring, her husband's mouth…they all fit perfectly.

And so, at long last, did she.

* * * * *

"She's paying attention, all right," Dante murmur...

Dante Raintree stood with his arms crossed as he watched the woman on the monitor. The image was in black and white to better show details; color distracted the brain. He focused on her hands, watching every move she made, but what struck him most was how uncommonly *still* she was. She didn't fidget or play with her chips, or look around at the other players. She peeked once at her down card, then didn't touch it again, signaling for another hit by tapping a fingernail on the table. Just because she didn't seem to be paying attention to the other players, though, didn't mean she was as unaware as she seemed.

"What's her name?" Dante asked.

"Lorna Clay," replied his chief of security, Al Rayburn.

"At first I thought she was counting, but she doesn't pay enough attention."

"She's paying attention, all right," Dante murmured.

"You just don't see her doing it." A card counter had to remember every card played. Supposedly counting cards was impossible with the number of decks used by the casinos, but there were those rare individuals who could calculate the odds even with multiple decks.

"I thought that, too," said Al. "But look at this piece of tape coming up. Someone she knows comes up to her and speaks, she looks around and starts chatting, completely misses the play of the people to her left—and doesn't look around even when the deal comes back to her, just taps that finger. And damn if she didn't win. Again."

Dante watched the tape, rewound it, watched it again. Then he watched it a third time. There had to be something he was missing, because he couldn't pick out a single giveaway.

"If she's cheating," Al said with something like respect, "she's the best I've ever seen."

"What does your gut say?"

Al scratched the side of his jaw, considering. Finally, he said, "If she isn't cheating, she's the luckiest person walking. She wins. Week in, week out, she wins. Never a huge amount, but I ran the numbers and she's into us for about five grand a week. Hell, boss, on her way out of the casino she'll stop by a slot machine, feed a dollar in and walk away with at least fifty. It's never the same machine, either. I've had her watched, I've had her followed, I've even looked for the same faces in the casino every time she's in here, and I can't find a common denominator."

"Is she here now?"

"She came in about half an hour ago. She's playing blackjack, as usual."

"Bring her to my office," Dante said, making a swift decision. "Don't make a scene."

"Got it," said Al, turning on his heel and leaving the security center.

Dante left, too, going up to his office. His face was calm. Normally he would leave it to Al to deal with a cheater, but he was curious. How was she doing it? There were a lot of bad cheaters, a few good ones, and every so often one would come along who was the stuff of which legends were made: the cheater who didn't get caught, even when people were alert and the camera was on him— or, in this case, her.

It was possible to simply be lucky, as most people understood luck. Chance could turn a habitual loser into a big-time winner. Casinos, in fact, thrived on that hope. But luck itself wasn't habitual, and he knew that what passed for luck was often something else: cheating. And there was the other kind of luck, the kind he himself possessed, but it depended not on chance but on who and what he was. He knew it was an innate power and not Dame Fortune's erratic smile. Since power like his was rare, the odds made it likely the woman he'd been watching was merely a very clever cheat.

Her skill could provide her with a very good living, he thought, doing some swift calculations in his head. Five grand a week equaled $260,000 a year, and that was just from his casino. She probably hit them all, careful to keep the numbers relatively low so she stayed under the radar.

He wondered how long she'd been taking him, how long she'd been winning a little here, a little there, before Al noticed.

The curtains were open on the wall-to-wall window in his office, giving the impression, when one first opened the door, of stepping out onto a covered balcony. The glazed window faced west, so he could catch the sunsets. The sun was low now, the sky painted in purple and gold. At his home in the mountains, most of the windows faced east, affording him views of the sunrise. Something in him needed both the greeting and the goodbye of the sun. He'd always been drawn to sunlight, maybe because fire was his element to call, to control.

He checked his internal time: four minutes until sundown. Without checking the sunrise tables every day, he knew exactly when the sun would slide behind the mountains. He didn't own an alarm clock. He didn't need one. He was so acutely attuned to the sun's position that he had only to check within himself to know the time. As for waking at a particular time, he was one of those people who could tell himself to wake at a certain time, and he did. That talent had nothing to do with being Raintree, so he didn't have to hide it; a lot of perfectly ordinary people had the same ability.

He had other talents and abilities, however, that did require careful shielding. The long days of summer instilled in him an almost sexual high, when he could feel contained power buzzing just beneath his skin. He had to be doubly careful not to cause candles to leap into flame just by his presence, or to start wildfires with a glance in the dry-as-tinder brush. He loved Reno; he didn't want to burn it down. He just felt so damn *alive* with all the sunshine pouring down that he wanted to let the energy pour through him instead of holding it inside.

This must be how his brother Gideon felt while pulling lightning, all that hot power searing through his muscles, his veins. They had this in common, the connection with raw power. All the members of the far-flung Raintree clan had some power, some heightened ability, but only members of the royal family could channel and control the earth's natural energies.

Dante wasn't just of the royal family, he was the Dranir, the leader of the entire clan. "Dranir" was synonymous with king, but the position he held wasn't ceremonial, it was one of sheer power. He was the oldest son of the previous Dranir, but he would have been passed over for the position if he hadn't also inherited the power to hold it.

Behind him came Al's distinctive knock on the door. The outer office was empty, Dante's secretary having gone home hours before. "Come in," he called, not turning from his view of the sunset.

The door opened, and Al said, "Mr. Raintree, this is Lorna Clay."

Dante turned and looked at the woman, all his senses on alert. The first thing he noticed was the vibrant color of her hair, a rich, dark red that encompassed a multitude of shades from copper to burgundy. The warm amber light danced along the iridescent strands, and he felt a hard tug of sheer lust in his gut. Looking at her hair was almost like looking at fire, and he had the same reaction.

The second thing he noticed was that she was spitting mad.

Silhouette®

Romantic
SUSPENSE

**Sparked by Danger,
Fueled by Passion.**

*This month and every month look for
four new heart-racing romances
set against a backdrop of suspense!*

Available in May 2007

Safety in Numbers
(Wild West Bodyguards miniseries)
by **Carla Cassidy**

Jackson's Woman
by **Maggie Price**

Shadow Warrior
(Night Guardians miniseries)
by **Linda Conrad**

One Cool Lawman
by **Diane Pershing**

Available wherever you buy books!

REQUEST YOUR FREE BOOKS!
2 FREE NOVELS PLUS 2 FREE GIFTS!

SPECIAL EDITION®
Life, Love and Family!

YES! Please send me 2 FREE Silhouette Special Edition® novels and my 2 FREE gifts. After receiving them, if I don't wish to receive any more books, I can return the shipping statement marked "cancel." If I don't cancel, I will receive 6 brand-new novels every month and be billed just $4.24 per book in the U.S., or $4.99 per book in Canada, plus 25¢ shipping and handling per book and applicable taxes, if any*. That's a savings of at least 15% off the cover price! I understand that accepting the 2 free books and gifts places me under no obligation to buy anything. I can always return a shipment and cancel at any time. Even if I never buy another book from Silhouette, the two free books and gifts are mine to keep forever.

235 SDN EEYU   335 SDN EEY6

Name _____ (PLEASE PRINT)

Address _____ Apt. _____

City _____ State/Prov. _____ Zip/Postal Code _____

Signature (if under 18, a parent or guardian must sign)

Mail to the **Silhouette Reader Service**™:
IN U.S.A.: P.O. Box 1867, Buffalo, NY 14240-1867
IN CANADA: P.O. Box 609, Fort Erie, Ontario L2A 5X3

Not valid to current Silhouette Special Edition subscribers.

Want to try two free books from another line?
Call 1-800-873-8635 or visit www.morefreebooks.com.

* Terms and prices subject to change without notice. NY residents add applicable sales tax. Canadian residents will be charged applicable provincial taxes and GST. This offer is limited to one order per household. All orders subject to approval. Credit or debit balances in a customer's account(s) may be offset by any other outstanding balance owed by or to the customer. Please allow 4 to 6 weeks for delivery.

Your Privacy: Silhouette is committed to protecting your privacy. Our Privacy Policy is available online at www.eHarlequin.com or upon request from the Reader Service. From time to time we make our lists of customers available to reputable firms who may have a product or service of interest to you. If you would prefer we not share your name and address, please check here. ☐

SSE07

HARLEQUIN®

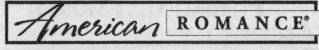

A THREE-BOOK SERIES BY BELOVED AUTHOR

Judy Christenberry

Dallas Duets
What's behind the doors of
the Yellow Rose Lane apartments?
Love, Texas-style!

THE MARRYING KIND
May 2007

Jonathan Davis was many things—a millionaire,
a player, a catch. But he'd never be a husband.
For him, "marriage" equaled "mistake." Diane Black
was a forever kind of woman, a babies-and-minivan
kind of woman. But John was confident he could
date her and still avoid that trap.
Until he kissed her…

Also watch for:
DADDY NEXT DOOR
January 2007

MOMMY FOR A MINUTE
August 2007

Available wherever Harlequin books are sold.